Beyond the Miniyar

A Tale of Hope

Joseph Michael Lamb

Contact the author at josephmichaellamb.com

Copyright © 2023 by Joseph Michael Lamb

Zero Bubble Press
Alpharetta, GA 30004

Contact the Publisher at zerobubblepress.com

First Zero Bubble Press edition: October 2023

ISBN: 978-1-961354-05-0   (Paperback Edition)

ISBN: 978-1-961354-04-3   (Ebook Edition)

ISBN: 978-1-961354-06-7   (Hardback Edition)

Editor: Bob Cooper (Bob-Cooper.com)

Cover Art by: MIBLart.com reproduced in any form without written permission from the publisher or author, except as permitted by U.S. copyright law.

No part of this work was created by artificial intelligence software.

This book is dedicated to my daughter Emily, who gives me hope for the future state of our world.

Chapter 1

INNAUGERATION

T he spirit in the air was celebratory. Balloons, banners, and posters littered the streets as people of all ages and backgrounds blended into a crowd that seemed to move like the waves of the ocean. They waited patiently with jubilant expectation. Families, large and small, were all in attendance to honor the inauguration of their first governor, holding tiny flags donned in red, white, and blue. At least eight other flags were displayed around the podium, blowing in the breeze, mimicking their tiny counterparts. The skies were clear, and while the temperature this time of year could fluctuate, the day was perfect.

Lieutenant Leena Zhen stood to the left of the platform. From her vantage point on the stairs of the Capitol building, she could see the masses collecting. Standing in the shadow of the great hall gave her some shelter from the sun, which was glowing as if to validate the sacredness of the day's activities. Zone 6 had never had a governor. After two long years of negotiation with the Aberjay, they signed a treaty that gave the Miniyar the ability to hold a free and public election. A month earlier, the masses had flooded the streets, casting their ballots to elect who they believed was the best candidate to lead them. Today, they put Joseph Hamrick in office and placed their hopes in his hands.

Hamrick was not a candidate of extremes. He played to the center. Many wanted to abandon all connections to the Aberjay—those who ruled over Zone 7 and, until recently, ruled them as well. Hamrick was smart enough to know a complete revolution would leave them in a vulnerable state. There were too many issues to work out before they could throw off the chains that bound them entirely. The Miniyar took for granted utilities like water, electricity, and trash service. Smarter minds understood they needed a plan for those needs before any full insurrection.

The democratic process was not the end of their struggle, but only the beginning. After the decisive train depot battle and many skirmishes that followed, the Aberjay asked for peace. The Resistance forces stood down long enough to set up peace talks and make their case for a new government. While it was their intention to dismantle the bodies that currently governed the state in response to the genocide they had witnessed, the mass execution of Zone 6 citizens was ultimately blamed on Sergeant McBride and a few overzealous Citizens Protection Unit (CPU) leaders, not a direct order from the top. The Miniyar contingent wanted to institute new government but had to settle for self-management of their zone as a first step toward total liberation.

With a roar, Governor Joseph Hamrick emerged from the Capitol building and walked to the platform with several other democratically elected personnel, including two new senators. The Miniyar had selected them to provide representation in the state's congressional sessions. The governor looked out over the crowd, happy that the people had well received his election. He waved, along with his wife and two children, who did their best to show the picture of a happy family.

Leena did not know the governor at that point but heard he was a good choice for the position. He had a history in the law and had been a judge for many years. There were attempts to dig up scandal during the election but to no avail. There were no skeletons to find in Hamrick's closet. He was clean.

It had been two years since Leena lost her mother in the tragic collapse of her building, along with Diego, her grandfather. She thought about them both often and felt if there was a place after death where they might see her, they would be proud of what she had become. After their passing, she fought for the poor and those who could not fight for themselves. She fought for the liberation of the Miniyar and the ability for them to determine their own destiny by governing themselves.

The scene before her was patriotic. Leena recalled the Declaration of Independence, which had meant so much to her during that time, and her foolish dreams of throwing off the corrupt government and being a part of something new. She was naïve. Change does not happen that quickly. She had taken a small role in assisting with the steps that led to the Treaty of Abignol, the small area of Zone 7 where they signed the treaty. She could be proud of that, even if she didn't think it went far enough.

The governor stepped to the microphone and began reading from the prompt. The crowd followed the words and cheered at the appropriate times. Leena didn't focus on his words as much as the sway of the crowd. Her job today was to ensure the proceeding was safe for everyone and, ultimately, protect the governor from harm. This was her last day of service in this role.

"Team 6, check in," she whispered into her radio.

One at a time, each person on her team of ten checked in to report their location and the status of the crowd from their vantage point. They looked for anything out of order. Security requires you to have a nose for the type of situations that lead to trouble: a change in the crowd's tone or someone who doesn't quite look like they belong. It was challenging as sometimes those you least suspected could be the antagonists.

Leena had spent the last few months on the campaign trail protecting the governor and, although there had yet to be a serious incident, recent intel indicated that some did not like the candidate. Many thought him too weak to stand up to the Aberjay. Most Miniyar wanted peace and were happy with the small steps toward freedom, but there was a group who wanted complete revolution and nothing less.

Two years ago, Leena probably would have agreed with the separatists. When her mother and Diego died, she was ready to topple the entire system. She saw no value in it. After negotiating for compromises from the Aberjay and small amounts of freedom, she changed her mind. Her life was not perfect, but she was seeing hope for her future. She had Jordan, a home, a job. Maybe that was more than anyone should expect out of this life.

Sergeant Liv Zolenski approached from the stairs, dressed in her finest fatigues. This rabble army could not afford formal dress clothes for soldiers, so they did the best they could to avoid fatigues that were blood-stained.

"Lieutenant," Liv said, giving a small nod to acknowledge her commanding officer and her best friend.

"Sergeant," Leena replied with a grin.

"The crowd is bigger than expected," Liv continued, "but I had some soldiers from Team Four posted at the back to help with security."

"Good call," Leena responded.

"So, what happens to us tomorrow?" Liv asked.

"New orders, I guess. The election is over. We are soldiers, right? We go where we are told."

"I just hope we don't get trash duty," Liv said with a chuckle.

"I am sure whatever the commander has in store for us will fit our skills. I can assure you *I* won't be given trash duty."

The crowd roared as the governor concluded his speech, but one person in the crowd stood out when Leena scanned the scene. A man wearing a green camo jacket moving through the sea of people, getting closer and closer to the stage.

"Liv, check that out," Leena said and then engaged her radio, which was no bigger than a watch, on her left wrist. "Team Six, we have a suspicious target moving through the crowd. Older man with red hair and a beard. He is wearing a green camo jacket and is about thirty feet from the stage."

Leena moved toward the governor while Liv walked toward the front of the stage to get in the man's path. The man raised his left hand and with a pointed finger began shouting at the governor, who had just finished his speech and was waving at the crowd. She could not make out the words over the sound of the crowd, but his body language displayed aggression.

"Take him, Liv," Leena said into her radio, knowing that Liv would not hear her over the shouting if she didn't.

Liv waded through the crowd and jumped at the man, placing two hands on his old fatigues. His resistance pulled them both back, falling to the ground at the feet of the cheering crowd. Leena strained to glimpse Liv and the perpetrator, but they were lost in the sea of people. She could not wait and, grasping the governor by his arm, led him, surrounded by soldiers and other politicians, into the Capitol.

As she entered the tall doors of the building, the governor turned to Leena.

"Trouble, Lieutenant?"

"Just a suspicious character, Governor. Better safe than sorry," Leena said.

The Governor nodded and led those surrounding him to the executive offices on the second floor as Leena walked out the front door to check on Liv.

"I lost him," Liv said as she climbed the stairs of the Capitol. "I had him in my grasp, but when we hit the ground, he broke free. Do you want me to put out a bulletin?"

"No, let it go," Leena replied. "If we arrested every spectator with a firm opinion, we would not have jail space."

Both Liv and Leena spent the day looking out for the governor as he made appearances at several locations around the city, including a charity dinner, a homeless shelter, and several meetings with the few wealthy residents of the zone. Leena drove home that night excited about what was next for her. The election was over. She was to report to her commander the next morning for new orders.

Leena woke to a tapping sound. Tap. Tap. She sat up in her bed and looked around the room to find the culprit. Jordan lay next to her, snoring slightly. Putting her feet on the ground and turning toward the window, she spotted the little blue bird. It had a red chest and bright blue wings. It fluttered about, tapping on the window. Repeatedly, it would fly off the sill and tap its beak on the window, then land back on the sill. Did the bird want to come in? Or did it think it was trapped and was trying to get out?

Leena waved her arms to scare off the little bird. The bird's antics agitated her, but she knew she had to get up anyway. She stood, stretched her arms, and let out an enormous yawn. She would let Jordan sleep for a few more minutes before waking him. He worked hard these days. She trudged into the bathroom to begin her morning routine. She was thankful for her little home on the south side of town. It was much nicer than the apartment she grew up in that had stained walls and holes in the ceiling. Although tiny, with only three rooms, this one was hers. She took great pride in her dwelling even though she didn't own it.

Leena put the kettle on the stovetop and prepared the tea bags. Jordan preferred coffee, but they played a little game with one another. On days that he got up first, they drank coffee. Most days, they drank tea. Leena placed the tea bags into the cups to steep and began to dress. Opening her drawers, she found several pairs of pants, all green fatigues. Choosing the top one, she moved to the closet where, peering in, she found five shirts of the same color. This made her chuckle. She was never one for fashion, but this was about as mediocre as one can get.

Leena grabbed her boots and laced them. She learned how to dress the army way in basic training. She was put through the program a couple of years before, after the two sides called for peace. She was already a ranking member of the Resistance, which became the People's Army, but her status was only provisional and only valid during times of war. She had to complete the training for it to stick. She had the option to leave the army, but she stayed because she enjoyed feeling like she was making a difference in people's lives. And there were no jobs to be had anyway.

Leena walked out her backdoor toward the garden. Their fenced backyard was a pleasant spot to grow much of the food they ate. The garden was about thirty by forty feet and took up most of the backyard. But this was not a hobby. She and Jordan needed the food the garden provided to live. Leena made little money as a soldier, and Jordan didn't do much better at the ironworks.

She walked to her dresser and put on her only piece of jewelry, a bracelet the Aberjay called the Tracker. A scar on her wrist revealed where it used to be implanted. Until recently, the Aberjay required every citizen to receive the implant on their tenth birthday. The device allowed them to be plugged into the Aberjay commerce system. It allowed residents to pay for services, apply for jobs, confirm their identity, and track vital signs and health issues.

Leena remembered getting her implant. It was something you looked forward to when you were approaching ten. It was a part of becoming an adult. First, you got your bracelet and, at eighteen, you got a driver's license. It was part of your coming of age. But once you realized that the health-related functionality never really worked and that the device was also a tracking device so the Aberjay could monitor your behavior—and that it was so well-made that a kid with a computer could hack it—it lost its appeal.

She remembered the farm where she had it removed. It was out in Tullian land, south of the city. A farm owned by her friend Jesse. His uncle—Barren Chief, as they called him—was one of the first designers of the implant. He worked for the Aberjay until they took the design from him to redesign it for their actual intent—tracking the citizens.

Based on the treaty signed with the Miniyar, the Aberjay stopped requiring the implant for Zone 6 citizens and created a design that did not require implantation. Leena ran her fingers around the smooth curves of silver on the bracelet. You would never know it had electronic components as it seemed like one solid piece of silver. Leena was careful to always remember it. It took some time to get used to a removable bracelet.

Today was the day. She would get new orders. Her last post ended with the election. For the last six months, she had been in charge of security for Joseph Hamrick. Now that the election was over, she had to return to receive new orders. She believed the commander would make her a part of his security detail once again. Leena was okay with that placement if that was the decision. She enjoyed the post. It kept her moving about, and her keen sense of any scene made her well-suited for it. She noticed things that others were prone to miss. A person in the crowd who doesn't fit. A vehicle that doesn't belong.

"Good morning, beautiful," Jordan said as he entered the kitchen. "Any coffee?"

"No," Leena said, smiling and giving him a tilt of her head. "Tea."

Jordan gave her a long kiss and then went to the refrigerator to pull out some vegetables for breakfast. Mung bean, tofu, some turnip greens.

"Tofu scramble?" Jordan asked.

"Yes, please," Leena replied.

Jordan was an excellent cook. He loved spicing things up with hot sauce, garlic, and peppers. Leena's palette favored blander food, but she kept it to herself. She didn't want to hurt his feelings and lose her chef. She did like to cook, but he was better at it, so she let him take the lead in the kitchen.

"Are you nervous?" Jordan asked as he set a plate down in front of his wife.

"No, not really. I will most likely get another security detail."

"Maybe he will make you an ambassador to the Tullian," Jordan joked.

"I would take it if it meant we could move to the country and live with cows and chickens."

The Tullian were those who lived outside of the city. It was a barren land filled with the worst types of people. True anarchy. There were no walls or police forces to keep you safe. You were on your own. On Leena's first trip to those lands, cannibals kidnapped her. They would have eaten her for breakfast if Jesse hadn't saved her. Jesse lived on a farm with fresh water, milk, bacon, and plenty of gardens for food. But his paradise was an oasis in a sea of danger. The surrounding lands contained all types of evil.

She had always thought when things settled down, she and Jordan could move out there and find Jesse once again. Maybe they would try farm life. But right now, there were more important matters. People who needed help. Their life was here in Zone 6.

Leena and Jordan enjoyed their breakfast together, laughing and talking about the future. They tried not to take what they had for granted as they both had less than most people but understood the richness of the life they were living. They had food to eat, a roof over their heads, and each other. That was enough. It had to be.

Leena drove to work in an old Jeep that the army assigned to her. It rattled and creaked like a rusty pogo stick and stalled often. But she was thankful. It got her to work every day and made getting around town easier than Jordan's motorbike. She had also learned, with Jordan's help, a good deal about auto mechanics. They could not afford a professional mechanic, so when it would need a repair, they had to figure it out. Sometimes Leena would take it to the mechanics on the base to get some advice or learn a new trick to get it running. That group was always one of the busiest trying to keep really old equipment in operation.

The town had changed significantly in the last couple of years. The streets used to be blocked by old burned-out tanks, relics of past wars, and abandoned vehicles. Fuel was so expensive that people often just left their vehicles on the road once they ran out of gas until they could buy more and rescue it. On this day, however, progress was becoming apparent. Even though the governor had not been sworn in yet, a temporary government had already begun making sweeping changes to beautify the city. In addition, after the Miniyar signed the treaty with the Aberjay, hope returned to the city. Many residents took pride in their homes once again and launched many projects to clear the streets, beautify the parks, and more.

Many of the streetlights that had not worked in years now burned bright at night. Simple items such as paint were now available in the zone, so residents could make their homes look new again. There was still much to do though. Trash filled the streets as the private company that used to perform the trash collection was Aberjay-owned. Because of the treaty, they pulled out, leaving trash collection and disposal to the residents. People had no idea where to take their trash, even if they did have a vehicle to haul it in. Piles of garbage was being stacked in alleys and on corners awaiting a new solution to the problem.

Most of the stores in commercial areas were still closed, left in ruins from prior conflicts, but some forward-thinking individuals had already begun investing in some sections of the city, bringing them to life once again.

Leena felt sorry for Joseph Hamrick as she drove. It was clear he had his work cut out for him. There were so many needs and so much suffering. The amount of work necessary to care for the residents seemed insurmountable. They needed clean water, which was still controlled by the Aberjay, trash collection, stores, food to buy in those stores, and homes that were not falling down. This was a tall order. Leena wondered where one would even start.

The headquarters for the People's Army was now a compound next to an old airport runway. It used to host commercial traffic, thousands of planes per day. Many years before, however, the Aberjay built an airport just north of Zone 7. They didn't want their residents making the trip through what they considered 'unsafe' areas. Now very few flights took off or landed on this runway.

Twenty-one large buildings housed training facilities, mess halls, barracks, offices, and even munitions dumps. Most soldiers lived on base. Officers and those who were married could live offsite. Small homes surrounded the base for this purpose. They offered Leena one, but she lived a little farther away so they could be close to Jordan's job at the ironworks.

Leena walked into the command room where Captain John Lewis sat at a table, drinking his coffee. He was a short man with dark curly hair. He had a firm jaw and was always clean-shaven. His muscular shoulders and wide frame provided evidence of his time spent in the gym.

The room was large, with room for more than fifty people. A large table in the center seated twenty-four comfortably. Maps of different parts of the city filled the walls. Communications equipment occupied some of the tables. On one wall hung the framed copy of the Declaration of Independence, which had always been the leading document of this army's rebellion against Aberjay rule. Leena read it often.

"Captain Lewis... reporting for duty, sir," Leena began.

"At ease, Lieutenant, have a seat," he replied.

The captain walked to the coffeepot and filled his cup, turning to Leena and gesturing to determine if she would like a cup. She waved him off, and he returned to the table to sit.

"Any trouble at the inauguration?"

"No sir, just a few outspoken citizens who became aggressive," Leena replied.

"Good. This is a new era for us. We have our own governor, recognized by the Aberjay," he said with a hint of sarcasm. "We need to ensure his safety and provide him with the opportunity to govern. No one knows what type of governor he will be, but until the next election, it's our job to make sure he has support."

"Yes sir," Leena replied.

"I wanted to let you know we are giving the security detail to Master Sergeant Liv Zolenski. I believe you two are close?"

"Yes sir," Leena said, "but I was not aware of her promotion."

"She isn't either, but she needs to be promoted to take on the role of protecting the governor. Do you have any reservations about her ability to do that?"

"No sir. Liv is quite capable." Leena cringed a little inside as this was the detail she thought she would be assigned to, which meant something new was in store for her.

"Good, then I will get her promotion processed."

"And for me, sir?" Leena asked.

The captain handed a manila envelope to Leena. "These are your orders."

Leena opened the envelope and pulled out the contents.

"Liaison to the Governor?" Leena said after skimming the document.

"Yes, Lieutenant, it's a new position we created. You will work with the governor as a liaison to the People's Army. The idea is to filter all communication between the governor and the army through you so we can speak with one voice. We need you to be in his meetings, understand the changes he is making, and speak up when you feel his decisions might negatively affect the army or our ability to keep people safe. You will also brief the press on questions and announcements that may involve the military."

"Yes sir," Leena replied.

The captain continued, "Things are tense right now. The Aberjay have given us a little freedom, but I don't think it will last. Not everyone agrees with me, but I believe they are just trying to find more creative ways to silence us. We have taken a few steps forward. I would like you to ensure we don't take any steps back. Can you do that?"

"Yes sir, I will do my best," she agreed.

"You also have Zolenski and the security detail under your command, so make sure the governor stays safe. You will need to go to Zone 7 for meetings, so there is a pass included with your orders that should give you free access to the zone. Questions?"

Leena's mind raced with questions. Not only was she arrested a couple of years back for breaking into a pharmacy, but her actions during the last two years put her on a wanted list. She didn't know of her status on that list since the treaty was signed, and she was not sure she wanted to find out.

"Sir, I am concerned."

"Yes, Lieutenant?"

"I was on a wanted list if you remember. Can I even enter Zone 7 without being arrested?" Leena replied.

"I wondered that myself. It should be okay. I had to issue your name to the CPU to get the pass for you, and they didn't mention you being on a list."

"Would they mention it, sir?" Leena said with a tinge of sarcasm.

"We will just have to take our chances with this one, Leena. I don't think they want any more incidents. They took too many losses, and they know our army now matches theirs in size. If you have any trouble, call me and I'll figure it out."

Leena stood at attention. "Yes sir."

"Okay then, soldier, report to the Governor's Office."

Leena drove toward the Capitol, about ten miles from the base. She was excited about her new position. It would put her in the room where decisions were being made. She was also anxious because the role was more political than tactical, and she was not sure if her skill set was strong enough in that area to do the position justice. Leena realized as she drove that she was now partly responsible for healing the city. She was not the governor, but she would be at the table when decisions were debated. She could change lives with her input.

Leena pulled into the parking lot of the Capitol and the soldiers saluted her quickly and waved her into the parking area. After entering the building, security handed her a badge that was waiting for her. It would provide top-level clearance to the Capitol. She walked upstairs to the governor's office to report to his Chief of Staff, which was the custom for new employees in the Capitol.

"Mrs. Arinson," Leena said as she walked through the door and into a large waiting area outside the Governor's Office.

"Hello Lieutenant, please have a seat, and I will be right with you."

Leena sat in a row of chairs and witnessed pandemonium. It was moving day, so employees were moving into the Capitol and setting up their offices to govern for the next six years. Boxes and crates littered the office and the hallways. Many movers in one-piece gray jumpsuits unpacked boxes and set up the office bookshelves, filing cabinets, desks, and other furniture. There had not been a working government operating in this building for more than fifty years, so many of the books, files, and maps were outdated. Leena assumed they wanted the appearance of a government even if the tools of the trade were too old to be of any use.

"Lieutenant?" Mrs. Arinson said to get Leena's attention. "Please follow me."

Leena followed close behind Tilda Arinson. They walked back toward the rotunda, crossing over the balcony that looked down on the lobby and then to the other side of the building. Workers had sealed many of the doors in the building years ago when the previous government moved the seat of power to Zone 7. They had recently opened up many of them to clean them and prepare for this new era, but most remained unused. Leena quietly wondered what the insides of those offices looked like. It bewildered her that many of these doors had been unopened since long before she was born.

Leena did not remember when the Aberjay moved the Capitol to Zone 7. She had learned the history of the event in school. When the area around the Capitol had become a cesspool of crime and violence, leaders felt it was safer to move north. That was their excuse anyway. After that happened, what remained of the wealthy in that area moved along with it. The departure of those families who funded so much of the taxes for the region caused it to fall. No taxes meant no police, no fire trucks, no parks. It also meant those who had businesses in the area were no longer protected from thieves. Once one or two stores fell victim to robbery or arson; the rest quickly closed their stores and moved to other areas.

"Here we are," said Tilda as she turned a key to a room with a frosted-glass door. When she opened the door, she was met with the sight of a small office containing a desk, a chair, several bookshelves yet to be filled, and an empty wastebasket. The large window allowed the sun's rays to stream in, illuminating the room, while the scent of lemon from the recent cleaning lingered in the air.

Leena was grateful for the space even though it was small. She'd never had an office before or even an actual job. She worked in a factory for one summer and did small jobs for her parents in their fabric store, but this was a new level. Leena walked into the room, trying to act like this was normal for her. She went to the desk and sat in the chair to see how it felt. It creaked as she leaned back, turning to face the window.

"Your nameplate will be ready in a few days. I will send over the meeting schedule as soon as we find my printer. Hopefully, it still works when they find it. If there is anything you need, let me know. We don't have much money, so try to make do with what you've got," Tilda said in a crass tone. "Here is your key," she finished as she placed the key on the desk.

Leena had just met her, but she thought Tilda was an odd bird. She had long gray hair she wore in a bun. It looked like a bird's nest. Her body was a strange shape, with breasts so large that it seemed like gravity would pull her from side to side as she walked. Her body was slender, yet her hips and backside were voluminous, giving her a unique hourglass silhouette. Tilda was most likely in her sixties and carried herself with an air of despondence as if she cared little about anything that happened around her. Despite all of this, she seemed to always have everything well in hand. She handled the administrative duties with finesse and the highest of competencies on the campaign trail. She followed the governor religiously, always there to hand him a file or a tissue, remind him of a name, or suggest a schedule change. She was quite capable, and it made sense she was now running his office.

Leena took a few minutes to enjoy her good fortune. She moved her chair close to the enormous wall of glass to look down on the city street. She watched the leaves on the large trees ripple in the wind, accompanied by the occasional passerby. Her mind got lost as she daydreamed about what her future might hold. She felt she could get used to this post and, even though it had not even begun, she thought it was a fit.

As she continued to assess her new situation, a flash of red near a tree caught her eye. Thinking she might have imagined it, she stood and stepped close to the window to look more intently. A large oak tree with long wispy branches was shielding something. Then she saw it again. It was hair. A flutter of hair in the wind. Stepping out from under the tree was a tall man with red hair and a red beard. Clothed in camo fatigues, this was the same man who was at the event the day before. He stood next to the tree, looking up at Leena. He seemed to look right through her.

Leena wondered if she should use her radio to have someone check him out, but as she raised her hand to call some team members who were scattered about the Capitol, the man stepped back behind the tree and was gone. She thought for a moment that he was still hiding behind the tree, but after looking for a few minutes, she did not see him again.

Leena had done enough daydreaming and was ready to get to work. She had a meeting scheduled with some of her staff, as well as Liv, to go over the plan for the Governor's security detail. They had processes to craft and code words to create. She was excited about getting started. Leena looked around for a pad so she could take notes and realized the office was quite barren. She didn't relish the thought of having to ask Tilda for paper but knew her day could not get started until she did.

Chapter 2

MEETINGS

Leena's first week as the People's Army's liaison to the Governor's Office was a whirlwind. The title alone was a mouthful. She didn't see the governor but met with her staff to get them started on developing processes for the security of the Capitol and the governor when he traveled. Liv was a good soldier, and there was no one Leena would have preferred to be heading up that security detail, but when it came to the administrative tasks of formulating processes and writing job descriptions, she was a bit lacking. Leena knew she would have to help her out in these areas, but she was okay with that as Liv was always supportive of her as well.

The weather had turned. It was rainy, which was common in the spring. No one minded the rain, knowing that many of the falling drops wound up in water collection receptacles and kept people alive. City water was a major concern, and the primary topic of meetings Leena would attend that day. The Miniyar, the poor who lived in Zone 6, always had to conserve. Water was expensive. Many homes didn't have any at all because they couldn't afford it. They collected water in rain barrels and boiled it to make meals, do dishes, and take baths.

It was a global problem and had been since before Leena was born. A warming planet was the culprit, according to scientists. The West was mostly desert now. They had much less rain than in the east. Leena was not even sure how they survived.

She had some cousins come through town when she was young who talked about living in Arizona. They said it only rained a few days a year out there. They collected what they could but made long trips to water stations for the rest. Some weeks, they lived on less than a gallon of water for the entire family. Planting was nearly impossible. Without rain, nothing grows.

Leena had heard stories of folks just dropping dead of dehydration in those hot summer months when the sun would beat down on them. The power company had become good at harnessing the sun for electricity, as most of the west received their power from solar, but the unrelenting heat created a love-hate relationship for residents. They had power to run the air conditioners, but the cool air removed moisture from the air, drying them out even more.

Leena remembered the stories because they intrigued her. She had traveled little, so how others lived was always of interest. She wondered how many of the stories were exaggerated. Those cousins ended up going further north, she believed. Pittsburgh? Or was it New York? She couldn't remember; she was quite young.

Meetings were on her schedule this week, but unlike the previous week, these were meetings with the governor and his staff and several committees where the two senators that represented their people managed different affairs of the zone such as sanitation, taxes, and education to name just a few. Leena was excited to contribute but knew she was not qualified. She had not gone to college, worked a proper job, or had any verifiable life experience that would make her opinions credible. She struggled daily with these thoughts, wondering when those who put her in this position would realize she had no business being there. Her lack of experience was not a secret. She did not know why the commander kept putting her in these positions of power.

"Good morning, all," Leena said as she walked into the large conference room. This was her first meeting of the week and would likely be an all-day affair. She received several nods from other members of the team, including Senator Lansom and Senator Chin, who were both already conferring with each other at the other end of the enormous room. She didn't really know either of them, but they were nice enough.

Vivian Lansom was an entrepreneur before she was elected as a senator. She led the few groups in Zone 6 that encouraged the growth of small businesses and helped with the development of several shopping districts. No one was sure where her wealth came from or if she was even that well off. Most people just assumed it because of the house she lived in and the car she drove. Leena liked how she dressed. She was always in a business suit, never a dress.

Senator Robert Chin she did not know as well. She believed he was a reporter on a paper up north before coming here. His dress was much less formal than Senator Lansom. He was short and quiet. People most likely voted for Senator Chin because he was Chinese, whose population comprised more than thirty percent of the zone, and because he was an unknown. After considering the alternative candidates, they took a risk on someone they didn't know rather than electing someone they did. Leena believed it was human nature. We are more inclined to accept strangers than family because we know our families' secrets.

Also in the room was Liv, who did not sit at the table but in the corner to provide security. Tilda Arinson sat next to the governor to take notes and provide staffing input. Viktor Brommel, a former fire chief and now appointed as the Director of Community Services, and Angela Schwimmer, a former teacher and now Director of Education, sat at the other end of the table. And, of course, the governor was there. Viktor and Angela were board members, along with the two senators. The governor served as the fifth board member and final decision-maker. Leena's input was welcomed, but she did not have a vote on the board.

They began the meeting with a check-in from each department. There were many things to build in a government so new. Those who sat at the table understood the tasks at hand were monumental but also knew the public was short on patience when it came to health and wellness. According to the agenda distributed by Tilda, water, food, education, and utilities such as electricity and trash removal were all on the table. So was zone security. The Aberjay had provided all of those things before the Treaty was signed but didn't do a great job of it. Now things were different. The newly elected government was responsible for providing for the people and had a short time to make everything right before the people would grow restless.

"Later this month," the governor said, "we will attend the congressional session in Zone 7 for the first time. We need to develop proposals that the authorities have asked for. They promised to hear us out. If this autonomy is going to last, we need to make reasonable requests of them. I will need reports from each of you this week detailing how you plan to develop those proposals. Just summaries. I don't need the entire report. But our goal should be to focus on three things: clean water, trash services, and property reclamation."

"Reclamation?" Viktor asked.

"Yes," Senator Lansom chimed in, "they took many of our homes and storefronts from us via eminent domain to build a factory before the transition. They never built the factory. We think it's only fair that we be allowed to reclaim them. We want to use them for redevelopment."

Everyone nodded as if they understood, but Leena was confused and didn't really understand the rules around eminent domain. She thought it was better not to ask questions at this stage for fear of looking uninformed. She figured there was plenty of time for her to educate herself.

"Do we have the votes for that?" Senator Chin asked. "It seems like a tall order, but I can make some calls to build support before the session."

"No, that's okay, Robert. I have already made several calls, and I think it will pass without an issue," Senator Lansom assured him.

"Viktor," the governor continued, "what is the status of water in the zone?"

Viktor shuffled through a stack of papers, looking for a particular report. "Water flow has slowed. We have issues with pressure in several areas of the zone. Only about one-quarter of residents still have water service and are making do with rainwater collection and what they get from the water stations. The army has a distilling machine, but even if we ask them to maximize production, it does not generate water fast enough to accommodate the need."

Viktor glanced at Leena to get her approval of his assumption. Leena nodded her assent but did not know how the machine worked or its production speed.

"Of the four water towers in the city, one is full, and one is at forty-five percent. The others are empty. I am working on getting the empty ones full, but with the lack of pressure coming from the plant, it will be a challenge to fill them." Viktor finished his report, removing his glasses and setting them on the table next to the stack of papers.

"What causes the pressure problem?" the governor asked.

"It's hard to tell. I have people working on identifying the issue, but if I had to guess, I would say there is an open line somewhere north of us," Viktor responded.

"In Zone 7?" Senator Chin asked.

"Yes. Either there is a hole they don't know about, or they are slowly rationing our water. The pressure seems to go down a little every day. We have been watching it for weeks."

"Okay, monitor that and let me know if it gets critical. We cannot survive without water." The governor finished his statement and dismissed the team for lunch.

Leena walked back to her office. As she entered, a new face startled her.

"Maggie!" Leena said loudly. "What are you doing here?"

Maggie Cho was an inmate at the prison where Leena was incarcerated for thirty days while awaiting trial for the pharmacy break-in. She ate lunch with her almost every day she was in lockup. Maggie was a short, quiet Korean woman and dressed modestly, with a long skirt and colorful top. She was young. Leena guessed about twenty or twenty-one. Her hair was long and black and as straight as a painted line, as if every single hair were glued together to form a single piece.

"Hello Leena," Maggie said as she stood to hug her.

Maggie was not an overly affectionate person, but a bond had formed between the two of them when they were in prison together. The CPU imprisoned her for stealing food from a bakery, and Leena knew she was not a criminal at heart, just a victim of circumstance.

Tilda walked in behind the two and said, "Oh, I see you two have gotten acquainted."

"Maggie and I know each other from..." Leena paused, not wanting to mention her time in prison. "Our parents are old friends."

"Well, that is wonderful," Tilda responded with sarcasm. "Maggie is an aide we just hired to help with administrative duties; feel free to make use of her services. I will leave you to continue the reunion," Tilda said with an edge of derision and quickly vanished from the room.

Leena and Maggie spent the better part of an hour catching up. They had not seen each other in years. Maggie was paroled from prison one month earlier after serving five years for stealing bread. She had applied for the position at the Capitol and beat out more than one hundred other candidates because she spoke several languages, including Chinese, Thai, and her native Korean.

After exchanging stories, Maggie went back to Human Resources to finish her paperwork while Leena rearranged some of the furniture in her office. She did not like the feng shui of the bookcases as they were different sizes and repositioned them to provide more balance to the room.

Leena sat at her desk to eat her lunch. She enjoyed her office despite the mismatched furniture. She unwrapped her sandwich of tomatoes and cucumbers on fresh sourdough she had made the night before. Everything she had for lunch that day came from her garden except the flour to make the bread. She usually added hummus, but she had run out of chickpeas. She had to settle for some balsamic vinegar.

Her eyes scanned her empty bookshelves, and she wondered where she might get some books to fill them. There was obviously no budget for it. She thought about several thrift stores that still had some old books. Maybe those would work. She thought about what might make sense. Maybe an atlas of some sort? A couple of books on recent history? A book on war and maybe something on ethics?

As she debated the creation of her library, her earpiece rang out.

"Lieutenant Zhen, come in," the voice sounded.

"This is Lieutenant Zhen," she responded.

"Lieutenant, please call Commander Johnson as soon as possible," the voice said.

"Will do," she said as she reached for her bag to retrieve her cell phone.

She always carried the phone around, but the tower structure in the zone was not optimal, so it often failed to work effectively. Calling in to command was not uncommon, and there were some old landline phones in the building she could use if her cell phone failed to connect. Landline calls were a necessity for private conversations that you didn't want to go out on the radio.

She dialed the number for the commander's office and was put through after briefly chatting with his administrative assistant.

"Commander, this is Lieutenant Zhen. Did you need me?"

"Yes, Lieutenant. How are you getting settled over there?" the commander asked.

"I'm doing great," Leena said, suspicious that the commander began with small talk.

"I have some intel I wanted to share with you so that you can inform the governor. Do you have a moment? Are you in a secure location?"

"Yes, Commander, go ahead."

"The Chinese army in the Federated States has mobilized. They are gathering on their borders. It looks like they plan to make a push. They have a lot of land to cover before they might reach our doorstep, but the governor needs to know they are on the move so that he can determine his response to the Aberjay, who will likely ask for our help."

"What is our position, Commander?"

"We can certainly spare some forces if the governor orders us to do so, but it will leave us thin. Things are unstable right now, and our forces are tied up trying to build infrastructure."

"I understand, Commander. I will pass on the intel," Leena finished and went back to her sandwich.

The federal government had a small army. After cutting their budget years before to provide tax relief and reallocating funds to local governments, their ability to respond to threats such as the Chinese was limited without calling on local governments to help. The Aberjay had the Citizen Protection Units (CPU), who doubled as soldiers and police and would likely be called up to assist, but the People's Army of Zone 6 was a new entity. *Would they be called on to fight?* Leena didn't know the answer but knew this was information she needed to get in front of the governor. Fortunately, she did not have to make the final decision about their involvement.

Hanging up with the commander, Leena walked into the Governor's Office and asked Tilda for a couple of minutes with Governor Hamrick. After being ushered into the office, she informed the governor of the new intelligence. His response was unexpected.

"Hell no! We don't have time for this. I am building a city here. We can't go to war."

The governor was angrier than Leena expected him to get on receiving the news. She had spent considerable time with him during the campaign, but he had never become so angry so quickly. Either he was on his best behavior before the election, or he had reserved his outbursts for selective ears.

"Do you have any requests of the People's Army, Governor?" Leena asked.

"No, not right now," he said as he ran his hands through his thinning hairline. "We may need to select a group to send to the front, but we will cross that proverbial bridge when we come to it. Thank you, Lieutenant."

Leena woke to the sound of breakfast being made. It put a smile on her face. She was lucky enough to have a husband who liked to cook and looked forward to his artisanal breakfasts. Rubbing her eyes, she sat up and looked around the room. She came to bed late when Jordan was already asleep. She was working long hours. Jordan never mentioned that he was unhappy with it, but she knew she was pushing the boundaries. He seemed to understand, though; she was building something. She was a part of a new government. People were counting on her.

She rose and put on her robe before going to the window and checking on the garden. It was a bright morning, and the sun lit up the room. Her thoughts turned to the staff meeting the day before, where they discussed the upcoming congressional session. She would have to travel to Zone 7 soon.

She thought about her run-in with the authorities a couple of years earlier. Fernando Martinez, the previous zone advocate, had come to her rescue to get her a suspended sentence. That meant that technically she was still in danger of being jailed if she entered Zone 7. But that was years ago. She felt sure the time had run out on that. It would be terribly embarrassing to be arrested at the gate.

Leena walked into the kitchen to see Jordan plating her breakfast.

"Thanks, babe," she said with a smile and an air kiss. Leena sat and began spreading strawberry preserves on a toasted slice of sourdough. The strawberries she grew last summer. She loved strawberries, and turning them into jam was a good way to enjoy them year-round.

"You're welcome," Jordan responded. "You came home late last night."

"Yes, we were working on some new policies." Leena tried to read Jordan's face to see if he was upset with her for coming in late, but she couldn't decipher it.

"Are you headed back to work this morning?" Jordan asked.

"Yes, we gotta get ready for the trip. I have procedures to work on. How about you?"

Leena knew there was much more on her plate than the procedures, but because Jordan didn't have clearance, she could not share it.

"I have a second shift, so I'm going to clean a little and go to work about noon."

"Okay, I hope you have a good day. I'm running late. I need to get going." Leena finished her toast along with some mung bean scramble and scurried from the table.

Leena turned on the shower to get it warm and disrobed. Grabbing a fresh towel and placing it next to the shower, she stepped into the claw-foot tub and melted at the feeling of the warm water flowing over her body. Water was scarce, so she knew she had to hurry. They tried to limit their showers to five minutes at most. The water that ran the shower didn't come from rain barrels but from the city, which meant that high water usage meant a hefty water bill.

She quickly lathered her body and worked shampoo into her hair, letting the lukewarm water wash it clean. She turned to get the remnants of soap off her body when the water stopped. She reached down to turn the knobs to no avail. Grabbing a towel, she began wiping the water and the small bit of remaining soap off her body. She wondered if Jordan might have added a timing device to turn off the water after several minutes. They often playfully fought over how long five minutes really lasted as there wasn't a timer in the shower and Leena's five minutes always seem to be longer than Jordan's.

"Jordan," she called from the bathroom.

"Yes, darling?" he responded.

"The water stopped."

"Yes, I heard that. Maybe a line is cut somewhere. I'll look around the house to make sure it isn't us."

Leena finished drying herself and got dressed. She jumped when she saw a head walk by her window but quickly realized it was Jordan checking the water lines coming into the house. They met in the kitchen as Leena was preparing her lunch.

"I didn't see a problem, but I did see several neighbors looking around their house the same way, so it's obviously a water outage," Jordan said.

"I need to get to work," Leena said as she packed up her lunch. "I will check with Viktor when I get to the Capitol to see what's going on."

Leena gave Jordan a kiss and then headed off to work.

As Leena drove to work, it was clear the water issue was not only on her block. Clusters of people gathered at several intersections. Utility outages were common in Zone 6. The residents were used to brief periods without water, and rain collection was essential to ensure they had drinking water. Something about the people's response to this outage felt different though. Maybe it was the new government that was being put in place but seeing the residents already on the streets discussing the outage was not normal.

Leena went on her radio as she drove, calling out the areas that needed crowd control. Residents likely would overrun the few water stations scattered around the city. Panic and anxiety had a way of making people abandon their principles of nonviolence. Zone leaders set up the water stations more than fifty years ago when the first signs of water shortages hit the city. If the Aberjay ever cut off the water supply, the water stations provided the only place the residents could get water.

The water stations were placed above wells that city workers dug deep into the earth, usually one hundred yards or more. People had to bring their own containers, and soldiers would dispense one gallon per person, but you could visit daily. Assuming the well didn't run dry, there would be enough water to keep people alive.

As Leena drove past the 7th Street Water Station, she came upon a swelling crowd. Pulling her vehicle up onto a sidewalk, she stepped out to get a better assessment. She knew there were soldiers from the People's Army here to secure the water station but wanted to get an understanding of why this was escalating so quickly.

The water stations were just small glass buildings of only two hundred square feet. Inside each one was a counter and, behind it, a spigot that dispensed the water. It was a lousy design as water was one of those services that, when in low supply and high demand, caused riots. A rowdy group could easily destroy the glass and enter the building if it were closed, so having people manage the facilities was essential. Because of the glass walls, however, the buildings were non-defendable. If the residents wanted in, they would get in.

Leena assumed the bad design was an attempt at transparency, but she felt despite the reason, glass walls made no sense. She would make a note to suggest rebuilding them with concrete.

As she approached the crowd, she placed her hand on the small pistol she carried at her side. This was part of her training to ensure someone in the mob did not abscond with her weapon while she was moving through. She yelled at the throngs of people to make way as she covered her firearm with one hand and pushed with the other. The energy was high, but the crowd was not unruly. Leena had limited time to satisfy this group, or she would face a riot.

Two soldiers guarded the front of the building, but Leena did not recognize them. She could see through the glass that there were two more inside, but they were not dispensing water. Leena put her hands up with palms facing the people to communicate her desire for them to be quiet so she could assess the situation.

"What is the situation, soldier?" Leena asked.

"We were told to secure the water station, Lieutenant," the first soldier began. "There was already a crowd gathered, and it's tripled in the last twenty minutes."

"So, what's the problem? Is the pump working?"

"Yes, Lieutenant, it works, but we were told to secure it and wait for orders before we opened it up."

"Who gave you those orders?"

"Master Sergeant Bryant," the soldier replied.

Leena looked around and took a few seconds to think. She didn't understand why they would not want to open the water stations if the water had stopped. She assumed they just didn't know what was happening on the ground. Leena had to get this station open, or the people would take the water by force.

"Private, I am ordering you to open this water station. The people need water, so let's give it to them."

"Yes, Lieutenant," the soldier replied before opening the door and motioning for the first few residents to enter the building.

The crowd cheered as they saw the door opening and moved in closer.

"Let's limit those inside to about eight," Leena said to the private.

"Yes, Lieutenant," the soldier replied.

Leena spent several minutes speaking to residents outside of the water station as they waited to enter. Their fear, as she suspected, was a response to the change in government. In contrast to the outages that had been common in the past, most of them believed the shortage was intentional—retaliation by the Aberjay for holding free elections. Leena did her best to reassure them that the loss of water was only momentary, but she didn't really know.

Leena watched through the glass from the outside as they filed into the small, box-like structure, and the soldiers inside began filling their containers, one gallon at a time. As she watched through the glass, she saw something that drew her focus. The man with the red beard. He was on the other side of the glass walls and just stared at her. He stood out because he was not holding a container or trying to enter the water station like the others. The man just stood with his arms to his side, staring at Leena with a shy grin.

Leena questioned whether she might be in danger but felt that with this mass of people, she was relatively safe. She moved to the side of the building to get to his position. As she reached the area where he was standing, though, he was gone. She looked through the crowd, bending down and then up, even jumping to see the redheaded man from above among the throngs of people. Then she heard a voice calling out to her.

"You can't do it, Lieutenant!"

Leena looked in the direction of the voice but couldn't see anyone.

"You are only fooling yourself!"

She pushed into the mass of people, still waiting to enter the building, trying to get to the source of the voice.

"Your destiny awaits, Lieutenant!"

Leena pushed and pulled in multiple directions as the voice seemed to come from all directions. After a few minutes of struggling through the crowd, the voice stopped. Not wanting to be in a vulnerable position, she pushed through the masses and rushed back to her vehicle. She heard no more voices and felt that a continued search for the man who didn't want to be found was unwise. She didn't want to admit to herself that it scared her. *Who is this man, and why is he singling me out?*

Leena climbed into her vehicle and took a minute to collect herself before driving off the curb onto the street, which was now clear of people. She needed to get to work and put this strange occurrence behind her. Placing her hands on the steering wheel, she noticed she was shaking. It had affected her more than she had thought.

Chapter 3

DISTRUBANCE

L eena entered the conference room to attend the staff meeting. The usual attendees were present, including Liv, Tilda, the senators, Viktor, Angela, and the governor. Everyone was already at the table, and the energy in the room was electric. Viktor had a handful of rolled-up schematics.

"Let's get started," the governor said.

"Everyone has an agenda in front of them, but my guess is we want to fast-track the water issues to the top," Tilda stated.

"Yes," Viktor replied.

"Okay, let's have it," the governor said.

"We have yet to figure out why the water has stopped. It's not uncommon to have a burst pipe or a leak of some sort causing a problem, but we have traced the entire damn line in Zone 6 and found nothing. Either the stoppage is caused by a leak farther up the line in Zone 7 or..." Viktor stopped.

"Or what?" the governor prodded.

"Or they turned it off."

"Turned it off? Why would they do that? They have no reason to stop our water," the governor reasoned.

The door to the conference room opened slightly, and a small blonde woman with large glasses entered. Walking sheepishly toward Viktor, she handed him a note and made her way back out of the room.

Viktor opened the note and read it silently.

"What is it?" Leena questioned.

"They did it."

"They did what?" the governor demanded.

"They turned it off. I just received confirmation. They deny it, but my engineers have backchannels into the zone, and their confidants on the other side said they turned it off. They don't know why." Viktor finished his report and began laying out some of his maps.

"What is all this then?" the governor asked, pointing to the stack of maps Viktor had now spread out on the table.

"I went back and looked at the schematics for the water pipeline that runs through town," Viktor replied. "We have plenty of schematics, and all of them seem to tell the same story. The pipeline from Zone 7 is the only way water gets into the city."

"Well, that is depressing," said Senator Chin.

"But then I found these," Viktor continued, pointing to some older maps that had significant wear and tear and a tint of brown that showed their age. "My team found these in the basement of this building when we were cleaning it out. I had them stacked up in my office and hadn't looked at them, but this morning, out of curiosity, I opened them. All of them show another pipeline."

"Another pipeline? Where does it go?" the governor asked.

"Not where does it go, but where does it come from is the proper question," Viktor said with a smile. "They come from the east. From the ocean. A town called Port Loyal."

"I don't know anything about another pipeline. Have you ever heard of it? Is it still there?" the governor asked.

"I have never heard of it, but why would it be on the map if it didn't exist?" Viktor said.

"Is it possible it was drawn to show a future state and that the pipeline was never built?" Senator Chin asked.

"Anything is possible, but that isn't likely. The maps display dotted lines for pipelines that are planned for the future. In fact, the map shows the Zone 7 pipeline as a dotted line, so when these maps were made, our current pipeline had not been built yet."

"What is the likelihood it's usable?" the governor asked. "And would it bring in ocean water? What good would that do? We can't drink saltwater."

"I don't know, Governor. Maybe there's a desalination plant there that filters the water before it gets here. It seems strange they would pipe saltwater as corrosive as it is. I think we need to figure it out. If we could get water from another source, outside the control of the Aberjay, it would mean water independence," Viktor stated confidently.

"Wait," Leena chimed in, "if the pipeline goes all the way to the ocean, doesn't that mean it goes through Tullian land?"

"Yes, Leena," Viktor responded. "Almost three hundred miles of pipeline. Although much of it is probably underground, if it ever carried water, it's highly likely the Tullian have patched into it in several places or destroyed links altogether."

"Okay, get on that. Let's see if those pipes exist and how we might turn them on. For now, we will have to rely on the water stations and what residents have collected from rainwater to keep us going," the governor ordered. "Let's go on to new business."

The staff meeting lasted most of the day, which was quite common. The city had many problems that needed to be discussed. In long meetings, Leena would go numb after a while. She always tried to listen and learn, but some topics were painfully boring to follow, and she fell asleep often. She had learned to pull on the hairs of her arm when she was falling asleep during long meetings, and that seemed to wake her.

The next day, they were traveling to Zone 7 for the congressional session. She was excited but apprehensive as well. She had not been to Zone 7 since being arrested for breaking into the pharmacy. *Will they arrest me onsite? Am I still wanted for crimes?*

The governor would stay behind, but he asked Leena to attend the session to provide security for the senators. She wondered how it would feel being back in Zone 7. She had asked her Zone 7 liaison if wearing her uniform was appropriate, and the authorities allowed it. They even gave her permission to carry her weapon. She would bring her firearm, a 9mm pistol, along with a collapsible baton. She thought it would be silly to seek to protect the senators without weapons. Their permission surprised her a bit, but because firearms were legal for all citizens in Zone 7, it made sense they allowed it. Their rules around firearms had always differed from Zone 6, where gun control laws were strict.

Leena had not been to the northern part of the city for some time. She decided she would drive that way to check it out before heading home. It would take her over an hour to get up there and back home, but she wanted to put her eyes on the gate to see if anything had changed since she was last there. She also enjoyed driving past her old building. Even though it was just a flat piece of land now, it was where her mom and Grandfather Diego died. She didn't have the luxury of arranging for a gravesite for her mother as she never received her mom's remains from the Aberjay, but she would often drive past the place where her mom took her last breath to see if she could feel her.

As she approached the gate, she pulled to the side of the road and stopped. She exited the vehicle to walk toward the entrance to the tunnel that lay beneath the enormous stone wall towering above her. This wall had been there her entire life. She hated it. She blamed the wall for her poverty. It separated her people from opportunity. Jobs to feed their families. Access to safe streets and excellent schools. Deep down, she knew taking the wall down would not solve the problems between the two sets of people, but it was easier to cast blame on the wall.

A People's Army corporal noticed Leena standing before the great wall and came out from the guardhouse.

"Lieutenant, are you okay? Is there anything we can do for you?"

"No thank you, Corporal, just looking. Has it been quiet?" Leena said in response.

"Yes ma'am, it's been quiet," the soldier said as he walked back to his guard gate.

In the past, the CPU had always guarded both sides of the gate. After the treaty, they agreed to let People's Army forces guard their side of the gate. Traffic was considerably slowed when this change took place as each side was nervous and distrustful of the other. People still went to work each day, and work permits were still required to enter Zone 7, but fewer folks ventured through the gate without a good reason.

Leena walked back to her small truck and drove south. The feeling of dread she had staring at the wall seemed to tag along. Within minutes, she was in front of the site of her old building where she grew up. It used to be eight stories tall, made mostly of brick, with a glorious garden on the roof. She grew up tending that garden, along with all of her neighbors in the building. Leena missed that place. It was her happy place.

She had fond memories of her upbringing. Life was hard, but they had each other, and they made it work. The neighbors looked out for each other and helped when they could. They shared food and credits. Life was simpler. The problems seemed smaller. *Or maybe it's just my perspective that has changed.*

Leena walked to where the front stairs used to be and kicked at the few bricks that remained. An assault on the building had destroyed it. The CPU had infiltrated it to wait for her. But she attacked the enemy with two teams of Resistance fighters and, using explosives, took the building, but only moments before it fell. The building's age and the haphazard use of explosives were to blame, and Leena had struggled to accept those facts. She knew she was at fault but reasoned that if the CPU hadn't been there in the first place, she would not have had to invade the building in that way. She still felt guilty about it.

Leena drove toward home with tears in her eyes. She missed her mom terribly. Her mother Mei had always been her rock, her stability. She was proud of the life she was building, but not having her mom to confide in was something she didn't think she would ever get over.

Leena was about halfway home when she got the call on the radio. It was some sort of disturbance on the north side of town, near Banyan Park. She responded on the radio to let them know she was in the area, and even though it was not her responsibility to respond, she said she would check it out.

She turned her vehicle into a side street to head in the opposite direction. Her dispatcher did not mention the nature of the disturbance, only that it involved an explosion, so she did not know what she would discover.

Nearing the park, she saw smoke rising above the large banyan trees that filled the park. The park was green with growth. It used to be a nice place, but many years of neglect had turned it into a hangout for mischievous teenagers and even criminals. Leena used to play there as a child and had fond memories. But it didn't look as appealing these days as it did back then.

She steered her vehicle toward the smoke drifting into the sky, visible high above the trees and the great wall. The smoke did not appear to be coming from the park but from the wall itself, just east of where the park bordered a residential street. When she came within a half-mile of the enormous wall, she noticed two People's Army vehicles and several soldiers standing outside, staring at the commotion. *Maybe another team had gotten there first*, Leena thought.

She recognized Liv, leaning against her vehicle and laughing, as one of the soldiers. The other soldiers were smiling in kind. Leena exited her vehicle and walked to Liv, still confused about the source of the comedy.

"Master Sergeant?" Leena said as a question.

The soldiers, surprised by the appearance of a higher-ranking officer, quickly stood at attention and removed the smiles from their faces.

"Lieutenant," Liv responded with a nod, standing upright and showing respect for her superior.

Liv was Leena's best friend, and they were normally very casual with each other, but around other soldiers, they tried to play the part and respect the rank.

"What is happening here? And why are you even here? Don't you have a governor to protect?" Leena questioned.

"Just a fireworks show, Lieutenant. Some residents thought it would be fun to blow up the wall. I am not even on duty. I was on my way home and saw the smoke."

Leena looked down the street toward the wall and saw about eight figures shuffling about and packing what looked like dirt into holes in the wall with fuses leading to a triggering mechanism. The sight confused her. She knew this was terrorist activity, a serious crime, but wasn't sure why Liv was taking it so lightly.

"I don't understand, Master Sergeant. If residents are committing an act of terrorism, why are you not arresting them?"

Liv's face turned to an expression of wonder. "What do you mean? They are trying to blow up the wall," Liv repeated.

"I understand that, Master Sergeant," Leena said, continuing to use her rank to impress on her the professionalism of this conversation. "Why are you not stopping them?"

"They can't do much damage with those little firecrackers they're using," Liv replied. "Plus, why should we care if they blow up the wall? You and I have discussed doing that for years."

Leena reasoned they were having an issue communicating because the other soldiers were present.

"Take a walk with me, Master Sergeant," Leena ordered.

The two walked away from the group of soldiers to Leena's vehicle.

"Liv, what the hell are you doing?"

"Even if they had what they needed to blow up that wall, I don't care if they do it, and you don't either," she responded, raising her voice a bit.

"It's our job to keep order in this zone, Liv. We can't have rogue agents attacking the Aberjay, and that includes the wall."

"Why do you care so much?" Liv asked. "You and I have both talked about blowing up that wall."

"That was long ago. Things are not the same now. We have a treaty in place," Leena explained.

"To hell with the treaty. Since when are you a part of the establishment? Our fight is not over. We shouldn't even be wearing these uniforms. This army is a joke. It used to mean something. Now we are just police." Liv finished and turned her back on Leena to collect herself as the emotion had brought tears to her eyes.

"Liv, I understand how you feel. I have not forgotten what they did, but we are in a different place now. We get to govern ourselves. We win the war in small incremental battles, not full revolution."

"I don't agree. We need to be taking the fight to them until that wall comes down and they provide us with the same opportunities," Liv said with passion.

"And what of the treaty? Doesn't it mean anything?"

"The treaty was a mistake. The only reason they wanted it was because we were winning. Another few months and we would have taken control."

"Control of what, Liv?" Leena asked.

"Control of our lives. We would have won our freedom."

"Look around, Liv. Do you see any CPU? Don't you sleep better at night than you did? Don't you have a job and a place to live? You already have freedom."

"You know this isn't real, Leena. They could come marching through the gates at any moment and hit us again. They have turned off our water. What do you think is next? Food? Electricity?"

"Liv, we can only deal with the information we have, and many things are going on that you are not aware of."

"Oh, above my pay grade, huh?" Liv replied sarcastically.

"Frankly, yes, there are things I am privy to that you don't know, and I am telling you, we need to play by the rules right now. Now go do your job and stop that pitiful excuse for terrorism."

"Yes, Lieutenant," Liv said with the most sarcasm in her voice that she had ever heard her use.

Liv walked back to her vehicle and spoke to the other soldiers before grabbing rifles and climbing into a small truck to make their way to the wall. Leena sat watching in the driver's seat of her vehicle as Liv and her soldiers pulled up to the wall and chased the ruffians, who scattered. She could tell that Liv was making only a halfhearted effort and intentionally let them escape.

Leena hated fighting with her best friend, but she was responsible for Liv's actions. Liv didn't seem to understand the gravity of even minor attacks on Zone 7. Any attack on the Aberjay could violate the treaty and spur hostilities again.

Although that might be what some wanted, the People's Army was responsible for keeping the peace and ensuring that treaty tenants were maintained.

Leena drove home questioning herself and her position. *Maybe Liv is right. Is it possible we didn't go far enough? Is the treaty a mistake?*

She will cool off, Leena thought as she pulled into her driveway. She always thought Liv was a hothead. Even in high school, everyone knew she had the propensity to blow a gasket when she didn't get her way. Leena would talk to her when she returned from the congressional session to clarify her position.

Leena stepped out of her truck and grabbed her backpack from behind her seat. As she turned to walk toward her front door, she heard a sound. A buzzing sound. She was familiar with the sound. It was a drone.

The Federal Government had outlawed drones many years before with the passage of the Federal Drone Elimination Act. The government put controls in place after drone technology had advanced to placing weapons on them and using them for select assassinations. This development outraged most Americans, leading to their elimination. The skies were free from buzzing for more than twenty years. Two years before, however, the government had repealed the Act, giving states the ability to decide for themselves how they would handle drones, and the Aberjay took immediately to the development of killer drones once again.

Leena stepped toward the end of her driveway and looked up to see if she could spot what she was hearing. The altitude of the drone put it out of eyesight, but it was definitely a drone. She knew the sound they made. While they were legal and used regularly in Zone 7, the treaty that was signed with the Miniyar forbade them from flying in Zone 6. This drone was either a violation of the treaty or the act of a highly unintelligent resident. They could not buy a drone in any local store, but they were available if you traveled to Zone 7 and paid for the permits. Some built their own as well.

Leena stood for a while trying to glimpse the drone, but it never descended low enough to get a good look at it. They didn't really need to. The cameras on them could take photos at high altitudes. After about fifteen minutes, the buzzing subsided, and Leena went inside.

Leena entered the kitchen just as Jordan was pouring her a glass of homemade wine. Grapes were hard to grow in their climate, but with the right care, it was possible. The muscadine grapes were easiest, but it made a sweet wine that Leena didn't care for as much as the dryer ones. They made it in small batches and often would have to throw out the entire bottle due to contamination. When they got it right, however, the process made a fairly good glass of wine.

"Welcome home, my love," Jordan said with a smile, holding out a half filled glass of wine with a yellow tint.

Leena gave him a long kiss before taking the wine from his hand and dropping her bag. She returned to the living area and slowly settled into the couch, a hand-me-down from some neighbors a year ago. It was an old couch, but the previous owner had it re-covered recently with a blue fabric.

Swirling the wine in the glass, she placed her nose in it and inhaled deeply before taking a sip and rolling it around in her mouth. She was no connoisseur but had seen movies where the characters did the same thing, and it always looked so elegant.

"How was your day?" she asked Jordan.

"It was long. I had to go in early and work a little late. There was a large order that came in for hedgehogs, and Bryan was cracking the whip."

"What is a hedgehog?" Leena asked.

"It's multiple pieces of iron molded together to form a large star-looking thing about the size of a truck."

"A truck? What the heck is it for?"

"War mostly. Armies put them on the fields to prevent trucks and tanks from advancing."

"Who placed the order?" Leena asked inquisitively.

Jordan paused for a moment, contemplating whether he should divulge that information. Rules were important to him. After processing the question, he determined there was more risk in withholding information from his wife than betraying the company that employed him. Their client list was not really a secret.

"An Aberjay company ordered them, but my guess is the buyer is the CPU or possibly the Federal Government."

"Things must be heating up out west, huh?"

"It would seem so. If war breaks out, how do you think it would affect us?" Jordan asked.

Leena took a last sip of her wine before placing the long-stemmed glass on the coffee table. She looked to the ceiling to think about Jordan's question while her mind spun off a new thought trail regarding the lack of paint on her ceiling. They had started renovations a year earlier, but she could not remember why they stopped before painting the ceiling. Knowing Jordan was waiting for an answer, she forced her mind into submission.

"I would only be guessing, but off the top of my head, tightened food supplies and access to water. But war also means the need for munitions. If someone gets that old plant running again, it could mean a lot of credits flowing into our zone. I will ask the commander about it."

"Do you think they could push this far east?

"I doubt it. It's a long way to move an army. It will likely end like last time. We will give them a little more dry land, and they will stand down." Leena stood and gave her husband a gentle squeeze on the arm before venturing into the bedroom to pack for her trip the next day.

Leena tried desperately to tell herself she was not anxious about the trip. They would be in Zone 7 for a week, longer than she had been away from home in her life. She told herself what she was doing was important and that she must go. And if they wanted to arrest her for past crimes, they would have to deal with the governor.

She walked to the dresser and, pushing all of her clothes to the side, reached into the back of the drawer and pulled out a manila envelope. She removed the contents, a stack of papers, and slowly sorted through them. Locating her Treaty Provision Notice, she removed it from the stack and gently folded it, sliding it into her suitcase. Her commander gave her the letter.

Part of the treaty signed with the Aberjay included immunity from prosecution for all Resistance fighters for all crimes committed in the execution of their duties. Leena felt she should have the letter with her in case they tried to arrest her, though the comfort it provided was limited for two reasons. First, when Leena broke into the pharmacy to steal medications for her mother, it was not in the *execution of her duties*. Second, the Aberjay lied quite frequently and would often go against treaties or promises they had made just because it suited them. The drone she heard earlier, assuming it was an Aberjay drone, was proof of their treachery.

She would have to leave her fate to chance and hope that all would be well. Leena had to follow orders, and entering Zone 7 to protect the senators was an order. After struggling with anxiety a bit more, she was determined to put it out of her mind and enjoy her last evening with her husband. A cup of tea was next on her agenda, along with some quality time with Jordan.

Leena finished packing and closed her suitcase (another hand-me-down from a friend) before going to the kitchen to boil some water for her tea.

Chapter 4

SECURITY

Leena parked her Jeep in the secured parking area next to the Capitol building. She was meeting the other senators and traveling by van to Zone 7 for the congressional hearings.

She climbed the stairs to the Capitol and made her way to her office. She knew the delegation would leave soon, but a stack of reports was waiting for her on her desk that she needed to sign. The People's Army loved reports. Rather than scheduling a quick call to discuss everything that happened every week, the army required written reports to be filled out, copied multiple times, and sent to multiple offices. Leena thought it was a bit of overkill, but seeing that she would be gone for a week, she thought it was best to complete them before she left the zone.

Upon entering her office, she noticed a package—a wardrobe box. She walked to the other side of her desk to open the box and read the note. "I thought you could use this!" the note read, signed by Maggie Cho.

Leena opened the box to reveal a green officer's uniform. It included well-pressed pants, a light green button-up shirt, and a black necktie as well as a finely tailored coat with a matching garrison cap. The coat had four gold buttons on the front with patches on the side showing the rank of lieutenant. Removing the fine clothing from the box revealed a nametag that read 'Zhen' and a gold braided cord.

Her eyes welled up as she considered the generosity of her friend, Maggie. *How did she find this?* Leena was not sure the People's Army even made uniforms like this. Was it from an antique store? She ran her fingers across the fabric, stopping at the holes in the shoulders of the jacket that provided space for her silver bar insignia. She ran the gold cord through her hands, feeling the luxury of the braids and the smoothness of the material. *Is it made of silk?*

Leena gently placed the items back in the box and carried them to the restroom down the hall from her office. She was eager to get out of her worn fatigues. She wondered as she rushed down the hallway if Maggie even knew her size. Entering the restroom and turning to lock the door, she quickly undressed and put on the pants and the button-up shirt, both of which fit perfectly. Then, after affixing her insignia, she slipped into the coat and black pumps that also fit like they were tailored for her. Lastly, she donned her garrison cap and gazed in the mirror to admire her new look. She practically broke down as she looked at her reflection as she had never been so well-dressed in her entire life. She made a mental note to do something nice for Maggie when she returned. What she had done for her was way above and beyond even what friendship requires.

She knew the team would leave soon, so she put on the included belt, carefully adding the holster that held her firearm. Adding the collapsible baton to the other side brought balance to the ensemble. She hurried back to her office and placed her old clothes into her duffel bag, along with her boots. Hoisting the luggage over her shoulder, she left her office. For the first time in her life, her shoes clicked on the floor as she walked across the marble floors. The sound reminded her of the 'click-click' of the Aberjay in their fine shoes walking through the courthouse when she was in trouble years before. How she desired to have a pair of shoes that would make that noise! She lifted her head high with pride as she exited the building.

Leena walked toward the van parked in front of the Capitol to see if her counterparts were ready to leave. She stepped into the small passenger van, but no one was inside. The van would seat about twelve. Leena could see an open area in the back of the van where luggage was already in place. She set her bag down in that area and then did a quick sweep of the bus seats to ensure the vehicle was secure.

As she stepped off the van stairs, she saw a figure across the small parking lot standing by a large tree. It was the red-bearded fellow who seemed to be stalking her recently. She was armed and felt that minimal danger existed, so she walked toward the man. He showed no signs of evading her pursuit, so she increased the speed of her steps, slowing only as she came near enough to engage with him verbally.

"It is you," Leena said.

"Aye, it is," he replied.

"Who are you?" Leena asked.

The man leaned against the tree, picking at the bark and looking up at the leaves. He wore the same green camo jacket and dirty green fatigues she had seen him in before.

"I asked your name, sir," Leena said more formally.

"No, you didn't," the man replied. "You asked me who I was, and that is not the same thing."

"Well then, you may tell me either one."

"I may, but I don't choose to do so." The man spoke with a thick accent. Leena thought it might be Irish.

"Why are you following me? Will you tell me that?"

"I am following you to remind you who you are, Leena Zhen. It seems you have forgotten."

"What does that mean?" she responded forcefully, beginning to get agitated by this discourse.

"I know you think you are helping, but you aren't. What you seek will not find down the road you are currently on."

"Leena!" someone behind her shouted.

Leena turned her head to see two senators entering the small van and waving for her to join them. She signaled to them, acknowledging their request.

Leena turned back to the man at the tree, but he was gone. She looked around the tree but did not find him hiding. As it was an open parking lot with only a few patches of grass and benches, she was not sure how he could vanish. She looked feverishly as one of the senators called her again.

Walking back toward the van, she looked back and forth across the extensive area. She thought she could see the silhouette of the man walking toward a wooded area. She did not know who this man was or what his odd behavior had to do with her, but something about the man intrigued her. Like she knew him or had met him before. She was certain that if she did, she would remember. It was a mystery that would have to wait to be solved as she was under a time constraint.

Leena greeted the senators, who were both thoughtful enough to comment on her new attire, and after a quick sweep of the outside of the van, she boarded it with the others. She took a seat close to the front so she could be ready for any action that might require her to exit the vehicle.

The trip to the Aberjay capital would only take an hour. Leena grew nervous as they approached the north gate leading into Zone 7. She had not been into the zone since breaking into the pharmacy two years earlier. She reached into her pocket and grasped the permit the commander had given her. Placing the permit with its blue lanyard over her cap and around her neck made her feel a little better as they passed their side of the gate. It grew dark as they entered the tunnel. She knew the next test was imminent.

The van stopped as CPU soldiers signaled to the driver to open the door. When he did, a soldier entered, dressed in the familiar dark-navy jumpsuit with a thick black utility belt and a shiny black helmet that also served as a communication device.

Leena was not sure of the protocol but felt that because she was providing security, she should show a sign of being in control. She stood to her feet and stepped into the aisle to meet the guard, blocking him from moving closer to the senators. The soldier paused and looked Leena up and down.

"Identification?" he said.

Leena grabbed her permit and, without removing it from her neck, lifted it to the soldier's eye level. The guard reached down to retrieve a scanner fixed to his belt. He scanned the back of the badge while looking down at the screen.

"Purpose of your visit to Zone 7?"

"We are here to attend the congressional session," Leena said with an obvious shakiness in her voice.

"I need to scan their badges as well," the soldier commanded.

Leena stood her ground, turned slightly, and put out her hand to signal to the senators the need for their passes. Both senators complied and passed them forward.

"Everything is in order," the soldier said after scanning the passes. "You may proceed."

Leena sighed deeply as he turned and stepped out of the van. After closing the doors, the driver drove forward into the sunlight of Zone 7. Leena was conscious of her sweating as she slunk back into her seat. Despite having every reason to feel inferior to the Aberjay, she despised herself for doing so. In her mind, their place of birth or family did not give them superiority over others. Respect should be given, not taken.

The driver drove the van down a large street surrounded by bright, multicolored buildings. Leena had never been in Zone 7 legally, so could not help but do some sightseeing. She moved close to the window as the van passed through the residential area and then into a commercial area filled with shoppers.

Advertising was a stark contrast to her home zone. In Zone 7, everything with a flat surface had some sort of billboard or advertising slogan. The businesses paid for roads and bridges by branding them with their own logos and slogans. This lightened the tax load on the citizens. While effective, Leena felt the constant barrage of offers in every direction a bit overwhelming.

Leena also noticed that every store was open, offering so many goods and services: a dry cleaner, a nail shop, a cigar store, and many others. There seemed to be a coffee shop on just about every corner. The shops were full of consumers, and the streets were teeming with pedestrians.

Everyone had money in Zone 7. They lived their lives thinking of the next pleasure, in notable contrast to the Miniyar, who thought of only their next meal and how to otherwise survive. The coffee shops and restaurants had outdoor seating, and most of the tables were full of citizens enjoying their coffee and breakfasts.

Mechanically Intelligent Robotic Operators (MIRO) moved through the streets independently. The newest versions were almost lifelike, with organic matter covering the aluminum alloy construction. They were not unique as they all looked identical except for a number on their left shoulders that identified their owners. The MIRO did the shopping, cooked meals, cleaned houses, delivered goods—just about any job a human could do, Zone 7 used a MIRO to accomplish. They had trouble with critical thinking, so humans were still needed in some roles, but each software release brought them closer to matching human thought processes.

The MIRO were outlawed in Zone 6, so the sight of them running around town was odd to Leena. The argument for the Miniyar banning them was that robotic intelligence could not be trusted, but the real reason was likely financial. MIRO were expensive, and the Miniyar had no chance of affording one, much less an army of them, to do chores.

Leena felt angst looking at how the Aberjay lived. She yearned for the stability and luxury they enjoyed but recognized paradoxical feeling of dread and betrayal for desiring it. Most of the folks she knew had little. She didn't understand how there could be so much excess on this side of the wall while the residents on the other side starved. *Why is wealth concentrated here? Is there not enough food and work to go around?*

The van passed a high school where young adults were congregating outside. The size and cleanliness of their school amazed Leena. Her school was lucky to have books and never had the luxury of cleanliness. Rats and roaches crawling across her classrooms were a common occurrence. She recalled mischievous boys capturing the roaches and putting them down the girls' shirts to watch them scream and squirm.

In front of the high school was a line of yellow buses that brought the students to the school. The bright color of the buses was pleasant and seemed fitting to the learning environment. The Aberjay certainly loved their colors and contrasts: black and white, yellow and blue. It seemed they color-coded everything. Leena's world was mostly gray.

As the van turned onto a highway, Leena could not help but compare the clean roads to the streets of her zone that looked more like a war zone. These streets were free of any obstacles and surrounded by bright green grass on all sides. The overpasses were free of graffiti, and fences on each one prevented anyone from dropping objects onto the highway.

She noticed the tall video poles at just about every block. To someone who did not know what they were, it would just seem like a pole sticking up out of the ground or hanging off a building, but Leena knew they were cameras. The Aberjay used cameras everywhere. With the help of sophisticated software, they could reduce crime through predictive science and artificial intelligence. In Zone 7, a person could be arrested hours or days after an offense because they were captured on video. They had eliminated due process for the prosecution of crimes caught on camera as the technology used provided multiple angles and high-resolution photography, and correlated with the identification technology present in the bracelet everyone wore to almost eliminate the possibility of punishing the wrong person. The system was something like 99.8 percent accurate, and for the Aberjay, that was good enough to abandon lengthy and costly trials that just backed up the justice system.

The Miniyar could not afford cameras even if they wanted them but always stood firmly against the idea because of privacy concerns. They read the American Constitution a little differently from the Aberjay, who were more than willing to give up freedom for security.

Leena always thought it was odd that they had cameras everywhere but let anyone carry a firearm. Guns were illegal in Zone 6. If the Aberjay wanted to eliminate crime, why would they put so many guns on the street? It seemed backward to her. She didn't get it.

The van pulled into the parking lot of the Congressional Building. It was larger than the Capitol building in Zone 6 and was very suburban. It seemed the entire building was surrounded by open fields of green grass and park benches connected by winding sidewalks that meandered through the property. The building itself was huge, with a large dome roof and a tall spire. A cross was fixed to the top, some relic of an old religion the Aberjay claimed to follow in their lawmaking.

There were several floors and probably hundreds of offices. The entire building was white stone, possibly marble. It shone brilliantly as the sun, now high in the sky, clothed it in rays. Hundreds of people, dressed mostly in suits, were hurrying about the grounds. They talked in groups, sat at tables and benches, or were individually rushing to a meeting or some other important event. Leena had never seen this much activity or a government building of this size before; it was quite impressive.

The van came to a stop in a parking lot. The doors opened, and Leena exited the vehicle to survey their location as the driver of the van waved the senators toward the exit.

"I will deliver your luggage to the apartment down the street and come back to pick you up in a week. Just leave word with Tilda when you're ready, and I'll be here."

The senators thanked the driver, and he continued on his way. As he pulled away from the parking lot, the enormity of the Capitol beckoned, and Leena led the way toward the hundreds of stairs that led to the entrance.

It did not take long before Leena felt the stares of those committed to figuring out who she was and why she was there. It could not have been a pleasant picture, she thought. She was a small Chinese woman in an army outfit that did not match their CPU. All eyes were on her as she escorted the senators up the stairs and into the Capitol rotunda. Once through the doors, they were in a round room with a high ceiling. Paintings and what looked like important documents hung on the walls of white marble, drawing everyone's attention. The tiles of the floor formed a large star, and red, white, and blue American flags hung on flagpoles throughout the Capitol.

Leena was not sure where to go, but the senators had been here before and quickly took over navigation. They walked up the stairs to the second floor and stopped at a bench across from two large doors.

"The meetings will be in there each day," Senator Chin said, pointing to the two closed doors. "We appreciate you accompanying us to the sessions, but unfortunately, they are closed, so you will not be allowed into the room."

"That's fine," Leena said.

"The days are long, but we will need an escort to our sleeping quarters each night and an escort back to the session each day. Other than that, you are free to roam where you would like."

"Wow, really?" Leena asked as if she had won a prize. "Where should I go? Is it safe?"

"I would imagine you are safer here than you have ever been at home. If you follow the sidewalk across the park, it leads to a long street of stores and shops. You might find it enjoyable to just look around or get something to eat." The senator then immediately turned to greet someone and started a conversation.

Leena turned to Senator Lansom. "I think I will find the apartments and survey the security, then I'll check out one of their cafes to get some tea."

"Okay, Lieutenant, enjoy yourself. We are off to fight the good fight."

Once the Senators entered the congressional house chamber, Leena found her way outside to a bench and sat down to explore the materials she had received prior to the trip. A map of the surrounding area provided the location of the apartments where they would sleep, along with restaurants, coffee shops, and a pharmacy.

Leena sat on the bench for some time, studying the map and trying to determine what she would do for the eight-plus hours she had to wait for the senators. She had her face in the map when a voice called out.

"Leena?"

She pulled her face away from the map and looked up to see a familiar face. Panic coursed through her body as she realized who it was, and her emotional state quickly turned to anger and resentment.

"Vincent Ryder, what are you doing here?"

Vincent approached with an enormous smile. He had grown older since she had last seen him. He wore a suit and had his hair cut short. Vincent was always good-looking, but now he had the markings of a man, with fine clothing, the smell of cologne, and faint evidence of a shadow beard.

"It's good to see you. You look fantastic!" Vincent said as he sat next to her on the bench.

Leena had met Vincent on a field trip to Zone 7 when she was a teenager. They kept in touch and almost had a love affair. He gave her a place to hide when she broke into the pharmacy a couple of years before but betrayed her by turning her in to the authorities to save his own hide.

"I am still quite upset with you, Vincent," Leena said sternly.

"I know; I don't blame you. I was wrong. I admit I was wrong. I hope you will find a way to forgive me."

"You betrayed me, Vincent! You could have sent me to jail for life! Did you not think about what might happen to me when you turned me in?" Leena continued.

"I wasn't thinking. I was terrified of being caught helping you and ending up in jail. My parents would have lost their minds, and I would have blown any opportunity for a life. But it all worked out, right? Here you are, and you are doing fine."

"Vincent, I went to jail. It was a nightmare."

"How long were you in there?" Vincent asked.

"It was about a month, but that's not the point."

"See, so you beat the rap. Good for you. No harm no foul, right?" Vincent said dismissively.

Leena's fury boiled within her. It was everything she could do not to punch him in the face. *What a stupid boy*, she thought. After several minutes of silence, she calmed down and tried to be civil.

"What are you doing here? Do you work here?"

"Yes. Remember the internship I spoke to you about? My dad pulled some strings and got me in. I interned for Senator Rollins for about a year, and he hired me on his staff right after that."

"So, you're a politician?" Leena asked.

"No, I just work for one. But maybe someday. Senator Rollins is a great mentor. He's also the CEO of Giant Core, a big developer here in the zone. I have learned a lot from him already."

"What exactly do you do for him?"

"I keep his schedule, write up briefs, meet with constituents. Whatever he needs." Vincent reached into his pocket and retrieved two pieces of pink chewing gum, unwrapping the first and placing it in his mouth as he handed the other one to Leena.

"Thank you," Leena said with a minimal level of civility as she unwrapped the gum and stuck it in her mouth.

"What are you doing here? And what's with this stellar uniform?" Vincent asked.

"I'm a People's Army lieutenant. I'm a liaison between the army and the governor."

"Really? Governor Reynolds?"

"No, Governor Hamrick," Leena said.

"Governor Hamrick? He isn't really a governor," Vincent said.

"Of course he is. He's our governor."

Vincent smirked and turned away before continuing. "He is a puppet put in place to make people think they have power. He takes orders from Senator Rollins and Governor Reynolds."

"No, he doesn't," Leena said, getting angry.

"Yes, he does. I know because I set up the calls."

"That doesn't make any sense. We just had an election," Leena said.

"Just forget I said anything. I don't want to get anyone in trouble," Vincent said, trying to dismiss the uncomfortable conversation.

"I think you are mistaken," Leena said.

"Okay," Vincent said, feigning agreement. "Well, anyway, it was good to see you. You look great. Maybe I will see you around this week and we can get lunch or something."

"I'm not sure about lunch, but maybe I will see you around."

"Okay, bye," Vincent said as he headed toward the Capitol stairs and made his way inside the building.

What the heck does he know? she wondered. *The Aberjay cannot rig an election, can they?* Leena collected her map and other personal items before walking down the sidewalk toward the apartments. *Vincent must be out of his mind.*

Leena arrived at the apartment block shortly before eleven a.m. They looked like multiple large rectangles connected in a hodgepodge fashion, all painted different colors: bright blue, bright red, bright yellow. It was a quad of four apartments per structure and probably sixteen in total.

As Leena approached, a CPU guard was standing outside who noticed her.

"Can I help you find something, ma'am?" the soldier asked.

"It's Lieutenant," Leena said with slight sarcasm.

"Yes, Lieutenant, can I help you find something?"

"I'm providing security for Senator Lansom and Senator Chin. I'm looking for their quarters as well as my own."

"Yes, Lieutenant. I was assigned to this post to make sure you found your way." The soldier turned and walked toward one of the apartment entrances and then turned back toward Leena. "This is your accommodation. Theirs are over there," he said as he pointed toward the yellow door and the red door across a small courtyard from where they were standing.

"Do you have keys, soldier?" Leena asked.

"No, ma'am. I mean, no, Lieutenant. The doors are coded to your bracelet. Just swipe to enter."

Leena ran her bracelet across the contact of the door, only half-believing it would work because her bracelet was not like the others that were implanted. The door made a clicking noise, and a green light came on to indicate it was unlocked. Leena turned the handle and opened the door before looking back at the soldier.

"I will be out here all night, so just come get me if you need me, Lieutenant."

"Thank you," Leena said, a little shocked at the service. She had always seen the CPU as the enemy, so this exchange was surreal. She wondered secretly if the hospitality was only a ruse to ensure the CPU could keep track of their enemy.

Leena entered the apartment and closed the door behind her. It was small, with a living area that included a sofa and chair, along with a coffee table and a TV wall. She noticed a doorway leading to a kitchen area where someone had stocked the counter and shelves with various cereals and canned goods, and the refrigerator was full of fruits, vegetables that looked freshly picked, and beverages. A selection of salted meats and cheeses were on a lower shelf.

Across the living room was another door. She investigated and found it led to a bedroom with an enormous king bed. Her bag was waiting for her next to the bed, and all of her clothes had been removed from her luggage and placed neatly on the bed. She didn't know whether to be pleased by the customer service or offended by the lack of privacy.

She quickly forgot about the privacy issue as she looked into the ultra-white bathroom with a beautifully tiled shower and inviting claw-foot tub. Next to the tub was a selection of soaps, shampoos, bubble bath additives, and salts. Her heart leaped in her chest as she thought about the bath she would take later. She tried her best but couldn't remember ever taking a bath in her life. She knew her mom washed her in a bathtub when she was young, but she did not recall the experience. And it certainly did not include bath salts.

Leena ran her hands along the marble countertops and then the porcelain tub. It was clean. She had never felt surfaces so clean before. Her bathroom at home didn't have a tub, just a shower, and the tiles were probably fifty years old, filled with dirty grout and years of abuse. She had experienced nothing like this in her entire life.

Leena feared changing anything and messing up the beautiful space. She walked back to the front door and hastily exited the most beautiful living space she had ever seen.

"Soldier, what is your name?" Leena asked the guard.

"Private Michael Miller," he responded.

"Private, does my bracelet open the senators' rooms so I can do a security sweep and check that their luggage arrived?"

"I can assure you they are secure, and their luggage has been delivered, but yes, your bracelet will allow you to access their rooms. It's protocol for security to have full access."

Leena entered the other two apartments with a swipe of her wrist and found they were identical to hers. She confirmed that the windows were secure, and their bags were next to the bed, just as hers had been. She took a moment to enjoy a fresh banana before exiting.

"Thank you, Private," Leena said as she walked past him on the path heading back toward the Capitol.

Leena walked down the sidewalk that led to the Capitol but took a left before reaching the main area. According to her map, this led to the stores that Senator Lansom had mentioned, and even after the banana, Leena's stomach was growling.

The path led over a small hill and connected directly to a street lined with stores in both directions. A sidewalk on both sides was filled with pedestrians as far as she could see. Hundreds of people were out, walking the path, sitting at tables outside cafés, or moving in and out of the buildings. It was such a contrast to the Miniyar shopping areas to not only see many people but to see them clean and well-dressed. Their attire was so attractive that they almost shone in the sunlight. Bright summer dresses and shiny shoes filled these streets.

Leena had no idea where she might want to eat, so she began walking. She got many looks but tried to hold her head up, knowing she looked good in the outfit. Leena knew their concern was likely her race, not her uniform. While there are many Chinese in Zone 6, Zone 7 had a small percentage.

She passed a bicycle shop and stopped briefly to look in the window at the impressive selection of electric bikes. Leena had a bike when she was young but it was from a thrift store, had considerable rust, and a chain that broke frequently. It was nothing like these bikes she was seeing through the window. They were shiny and bright.

She moved on from the bike shop but could have stayed there all day. A few stores later, she reached a sandwich shop and decided it was less crowded than the others. She entered, and a bell rang as the door closed behind her. The inside was bright and decorated in reds and whites. More than ten café tables were set inside with a small path between them to the counter. She made her way to the counter as a teenager of about fourteen stepped toward the register.

"What can I get you?" the teen asked.

"What do you have?" Leena asked awkwardly, unsure of how the process worked.

The teenage girl handed her an electronic tablet with a menu of items. Leena had never seen such a selection. In her zone, the few restaurants had two, maybe three options, but that was it. This menu had more than fifty items to choose from, each with a detailed description of the food and how it was prepared. *This could take a while,* she thought.

The cashier sensed it was overwhelming and recommended a few options. "The chicken salad is good today, and so is the cucumber sandwich."

"Do you have anything with bacon?" Leena asked.

"A BLT? Sure. Anything else?"

"Do you have tea?"

"Yes, hot or cold?" the girl replied.

"Hot, please," Leena said as she handed the tablet back to the girl.

Leena swiped her bracelet, again only half-believing it would work here, but to her surprise, it made the familiar beep and completed the transaction. She walked outside and sat at one of the outside tables so she could people-watch. The café filled up as more people came in to order. Within a few minutes, the girl delivered her sandwich, and she enjoyed her lunch.

As she ate, she noticed a well-dressed Chinese man across the street. He seemed to be looking in her direction. His suit was pinstriped and looked expensive, and he wore sunglasses. He was short and a little heavy. He sauntered across the street and seemed to head straight for Leena's table. As he approached, he gave a subtle bow.

"May I join you?" the man asked.

Leena looked around, trying to determine if he knew her or if he was just asking to share the table. The outside tables were not all occupied, so his inquiry confused her.

"I suppose so. Do I know you?" Leena asked.

"We have not had the pleasure of meeting, but I do know you, Leena Zhen. I have had an eye on you for a while."

"Is that so? Who are you?" Leena said, feeling nervous.

The stranger picked up on her nervousness and crossed his legs, leaning back at the table to use his posture to attempt to disarm her.

"Calm your nerves, Ms. Zhen, you are quite safe. My name is Feng Lao. I am the Chinese Ambassador to the United States."

Leena took a last bite of her sandwich and chewed slowly, waiting for more, but Ambassador Lao stayed silent.

"How do you know me, Mr. Lao?" Leena asked.

"It is my business to know things. I know your senators as well. I know you work for Governor Hamrick. I know your husband is Jordan Lin. I know your mom died a couple of years ago." Feng removed his sunglasses and placed them gently on the table before continuing. "I think we have a lot in common, Ms. Zhen."

"Because we are both Chinese?" Leena asked with some sarcasm.

"There are many commonalities. We are both Chinese, of course. We both lost our mothers to a dreadful disease. We both love our families. And we both want what is best for our society."

"That is pretty weak," Leena said. "Most people want what is best for society."

"See? There is an optimist viewpoint we also share."

"Mr. Lao, why do I feel like you are about to sell me a box of treasures?" Leena asked.

Feng chuckled. "I enjoy your sense of humor, Ms. Zhen. No, I am not here to sell you anything. I am here for the congressional sessions, just like you. I just thought that since we both have so much in common, we should get to know one another. You cannot have too many friends in this world, can you?"

"I suppose not, but aren't your soldiers currently marching on American soil? Doesn't that make you the enemy?" Leena said honestly.

"Do you know what is so sad about the one-eyed frog, Ms. Zhen?"

Leena paused, wondering what that had to do with anything they were discussing. His banter did remind her of Diego though. Her grandfather would often go off in another direction to tell a story or prove a point through parables or metaphors.

"No sir, what is so sad about the one-eyed frog?"

"He has no perspective. He can only see things one way. But we humans can get up from our chairs and see things from a different perspective. You may have been told we are moving some troops here or there, but from our perspective, we are liberating your people from centuries of oppression. Everyone values freedom, do they not?"

"You are offering them freedom?"

"Why yes, Ms. Zhen, that is all that we offer. Freedom from this corrupt system of haves and have-nots. Freedom to thrive instead of just surviving. Freedom to pursue what you are passionate about instead of just clawing your way through life, surviving on crumbs from a rich man's table. America makes everything about power and control, but that isn't who we are. Chinese citizens cherish their government. They live fruitful lives, have hobbies, watch their families grow without fear of starvation. In China, everyone has a job. No one is greater than anyone else. We all work for each other."

"The Miniyar are similar," Leena said, defending her people.

"Yes, I know," Feng responded. "Another commonality."

Leena put her cap on her head, preparing to leave. Feng Lao stood and put his sunglasses back on.

"Ms. Zhen, it was a pleasure to meet you. I do hope we meet again soon. Maybe we can find a way to help each other one day."

"Thank you. It was nice to meet you as well, Ambassador," Leena said sincerely as Feng turned and walked away.

Leena was not sure what that was all about. Politics was new to her, and she was just learning to navigate those waters. What she had learned was that every person has an agenda, and nothing happens by coincidence.

Chapter 5

POLITICS

L eena woke early, as she had the previous few mornings. It was Thursday, and the congressional session would continue through Friday, after which their driver would pick them up to return them to their world. She sat in her room enjoying a delicious cup of coffee. Leena was not normally a coffee drinker, but the provided ground beans were especially tasty. She wondered if the reason she grew fond of tea was the lack of good coffee in Zone 6 her entire life. Or maybe she just missed her husband, who always preferred coffee to tea.

She had enjoyed her stay in Zone 7 but felt guilty at the same time. The luxuries available to her over the previous few days were trivial to most Aberjay, part of their everyday life, but represented a quality of life that most Miniyar would never see in their lifetime. The soap, the clean water, the soft bed sheets, and the room free of insects and unpleasant odors were all strange and surreal experiences.

The luxury made her want to run back home and tell everyone how things could be. Only she knew the next question would be 'how,' and she had yet to figure that one out. She knew it had to do with education and jobs. Most Aberjay were highly educated and had a good income, allowing them to grow wealth and afford the nicer things in life. *But was that it? Was that the only differentiator?*

While an occasional Miniyar was accepted to a good school, it was rare. After years of applying and always being denied, most parents didn't even encourage their children to apply for entry as they knew it would not happen. And even if it did, college was expensive. Leena had read stories of a time in history when scholarships were common, and anyone could go to school who wanted to do so. *Where did the scholarships go?*

Leena finished the last sip of coffee and set the cup on the credenza. She knew housecleaning would be in the room shortly to provide clean mugs and make her bed, which made her feel quite uncomfortable, but she didn't know why. Having someone clean up after her just didn't sit right with her. Putting on her cap and checking her uniform in the mirror, she did a final check of her weapon and, after holstering it, made her way outside to meet the senators.

Senator Lansom was the first to meet Leena by the sidewalk. Private Miller had been relieved by another CPU soldier who was less friendly. He stood about twenty feet away wearing a slight smirk. Leena nodded in his direction to acknowledge him, but he failed to return the pleasantry. Senator Chin joined them a few minutes later and began the long walk to the Capitol building.

Leena always walked in front of the senators to ensure she could spot any threats that might come at them from the front, but being alone, she also needed to scan the perimeter frequently to ensure their rear was covered as well. There was minimal risk of an incident, but she still felt strongly about doing the job well. Leena kept her mind on the job at hand but could still hear the senators chatter as they walked.

"What do you think we are in for today, Vivian?" Senator Chin asked.

"More of the same, I'm afraid," Senator Lansom replied. "They still refuse to admit they cut off the water. I'm not sure how we will proceed until they do. We can't negotiate if they won't admit to doing it."

"Let's hope Viktor comes up with a solution soon. We may have to forego any help from the Aberjay."

"I agree. I can't imagine it doesn't have to do with money. Everything seems to revolve around money and business for them. If they would just give us a price, we could start a conversation, but it seems they are not selling." Senator Vivian Lansom stopped for a moment to adjust her high-heel shoes that were obviously uncomfortable.

"Did we get the eminent domain reversal approved?" Leena asked, hoping she was phrasing it the right way. "I would love to see stores opening up again in my old neighborhood."

"No, they outvoted us on that one," Senator Chin answered as he leered at Senator Lansom.

"We can bring it up again next session. I will try to make some calls and get some more support for it before they sell off the entire lot," Senator Lansom said.

Something about the interaction between the two senators around the topic brought tension into the air. Leena was not sure why, but she did recall Senator Chin suggesting he make calls to build support for the issue and Senator Lansom told him not to do so. *If this were an issue they both favored, why would Senator Lansom tell him to stand down?*

"They're selling the stores?" Leena inquired.

"Yes," Senator Chin chimed in, "the CPU wants to sell the entire area as one giant package. They say it encourages developers to implement large mixed-use construction, but it really just ensures that only Aberjay will own the property. No one in our zone would be able to afford to buy the entire area."

"Let's hope it doesn't sell before the next session. We can address it again," Senator Lansom said.

"Did you hear the selective service comment?" Senator Chin asked his colleague as they approached the stairs to the congressional building.

"Yes, and I believe it's a topic of discussion for tomorrow. They don't want to drop that bomb on us and give us any time to really discuss it. I'm afraid we are being ambushed," Senator Lansom said.

"What is selective service?" Leena asked. She tried not to get involved in their discussions, but they both made it clear they didn't mind sharing. Leena had the same security clearance level and, although she was only a liaison, they treated her as part of the team.

"It's a draft," Senator Chin began. "There is an old law on the books that allows the federal and local governments to draft young people into the army to serve during times of war. It has not been used since the twentieth century, but the fear of war and a constricted Federal Army may leave them with no choice."

"So, they make regular citizens fight? That seems so..." Leena struggled with the word she was searching for to complete the sentence. "Barbaric?"

"That's not the worst part," Senator Lansom added. "If history is any guide, they draft the young people. Normally ages eighteen to twenty-one."

Leena thought through it and was thankful she was twenty-two and Jordan was twenty-three. She had enough troubles of her own to pack up and go fight a war she knew nothing about.

"A draft can only be ordered if we are at war though, and although there is some risk of conflict with China again, most experts believe their latest moves are just posturing. They have little to gain by attacking America again."

Leena thought about what the ambassador had told her a few days before. She understood from that conversation that they didn't look at conflict as a means to 'get' anything but rather a liberating activity. She had not mentioned the meeting with the ambassador to the senators as it was not official and was only a short conversation that had no political implications that she was aware of. She did plan to tell her commander in her weekly report once she was back on Zone 6 soil.

The senators reached the congressional house chamber and entered without instruction to Leena, so she reasoned that today would be like any other and she had eight hours to kill before she would return for them.

Leena visited a coffee shop she had grown fond of the previous few mornings and had another cup of coffee along with a croissant, a delicacy that wasn't available in her zone due to the lack of real butter. Vegan butter just doesn't work as well in pastries.

Upon finishing her breakfast, she walked down the street to visit a bookstore. She had spent many hours there waiting for the senators. The two-story store was full of dark-wood floors, walls, and ceilings, giving the space a very studious look. She loved the smell of the air as she entered. It was a fragrance of musty books and lemon polish that was used on the wood tables and chairs that filled the place.

She read once that the world was filled with public libraries, where a person could check out any book they liked and return it when they wanted, all free of cost. She wondered why anyone would ever do away with something so ingenious and vital to the community. Leena didn't understand many of the things the Aberjay did.

This store allowed you to sit and read if you purchased the book. Otherwise, they charged a reading fee to read any book. Leena spent almost the entire first day just trying to decide which book to purchase as she wanted a memento and something she could share with Jordan. Books were not cheap, and although any of them might cost an entire day's wages, she felt that Jordan would approve the purchase.

Leena walked to the back of the store, where she felt the light was the best, and sat down, pulling the book she had purchased several days before out of her backpack. It was a history book focused on the twenty-first century. History fascinated Leena. She enjoyed learning how things used to be.

She learned that in the previous century America, many decisions and responsibilities were handled at the federal level rather than at a local level. Citizens used to vote for representatives to be their voice in a national congress. Those representatives would then vote on laws based on the best interests of their constituents. According to the author of the book, the system was replaced when businesses were allowed to vote. The weight of their vote was determined by their contributions to pay down the national debt. The largest corporations came together and put their people in the seats of power. A short time later, they simplified Congress to lower costs by having a group of fifty people—one from each state, replacing both houses of Congress—do all the voting.

This new Congress, made up of business professionals from the largest corporations in America, sought to further reduce taxes and government spending. They stripped the budget down to a handful of administrative costs and military spending, pushing the remaining concerns down to each state. The National Park Service, the Food and Drug Administration, the Social Security Administration, and many others Leena had never heard of were casualties of these new policies to cut costs. Even the military took some large hits to their budget.

Once China invaded the West Coast years later, the army that remained had little chance of defeating the Chinese war machine, which had grown to more than twenty million troops. They halted the conflict with an armistice that ceded land to the Chinese, which included California, Oregon, Washington, Nevada, and parts of Arizona.

According to the book, many believed the Chinese only agreed to the armistice to buy time to build troop counts and plan another assault, but it never materialized. No one knows why that didn't happen. It was only a theory. Both sides had lived in relative peace since the end of the war in the late twenty-first century.

Leena studied her precious book for a few more hours before packing up and heading to lunch. She had tried several restaurants as there were many to choose from in that neighborhood. On this day, she planned to eat pizza, but the pizzeria was on the far north end of the street and would be about a one-mile walk. It was a clear day, so she decided it would be worth it.

Leena walked for about twenty minutes, passing store after store, all open for business. She crossed a small bridge that covered a creek and then ascended a steep incline. She could feel the pain in her calves as she walked up the hill with her backpack pushing down on her. As she made it near the top, the land leveled off and she could see across a large parking lot to a small shop with the image of a pizza on top.

She had heard about the pizza spot from Private Miller, who had conversed with her almost every day she had been there. The unexpectedly friendly CPU soldier told her about all the nice places, including the bookstore and the coffee shop that she had grown to love.

Crossing the parking lot, Leena could see many cars and about thirty motorcycles. On and around the bikes were rough-looking characters, all men, all dressed in denim pants and leather vests. Many wore blue headscarves. The motorcycles were impossible to go around, so she was forced to walk through them to get to the door of the pizzeria.

As she approached, several of the guys noticed her and stepped off their bikes, pointing at her and signaling to their friends. As she drew closer to the group, they formed a wall of bodies that was impassable.

"Look at this," one of them said.

"We found a China girl," another called out.

Leena stopped about eight feet from the wall of men and placed her right hand on her firearm. As she did, she could see several in the group reach into the inside pockets of their jackets or inside their saddlebags to pull out firearms of their own. She did not want a conflict and felt she should turn and walk the other way, but at that point, she was certain they would follow.

"Can I please get by?" Leena said to the bikers.

"No ma'am," the larger of the group said, clearly the leader based on his posture and the way the others gathered behind him. "You have to pay the toll, little girl."

"And what would that be?" Leena replied.

"Just a little kiss, China girl." The men laughed in support of their leader's verbal condescension.

"That won't be happening. I suggest you move out of my way or there will be trouble," Leena said with confidence, hoping it would earn her a little respect.

"Why don't you go back to where you came from, China girl? We don't want your tea and chopsticks here," the leader responded.

Leena turned to walk back to where she came from, hoping to de-escalate the situation, but as she walked away, she could hear footsteps behind her that indicated they were not going to let her go that easily.

She managed to get her hand on her baton and removed it from the sheath as someone took hold of her backpack and threw her sideways so fiercely that her feet left the ground. She was slammed into the side of a car. She felt pain in her left shoulder and a rib that took the brunt of the impact with the car. She lay on her belly with the baton in her hand and quickly went through her options.

Leena stood and extended her baton with a quick throw of her wrist as two bikers reached for her. She easily landed a blow to the first one's head and threw her body against the second to push him back. She then spun the baton as she arose, landing a strike against the man's groin area. She took a third one down with a strike to his ribcage and a knee to his head, but the fourth attacker was too much for her, and within seconds she was being held above the ground in a bear hug and was thrown onto the hood of a parked car. Leena cried out in pain as three more men surrounded her, some bleeding from her attacks, and constrained her arms and legs.

"I am going to teach you a lesson, China girl," one biker said as he repeatedly landed his fist on Leena's stomach, further injuring her ribs. Getting a hand free, she reached for her firearm, but it was not there.

Then she heard a shot. It startled the bikers as they turned to see the pizzeria owner in an apron with a short shotgun that he had fired into the air.

"Dammit, Lenny," the shop owner shouted, "leave that poor girl alone!"

"This bitch just attacked us, John," the lead biker said in defense.

As they were talking, a CPU truck entered the parking lot with blue lights flashing. The truck pulled close to where they were, and several armed CPU soldiers exited.

"What is going on here?" the CPU soldier asked, addressing the owner.

"These fellas are having a bit too much fun, I would say," said the shop owner.

The soldier walked over to the biker leader as his buddies loosened their grip on Leena.

"What is going on here, Lenny?" the soldier asked again, now addressing the leader.

'Lenny?' Are these guys old friends?

"A Chinese invasion, officer! We saw this China girl come running at us with a weapon. We had to defend ourselves," Lenny said.

The soldier walked over to Leena and helped her off the hood of the vehicle. He sternly grabbed her arm and walked her back to the CPU truck, where another soldier took hold of her. The soldier turned back to Lenny.

"Thirty to one, Lenny? You must have been terrified," he said with sarcasm.

"She had a gun, Jimmy," Lenny said.

"Let me have it," the soldier said as one biker produced it and handed it over. "Stay here while I question the terrorist."

The soldier walked back to Leena. The shop owner went back into his establishment, seeing that the issue was under control.

"Ma'am, can I see some identification?"

Leena handed over her pass, which was still hanging from her neck. He scanned it with his handheld device.

"You are People's Army?" the soldier questioned.

"Yes, Lieutenant Leena Zhen."

"Were you razzing these guys as they said?"

"No sir, I was just trying to get a slice of pizza, but they would not let me enter. I tried to walk away to avoid conflict, but they jumped me."

"Okay, these credentials check out. Here is your firearm," he said as he handed her the weapon. "You are free to go, but I would try to avoid these guys in the future. They don't have much love for those who don't look like them. You should eat elsewhere today."

Leena walked sheepishly toward the men in leather as they stiffened up. She located her baton on the ground and retrieved it, placing it in her belt sheath. She managed a vindictive look as she turned to walk from the parking lot.

"Jimmy, you're going to let her go?" Lenny shouted. "She attacked us. You're not going to arrest her?"

"She has diplomatic immunity, Lenny; she's an American for God's sake. How about you guys stay out of trouble for once?"

Leena walked briskly toward the street as the grumbling of her enemies subsided. She hurt terribly around her ribcage but did not want to give them the satisfaction of seeing her limp away, so she swallowed the pain and made her way down the hill to what she now learned was the safer side of the neighborhood.

The gang of bikers who attacked her didn't seem like the kind of people who would live in the zone. She thought they were more of a fit for Zone 6 than 7. Even though they seemed out of place based on their dress, their violence and intolerant attitudes made them Aberjay to her. They looked down on her because of her race. This type of discrimination was not common in Zone 6.

Leena returned to the sandwich shop where she had first dined earlier in the week. She ordered another BLT and sat outside.

Within moments, her food arrived, and she savored the familiar bacon flavor. Every bite reminded her of Jesse and his Uncle Bill, her Tullian friends who raised cows, pigs, and chickens on their farm down south. She wondered often how he was doing and what their life was like compared to hers. She would visit, but the trip south was perilous without a large armed escort. There were so many raiders and cannibals living in the Tullian lands that any travel through there without a heavily armed contingent would be quite mad.

As she enjoyed her sandwich, only slightly aware of her surroundings as she daydreamed of the farm, a familiar man stood in front of her.

"Lieutenant, how are you on this fine day?"

Leena looked up to greet the ambassador once again. With a slight grin, she replied, "I am doing well, Ambassador. How about yourself?"

"I am also well," he said as he gestured to the chair in front of her, pulling it out and sitting before she could even gesture approval. "I am glad I could see you again. We had a friendly chat the other day. I was looking forward to continuing our conversation and learning more about you."

"Forgive me if I find that hard to believe, Ambassador."

"Why is that? I have many friends and always enjoy getting to know them."

"Is that what we are—friends?" Leena asked, still holding the grin on her face.

"We are friends if you want to be friends, Lieutenant. I can assure you that you don't want me as an enemy," the ambassador said without smiling.

They sat in silence for a few moments as Leena continued to eat her sandwich.

The ambassador smiled once again and broke the silence. "This is nice, isn't it? Sitting outside on this fine day, eating high-quality food, spending time with friends. Are you enjoying your visit to Zone 7?"

"Yes, it has been nice. It's different from where I live."

"Yes, I imagine so. I do plan to visit your home soon. Now that the Aberjay has given you control of your zone, I need to visit your new governor. Hamrick, is it?"

"Yes," Leena replied.

"Lieutenant, have you thought any more about our conversation the other day? About our commonalities?"

"Yes, I see some commonalities. But I am not a communist," Leena said.

"Labels, labels. Everyone gets caught up on labels. Your government has vilified the communists for over a century. Why? Because we believe in community? Because we believe that one person is not greater than the whole? Because we are not selfish and live our lives for each other rather than for ourselves? Yes, we are monsters indeed!"

"I think it's more complicated than that," Leena said quietly, knowing she did not have the political acumen to have this conversation.

"Is it though? Or is it possible the Americans are terrified that if we infect your people with our communal ideas, they will give up their selfish drive for monetary gain and topple the oligarchy?"

Ambassador Feng Lao waited for a response but did not get one, so he continued.

"No one knows if war is to come, Lieutenant. But if it does, I would like to think that your people will consider their commonalities with my people."

"You want us to fight with you against the Americans?" Leena questioned. "We are as American as they are, you know."

"No, no, we would never conceive of that. Your army is larger than federal troops in this area or the CPU. We would like you to stand down. Refuse to fight for a system and a people who don't treat you with respect." The ambassador motioned toward his surroundings. "Do your neighborhoods look like this? Do your children go to the same schools or graduate from the same colleges? Where do the jobs go? To your people?"

The ambassador was pushing all the right buttons. Leena knew this was an attempt to manipulate her. She was also thankful at that moment that the decision was not hers to make as Ambassador Feng made a compelling argument and was highly persuasive.

Leena finished the last bite of her sandwich and stood to leave. She extended a hand to the Ambassador to show their meeting was over. He reciprocated.

"It was nice to chat with you, Ambassador. Obviously, I cannot make any decision regarding our support during any hypothetical war. And I am obligated to report this conversation to my superiors."

"I understand, Lieutenant, I would expect nothing less. Please enjoy the rest of your stay in Zone 7. I am headed back to Washington but will return soon to visit your governor. Maybe we will see each other again."

"Goodbye," Leena said as she walked toward the safety of the bookstore.

Leena slowly packed her suitcase, preparing to leave what had been her home for the last five days. It was sad as she had enjoyed it very much, but she was looking forward to getting back home. She missed her neighbors, her tea, her home, and most of all, her husband.

She checked all the drawers and the bathroom to ensure she left nothing behind, then zipped the bag closed and turned off the lights.

Leena was pleased to see Private Miller was still on duty.

"I appreciated your hospitality, Private Miller," Leena said, addressing the young man standing near the sidewalk.

"My pleasure, Lieutenant. I do hope you enjoyed your stay."

"Indeed, I did," Leena responded as both senators exited their apartments with bags in hand.

Leena and the senators thanked the private for his service protecting them before the three of them trudged up the hill once again to the Capitol for the last day of meetings. Once inside the building, they dropped their bags off with a valet and made their way to the congressional house chamber. They made plans to meet in the same place later that day for the trip back home.

As the senators walked into the chamber, Leena took a minute to sit on the bench outside. She had taken her history book out of her luggage to ensure she had something to pass the time. Leena clung to the book as she stared at the American flag hanging from a flagpole just outside the chamber. The red, white, and blue brought powerful feelings to her mind. She had always considered herself a patriot. Leena slowly counted the forty-six stars embroidered in bright white that represented the United States of America. She thought about all the history that had taken place in America's three-hundred and seventy years of growth, starting with the Declaration of Independence, the industrial revolution, the wars, the Chinese invasion, and the development of synthetic life forms such as the MIRO.

Leena took a walk outside and found a quiet tree a few hundred feet from the Capitol building where she could sit and read and enjoy the beautiful weather. It was not long before she was interrupted.

"Hi Leena," Vincent Ryder said as he stepped between the sun and the tree, casting a shadow across her face.

Leena looked up and greeted her visitor. "Hello, Vincent."

"May I sit with you?"

"Yes, I am just reading."

Vincent grabbed the book from her hands and gave it a quick perusal. "Looks like some heavy stuff."

"I enjoy reading about history," Leena said as she grabbed it back from his loose grasp, sneering at him to express her consternation.

"I could never get into stuff like that—too boring," Vincent said.

"It's odd for someone working in politics to hate history," Leena shot back.

"I don't hate it; I just hate reading about it. Dates and times and places. It just doesn't excite me. I prefer to be in the action."

"What excites you?" Leena asked sincerely.

"I don't know—being someone important. Doing something great for the world. Making a ton of money."

Leena now remembered how shallow Vincent had always been. She did not see it when she was younger, but as she had become more of a critical thinker, she picked up on his lack of depth.

"How is your family, Vincent?"

"They are good. Dad has had some health trouble, but he is back at the restaurant now. We own three of them now."

"You don't want to run them when your father passes?" Leena asked.

"No, that is way too much work. Even with help from the few MIRO he bought, he still spends twelve hours a day managing them. I want to accomplish more than that—something that will change the world."

"What if changing the world doesn't pay well? What if you have to choose between making money and changing the world for good? Which would you choose?" Leena said.

"I am not sure why I would have to choose, but I'll play along. I think I would probably choose the money. Not because I'm greedy but because with the money, I can still get what I want and help others. You can't give to others if you don't have anything to give, right?"

Leena paused to see if he would offer any more philosophy to justify his decision, but he didn't. He had revealed his true colors.

"What do you think about the Chinese, Vincent?"

"I think they're getting ready to make a move. They've already massed troops on the border. Some say they will be in Salt Lake City before Christmas—oh shit, I probably wasn't supposed to tell you that. I forgot you don't have clearance."

"That really isn't news to me," Leena said, even though she had not heard about the troop movement in any detail. "Why do you think they would want war with America?"

"Because they're greedy and want everyone to think and live like they do. Every step those communist bastards take is a little more freedom taken from our people. They want us all to look the same and act the same. They want to take away our guns and make us slaves to their liberal agenda."

"Their liberal agenda?" Leena asked.

"We spent decades getting rid of stupid liberal ideas like gun control and equal opportunity, big government and gay rights. If the Chinese have their way, our entire way of life will be destroyed."

Leena considered herself a liberal and found his rant contrary to what she believed was moral, but his opinion was consistent with most Aberjay, so she was not shocked by it. Their TV news programs, books, and other media supported those conservative ideals with no room for disagreement. The only alternate opinions were found in the few voices of people who remembered when society was more equitable. Many lived in Zone 6. Now those voices were but a faint whisper. The Aberjay controlled the media, and no one dared speak out against the predominant opinions of those in power.

They talked for another twenty minutes before Vincent's employers summoned him to a meeting. Leena was happy he had been called away. She questioned what she ever saw in him. He lacked substance. His values were certainly not in alignment with her own.

Leena continued to read her book until lunchtime, when she went to eat what would be her last BLT for some time.

Chapter 6

UNREST

The van they were traveling in came to a stop in front of the Capitol building in Zone 6. Leena went to retrieve her duffel and help with the other luggage, but the driver stopped her.

"I'll take care of the bags, Lieutenant," the driver said as he reached to take her duffel from her hand. "You three go about your day. I will bring these up to you and put them in your offices."

The two senators and Leena exited the van without their luggage and made their way up the stairs. About halfway to the front entrance of the Capitol, an explosion behind them threw the three of them to the ground. Smoke and ash filled the air as metal and rubber parts of the van fell to the ground. Leena's ears rang loudly from the blast as she turned onto her back, reeling from the pain of being thrown by the force of the explosion. She attempted to sit up, but pain in her chest and arms, which took the brunt of the fall, made it a challenge. She looked around to determine if anyone was injured. Both senators were trying to stand as they picked pieces of metal and glass out of their hair and clothes. Senator Lansom's head was bleeding slightly from the shrapnel.

Leena looked back at the van, which was in an inferno. Only the undercarriage of the van remained, and a raging fire billowed smoke from the two remaining tires that were melting from the heat. She handed a handkerchief from her pocket to Senator Lansom.

"Put this on the wound and hold it," Leena said as she turned stumbling toward Senator Chin.

"You okay?" she shouted due to the ringing in her ears.

"I'm okay. Go check on the driver," Senator Chin said as he checked his body for injuries.

Leena turned toward the van and got as close as she could in the face of the heat radiating from the destruction. She rounded the front of the van trying to assess what had happened. *Was it an accident that the gas tank of the van exploded?* Leena could not find the driver. He had been unloading the bags next to the van when the explosion occurred, and now all that remained in that area was a dark spot. Blood spatter was visible on the sidewalk, evidence that the driver was likely torn to pieces by the blast. The damage to the van revealed that the explosion came from the side, so it appeared that one of the bags contained explosives.

People's Army soldiers and several members of Liv's team came running down the stairs, weapons drawn, to assess the risk. Leena put up her hand, ordering them to stand down. The team stopped on the stairs as Liv ran by them to reach Leena.

"What happened?" Liv asked Leena.

"I don't know, Liv. It happened so fast. I think the van had a bomb in it."

"What? Who the hell would do that? Why?" Liv searched for answers. "Are you okay? Any injuries?"

"I'm fine. Go check on Senator Lansom. She cut her head."

Leena continued to survey the wreckage and could not get the thought out of her mind that if it had happened a few minutes earlier, they all would have been dead. She looked at her hand, which was shaking. She was in shock. Leena had to figure out who did this. If one of them was the target, there would certainly be more attempts.

Leena walked toward the Capitol building to get some fresh bandages and clean up, leaving Liv in charge of the site until a team from the army could assess the situation and take over the investigation. Maggie met her in the hall outside the restroom.

"Oh goodness, are you okay?" Maggie asked in her quiet, mousy voice.

"I'll heal," Leena said as she limped toward the bathroom entrance.

"I heard the blast; I hope everyone is okay. Do you need anything?"

"Liv has it under control," Leena said as she removed her jacket, which Maggie had made for her. It had several tears in it from the fall to the stairs. "I'm sorry about my uniform."

"Don't worry about that. I will have someone fix it. Let's get you out of those clothes." Maggie helped Leena to the restroom to undress and put on her more comfortable fatigues.

"Who did this, Leena?"

"I don't know, but we need to find out, or none of us are safe."

Leena pulled into the People's Army headquarters and, after parking her Jeep, walked toward the command building. Commander Johnson had summoned her to a meeting. It had been two weeks since the bombing and her visit to Zone 7. Leena had written detailed reports about the terrorist attack, as they were calling it, in addition to her time in Zone 7. The commander could be summoning her to discuss either or both.

Walking into the familiar command room, Leena was shocked to see it was mostly empty. A couple of communications officers were working on the equipment, the only ones in the room besides the commander.

"Reporting as ordered, Commander," Leena said formally while giving a salute.

"At ease, Lieutenant. Please follow me to my office, where we can have some privacy."

The commander led Leena down the hall to a large room in the corner of the building. It had a small couch, two chairs, a round conference table, and on one side, an enormous desk covered with pictures. The walls displayed photos of the commander in his younger years, always in uniform. Based on the photos, he had served in the Federal Army.

"Take a seat," Commander Johnson said as he pointed to the couch. He sat across from Leena in a large leather chair and reached for a pipe resting on a floor-mounted ashtray. He lit the pipe, staring intently at the glowing tobacco before looking back to Leena.

"I heard about the explosion. I do hope you are okay. We have people you can talk to if you need it."

"I'm fine, Commander. It was definitely a close call, but I'm processing it," Leena said.

"Okay, but let me know if I can be of assistance. Incidents like that can be traumatic. Any leads on the source of the bomb?"

"No. Investigators are certain it was in our luggage, but we don't know which bag or when it was placed there. The driver was likely not in on it, or he would have lived. The explosives had to have been added on the last day when the bags were with the valet. But the trail runs cold there because we can't conduct an investigation on Aberjay land."

Leena thought about that day as she relayed the status of the investigation. She had not really thought about it up to that point, but when her bags were with the valet, she was with Vincent under that large oak tree. *Was he a plant? Sent there to distract her or keep her from the valet station?*

"Okay, well, keep me posted if there are any developments."

"Yes sir, will do," Leena replied.

"Also, I read your report on your week in Zone 7, Leena. Excellent work. I am a little concerned about your conversation with the ambassador and wanted the chance to discuss it with you. Can you give me the details of that conversation?"

"Yes, Commander. The ambassador approached me outside a lunch café where I ate most days. He told me who he was and spent significant time trying to convince me how alike the Miniyar were to his people." Leena paused.

"Is there more?"

"Yes, he met me another day and said that if war came, the Chinese would appreciate if we would stand down and not fight with federal troops."

"Wow, the gall of that man. Does he think we will dispense with our patriotism that easily? He must not know Americans very well. Do you think he knew you would report this?"

"Without a doubt. I told him I was under obligation to do so, and he said he expected nothing less," Leena said.

"So, he wanted to get the message to us. What do you think that means?"

"I don't know. Maybe he's planting a seed, hoping our hatred for the Aberjay will make us allies. Will the Chinese attack us, Commander?" Leena asked.

"They *are* massing troops on some borders. They will likely make a push soon, but that would be out west. There has been some tension between us lately, but no one knows what provoked it."

"Who would even make that decision to stand with the Chinese?" Leena asked.

"This is unfamiliar territory for us, but I would say Governor Hamrick would have to make that call—although he would never be elected again if he did." The commander tapped a button on his desk and a young man, unknown to Leena, entered the room. "Corporal Mitchell, please set up a call with CPU Commander Lawrence for later today."

The Corporal typed the request into his tablet and then left the room with a nod.

"Commander Lawrence?" Leena posited.

"Yes, if we're going to go to war, we need to coordinate with the CPU to ensure our troops are ready to ship out. I also want to see if they can provide help with the investigation."

"How many troops can we spare?" Leena asked.

"I think we can spare about twenty percent of our force. Let's hope it does not come to that."

After an awkward pause, the commander continued, "Thank you for your report, Lieutenant. Please share it with the governor's team as soon as possible. You are dismissed."

Leena drove to work with significant anxiety. The weeks since the explosion had her on edge. *Am I the target? How will they strike next?* The questions piled up in her brain, making any thoughts of the future cloudy. She found everything harder to do. Meetings seemed meaningless. Reports were challenging to write. She knew logically that these were symptoms of posttraumatic stress disorder, but she wasn't quite ready to talk about it. A headache had plagued her for weeks since the event, along with nausea and a tension that felt all-encompassing. She even threw up twice in the previous week. The idea of adding the stress of war was enough to push her over the edge.

As she rounded the corner to enter the Capitol grounds, she spotted a large mob. They held signs that were too far away to be legible as she parked her Jeep. As she walked toward the Capitol, she passed the guard gate.

"What is going on, PFC Gibbel?" Leena asked.

The guard snapped to attention when she noticed Leena approaching and gave a quick salute. "They were here early this morning. It seems highly organized. They are protesting the lack of water, I believe."

Leena thanked the soldier and walked toward the Capitol stairs, stopping only to glance at the throngs of protesters. The signs read, 'Water Now' and 'Hands Off Our Water' as well as similar sentiments. Leena surmised that the crowd numbered about two hundred.

Looking past the mob, standing on the grassy area about a hundred feet from the commotion was the red-bearded fellow she kept seeing all over town. She recognized the red hair and beard immediately and tried hard to remember his name, but she wasn't certain she ever knew it. She wanted to engage him but didn't have the time. Turning, she walked into the Capitol building to attend the governor's staff meeting.

Leena had asked for a few minutes of the governor's time from Tilda before the staff meeting and used the time to brief him on her latest report. They discussed several issues, including troop assignments and water station security status, and revisited a report regarding her interaction with the ambassador.

"There is one more thing, Lieutenant," the governor said as they concluded the brief meeting. "The north property is under contract. The CPU sold it to a developer from Zone 7, a company named Giant Core or something like that. I thought you would want to know since it includes the property where you grew up."

"Any idea what they are going to do with it?" Leena asked.

"Homes, I believe. Just another way for the wealthy Aberjay to siphon what little money we have."

"It's a shame we could not have purchased it. I would have loved to see Miniyar start businesses through some of our new programs."

"That is not likely now. They will no doubt make the properties unaffordable for most."

"Thank you for letting me know, Governor."

The usual group was gathered around the table. Leena looked at Senator Lansom and, although the bandage was now gone, she could see the large gash on her head from the explosion that would certainly leave a scar.

Governor Hamrick began, "I am going to make a speech after this meeting to the group that has gathered outside. Local media has been informed and should arrive shortly. I want to try to address their concerns."

"I am not sure I recommend that," Leena said.

"This administration must be transparent. We cannot leave them in the dark," the governor responded.

"But we don't really know anything yet," Senator Chin chimed in. "We don't know why we have no water, and we have no plan to fix it. We had an assassination attempt and have no idea who ordered it. We are really in the dark."

"Yes, I understand, but the public won't patiently wait. In the absence of information, people tend to make stuff up, and we cannot have the rumor mill taking over. I need to say something to calm them, to let them know this government is still in control." The governor then pulled a handkerchief from his pocket to wipe sweat from his brow. Then he continued. "Viktor, where are we with the water?"

Viktor glanced around the room at the faces, knowing they expected a solution to the problem plaguing the city. "We have found the pipeline coming into the city from the east. It runs through an old sewer tunnel. The pipe appears to be intact, so we should be able to get water flowing through it."

"What do we need to do to get it going?" Senator Lansom asked.

"We need to go to the source and find out why it's not in operation. We believe it's an old desalination plant."

"Is there a city nearby that we might work with to get it up and running?" Leena asked.

"The closest occupied city is Charleston, but that city is completely under Aberjay control and not likely to be of any help. They probably don't even know it's there. If they did, they would likely be using it," Viktor said.

"For all we know, they are," Senator Chin said, bringing some additional gloom into the room.

After a brief pause, the governor turned to Leena. "Lieutenant, what would it take for us to send out a group to investigate and get the plant up and running?"

Leena thought about the question for a moment, feeling she was probably not the right person to supply that information. She knew time was of the essence, and asking the team to wait while she contacted her commander would only slow things down. They heard the protests outside getting louder, and her massive headache had not subsided.

"I would say we need about thirty soldiers and some engineers from Viktor's team to get the plant going once we get there."

"I can give you five engineers. They should be able to fix any damaged pipeline and get the desalination plant fully functional, assuming we have the parts," Viktor said with confidence.

"Okay, let's do it," said the governor. "And Viktor, you go with them to ensure Leena has everything she needs."

"Wait, you want me to go?" Leena said louder than she expected.

"Yes. Is that a problem? I need the best people on this, Lieutenant."

"No problem, sir. I will make it happen," Leena said, her voice laced with resignation.

Leena returned to her office to begin making preparations and inform the commander of the governor's request. She hoped her commanding officer would not chastise her for committing troops without approval. She was not sure if she had the authority but felt at the time it was the best decision due to the needs of the city.

As she began making calls, she could hear the microphone being tested on the makeshift podium that was being set up for the governor to address the crowd that had gathered, which included the protestors. She knew she probably should be outside but felt that planning the trip to the east was more important.

She got the commander on the phone and, contrary to what she thought he might say, he congratulated her on her quick thinking and the needs assessment she provided for the governor. The commander further said he would have the team ready to go in twenty-four hours.

Being able to make things happen made Leena feel good about her position. She had the respect of the army and the commander as well as the governor and his staff. And she was only twenty-three years old. She continued to wonder when someone was going to wake up and see that she was not qualified for any of these positions, but each day seemed to go by without her being called out. In fact, as each day went by, she was becoming more qualified for her role. She wondered if this was what all successful people did. Did they just 'fake it until they make it' as some were fond of saying?

Leena could hear the governor beginning to speak to the crowd and went to the small television in her office. Turning it on, she switched to channel eight, the only Miniyar news station.

She watched as the governor spoke, trying to persuade the people that things would get better. He did not mention the newly discovered pipeline to them or the fact that the Aberjay had intentionally cut off the water supply because the team decided to keep both a secret until they needed to share them. He talked about sharing water, the use of water stations, the importance of water collection, and that his staff was diligently working to get water flowing again. Leena cringed as he delivered the next statement: "We plan to have water flowing within a week."

A week? Is he nuts? Has the governor now committed them to something that would be impossible to pull off? How could we get things flowing in a week? We don't even know what we'll find when we get out there. Leena's thoughts raced in response to the governor's words as she thought of all the repercussions.

She was so deep in thought that she barely heard the first gunshot. The sound startled her. *Is that a gunshot?* And then two more rang out from outside, accompanied by screams in the crowd. Leena turned on her radio to hear Liv's team shouting at each other: "The governor has been shot! The governor has been shot!"

Leena ran to the building entrance. Bursting through the front door, she was thrust into pandemonium. Protestors were scattering while Liv's team was on alert with weapons drawn. A group of people hovered over the fallen governor behind the podium. He had taken a shot to the chest.

"No contact, no contact," Leena heard on her radio, indicating they did not know where the shooter was located.

Several soldiers pointed to a man running from the scene. It was the red-headed man with the beard. Several soldiers took off after him, sprinting across the grass toward the trees, where he quickly disappeared.

An ambulance pulled up moments later with sirens blaring and cleared the area around the governor. They applied gauze to the wound and moved the governor to the ambulance with haste. Zone 6 didn't have a fully functional hospital, only clinics. If any invasive surgery was necessary to save him, he would need to go to Habersham Memorial, a hospital on the other side of the wall.

Leena ran to Liv. "Go with the governor," she ordered.

Liv gave some final orders to her team and then ran to the ambulance, ducking inside. The driver gunned the engine of the ambulance the moment she was inside as they headed north while onlookers shouted and cried around the podium.

Army investigation units were on the scene within thirty minutes. Leena stayed long enough to get resources engaged in assisting the investigators and cleaning up the site, but she needed to move away from the venue due to nausea that overcame her. She ran to the upstairs bathroom just in time to vomit again. She was overwhelmed with grief for the governor and the devastation of another tragedy taking place before her eyes. Her whole body seemed to hurt. She questioned whether she was getting the flu or if the posttraumatic stress might have had physical manifestations.

Once she pulled herself together, Leena made her way to the governor's office. The leadership team was already inside. She sat at the big table as they discussed successors in case the governor didn't make it.

"Someone needs to be in charge," Senator Lansom exclaimed.

"We don't have a succession structure," Senator Chin said. "We haven't really got that far."

"I think the logical thing is to have a vote," Leena said.

"We don't have time for another election," Viktor added.

"No, not an election. The people in this room need to vote. The people on the board, I mean," Leena clarified.

"There are only four of us, so what if it's a tie vote?" Senator Lansom asked.

"Then Leena will cast the deciding vote," Angela declared.

Everyone looked at each other around the table and seemed to be in agreement. Leena secretly hoped it would not come to that. She did not want to shoulder that responsibility and certainly did not want to be blamed for making the wrong choice. It was too much pressure.

Angela tore some paper into small squares and handed them out, along with pens. "Write the name of who you want to be the acting governor. It must be a board member."

"Can we vote for ourselves?" Senator Lansom asked.

Angela thought about it for a minute before answering. "Yes, you can vote for yourself, but I am hoping no one will do that," she said as her eyes moved around the table to look at each voting member.

Angela collected the ballets and unfolded them, stacking them in front of her.

"One vote for Senator Chin," she said as the senator remained stoic.

"One vote for Senator Lansom. Another vote for Senator Lansom."

The air was stiff as Angela opened the last ballot. She looked around the room before reading it, adding to the suspense albeit unintentionally.

"The last vote is for me," Angela said blushing.

"Okay then," Viktor said, "Vivian is the acting governor until Governor Hamrick gets out of the hospital. What do you want us to do, Vivian?"

She stood and pulled at her business suit to remove the wrinkles from sitting. She walked toward a window and looked out. She then turned to the staff to provide instructions.

"Leena, we need to know about the water sooner than later. Get your team ready and get on the road as quickly as you can. Robert, can you go to the hospital and be with the governor so you can relay information back to us about his condition?"

Senator Chin nodded in agreement.

"Liv is there as well," Leena added.

"Good, then he will have some security." Senator Lansom continued, "I know we have some security issues, but water has to be our primary goal right now. Did we catch the shooter?"

Leena had been listening on her radio during the voting. The soldiers did catch up with the red-haired man, and he was in custody.

"Yes, well...we caught someone. The man we think did it is in custody, but when we arrested him, he did not have a weapon," Leena said, expecting a sigh of relief from the board members though none came.

"As far as the public knows, we caught the shooter. We don't need a panic. Lieutenant, would you take charge of the interrogation to ensure we get all information that is relevant to the case? I don't want to mess this up."

"Yes, Senator, I mean Interim Gov...um, what do we call you?" Leena said.

"Let's just stick with Senator for now." Senator Lansom walked to the governor's office and asked Tilda to start writing a press release.

The team left the room to get to work. Leena met up with Viktor on the way out.

"Will you have your team ready to go day after tomorrow about seven a.m., Viktor?"

"Yes, that will be fine, assuming no other catastrophe hits in the interim. I will make sure we bring the equipment we need."

Leena returned to her desk to make some calls. She had to requisition the equipment she needed, including the trucks. Her radio would not work in the Aberjay zone, so she needed to wait for Liv or Senator Chin to phone in updates regarding the governor. She figured it would be a while before those details came in, but she left her television on just in case the news station received the information before her team did.

While Leena was typing out a report, a news bulletin appeared on the news station. She stopped what she was doing to stand and walk toward the TV.

The news anchor began the story with a still photo of a fighter jet on the screen.

"We are just receiving news that a Chinese aircraft has crashed in U.S. territory near Phoenix, Arizona. We don't have any video of the crash site but should have something very soon. Once again, a Chinese aircraft has crashed in U.S. territory near Phoenix, Arizona. We don't know what caused the crash, but we are monitoring details and will bring you the latest as soon as we know more."

Leena wondered about the significance of this event as Senator Chin lightly knocked and then entered her office.

"Did you see it?" Senator Chin asked.

"Yes, I just did," Leena replied.

"This is bad, this is very bad."

"Why is this bad?"

"The Chinese will blame this on America. If we shot it out of the sky, or if they crashed it and think we shot it out of the sky, we are at war. This is the pretext they need for their invasion. We all know they were planning it."

"Okay, I see how that could be bad," said Leena, now convinced that they were on the brink of war.

Soon joined by Tilda and Angela, they discussed the impact of the event for about an hour before the news broadcasted an update.

"We are now bringing you the latest regarding that downed Chinese aircraft. It was a J-35 fighter jet. Here is some footage showing the desert littered with parts and the fuselage still smoking from the crash. At this time, the Federal Government is claiming they have no involvement in this accident while the Chinese have already issued a statement blaming the United States for downing the aircraft. Escalating tension between the two sides seems unavoidable. We will keep you updated as new developments arise."

"And there you have it," Senator Chin said.

"Does this mean we are at war?" Leena said.

"We likely will be soon," Angela responded.

It was nearing the end of the workday as Leena pulled her Jeep into headquarters. The base had a small building used for detaining and interrogating prisoners. She had been asked by the acting governor to take over the interrogation of the prisoner, at least until she had to leave on her trip to the coast.

She stepped into the Quonset hut that clearly used to be used as barracks. The roof of the building was curved, and the walls were made of aluminum. Every sound inside produced an echo, including footsteps. The makeshift jail was comprised of about eight rooms, each with an almost indestructible glass door. The doors were controlled by magnets and, once it was shut and the magnet was engaged, a herd of elephants could not have opened the them.

Leena came upon two soldiers guarding access to the hallway that held the prison cells. Each stood at attention when she arrived as she was not only a lieutenant but quite a legend on the base due to her battle experience fighting the CPU and her prominent position serving the governor.

"At ease, soldiers," Leena said as she entered the area. "Do you have the prisoner secured?"

"Yes, Lieutenant, he's in cell four," one soldier responded.

"Okay, I am going in to speak with him. Would you please secure my firearm and baton?" she said as she handed him her weaponry.

She was escorted to the cell. As the soldier searched for his keycard to open the fortified-glass door, she peered inside at the red-haired man. He had a bloody nose and a slight bruise over his left eye. They must have roughed him up a little after the chase.

She entered the room and sat in the metal chair. The prisoner's hands were chained to the table to prevent much movement. The guard who let Leena in the room closed the door and reengaged the lock.

"We meet again, Leena Zhen," the prisoner said.

Leena took a long look at this bearded fellow, trying to intimidate him as much as she could with her stern expression.

"You know my name, but I don't know yours."

"That's because I haven't told it to you yet," the prisoner replied.

"Well, would you do me the honor?"

"My name is not important, but to save you from using unrelenting labels, I will tell you. My name is Nolan."

"Nolan, do you know why you are being detained?"

"Oh, I am not detained, young lady," Nolan said with condescension. "I can escape this place any time I like."

"Is that so? Do you know why you were brought here?"

"Because you think that I shot the governor." Nolan leaned his face down to his hands, which were chained to the table, and scratched his nose, peeling some blood from the tip.

"Are you saying you didn't shoot the governor?" Leena pressed.

"Did you see me shoot the governor?"

"You were there, were you not?"

"Lots of people were there. Did they all shoot the governor?"

"You claim your innocence then?" Leena asked.

"I don't think any of us are innocent, but I didn't shoot the governor any more than you did. Did you shoot the governor, Leena?"

"Please address me as Lieutenant. Did you or did you not shoot the governor and then run away?"

"I believe I have already answered that question. Why don't you ask me another? I'm bored with that one."

"Why do you think you are here if it isn't to answer for this crime, Mister..." Leena paused, hoping he would reveal his last name.

"Nolan will be fine. I think we should be on a first-name basis, don't you?"

"No. I don't know you."

"I am you, Leena Zhen. At least, I am who you were two years ago. But I'm not sure you are that person anymore. You're a soldier now. Following orders. Doing what they tell you."

Leena paused, feeling that the conversation was not progressing as she intended. She needed a way to reset. To get him to talk.

"Why don't you tell me who you are, Nolan?"

"I have already answered that question too. C'mon, Zhen, you are better than this."

"Why do you act like you know me, Nolan? I'd never met you before that day outside the Capitol building."

"I heard stories about you from my sister for years. She served under you and fought side by side with you, shedding her own blood on the same ground as yours."

Leena thought for a moment to try to solve the riddle. Who had she fought with who could be related to this wild man? Then she looked at his red hair and beard and it reminded her of someone.

"Tina Redmont! You are Nolan Redmont, her brother?"

"Very good, Leena. See, I knew you were smart."

"How is your sister?"

"She is not with us," Nolan said matter-of-factly.

"I am sorry to hear that."

"You should be. I blame you for her pain."

"Me? Why me? I have done nothing to Tina."

"You have done nothing, that is true. This war you started with the Aberjay affected her greatly. She believed in you. She believed in the cause. And you let her believe it. And then you gave up. You accepted their compromise treaty and became one of them."

Leena stood and slammed her fist on the table. "I am not Aberjay."

"Are you sure?" Nolan said to antagonize her. "You stopped fighting, and the wall is still there. Our people are still deprived of freedoms. What have you really done to make things better?"

"Things *are* better; we control our own lives now."

"Ha! That's a joke. You can't even travel without a pass. You can't eat until they let food in. You can't send your kids to school unless they fund it. How free do you think you are? You're living in a dream world. The war still rages, but you're sitting it out because you found a little bit of comfort. Open your eyes; you are being thrown crumbs from the table."

Leena thought about that phrase, 'crumbs from the table.' She thought back to her conversation with Ambassador Lao. He had used the same phrase. *Had she settled for crumbs?*

"I would love to continue this nonsensical discussion with you, but I have things I must do to help my people." Leena turned her back and walked to the door.

"Yes, that water, what would we do without water?" Nolan said, taunting her further. "You will find the desalination plant just as inaccessible as your freedom, Leena Zhen. They won't let you win."

Leena motioned for the door to be unlocked and stormed out in anger on the brink of tears. *How did he know about the desalination plant?* She strode briskly to the front of the building out of sight of the soldiers and began to cry. He had gotten to her. He had rattled the foundation of her faith in herself and what she thought was right. *Is he right? Have I become soft and allowed an image of freedom to take the place of real liberty?*

Leena composed herself and then met with the duty officer to report she had not made progress on a confession and, in her mind, felt he was probably not the shooter. She thought it was certain he wanted us to think that so he would be detained, but the lack of a weapon or gunpowder residue on his hands, which they had tested for on his arrival, led her to believe it was not likely he was the shooter. Despite this, she felt there was something off about Nolan and was not sure why he seemed to have an obsession with her. He might be blaming her for his sister's death. That would make sense, but was there more? Something else was tugging at her, and she could not put her finger on it.

She interviewed him again the next day but did not make any more progress. He just repeated the same things. That she was at fault. That she had let the Aberjay win. As much as she hated to admit it, he did remind her of herself several years earlier when she first began fighting alongside the Resistance fighters. The vitriol she felt during that time seemed consistent with his passion for revolution. It was hard to ascertain whether Nolan was an ally or an enemy. He was obviously sore about his sister, but some conversations seemed to indicate his willingness to help her if she would return to fighting the Aberjay. *Is he trying to get me to lead?*

Chapter 7

TRAVEL

Leena woke early enough to have breakfast with Jordan. He was not supportive of her trip and always worried when she was sent on missions that might be dangerous, but he had learned over the years that fighting her on it was pointless. She was going to go because she was ordered to go. She had a sense of duty that he didn't really understand. Even if she was not ordered to do something, her stubbornness would not stand in the way of letting anyone thwart what she thought was right.

Although it was quite early and still dark out, they enjoyed the time together. Leena informed Jordan of all the recent events leading up to this trip and why it was so important that she go. Jordan was already aware of the rising tension with the Chinese as his job had him building armaments for the army for the last month.

As they finished their beans and greens, along with a small piece of salted pork Jordan kept in the freezer for special occasions, the tension of the moment became too much. They embraced and held each other, weeping together. They always knew her job was dangerous but venturing into Tullian territory brought back bad memories. They had been kidnapped the last time they went into those barren lands where ruffians, thieves, and cannibals were commonplace.

This trip felt different than previous trips though. Or maybe it was just the tension of inevitable war, the governor being shot, or the near-death experience that had them on edge. All of it was enough to weaken even the strongest.

"Why don't we just run away?" Jordan said. "We have always discussed running away and finding a place that is just ours, away from all of this bullshit."

"I want to... I really do," Leena responded. "I just don't think I can. People need water, and I am the one tasked with getting it."

"I know. I was just hoping for a miracle. That maybe you would change your mind."

Leena pulled away from Jordan's embrace. She knew if she didn't, she would be tempted to stay. She walked into the bedroom and picked up her duffel bag and then walked out to the Jeep. Jordan was in the doorway as she prepared to leave. They were both still crying. She opened the Jeep door but then ran back to Jordan to hold him once more, hoping it would not be the last time.

The base was full of activity. The commander had obviously begun preparing for war. The rhetoric between the powers was escalating due to the aircraft that was down. The Chinese blamed the Americans for shooting it down. and the Americans blamed the Chinese for implicating the innocent. The plane did crash, but there was no evidence it was shot down. Who knows, it could have been an overzealous Tullian with a rocket launcher. It didn't matter. The countries were on a collision course.

Leena entered the designated hanger to see her troops loading the trucks. She was taking four trucks, three loaded with ten soldiers each and one with Viktor and five of his engineers. She saw them loading all types of pipes and equipment she figured they would use to fix the plant. Standing near the trucks were Liv and Viktor.

"Are we ready to go?" Leena asked.

"Yes, Lieutenant, we will be loaded in minutes," Liv replied cheerfully. Liv liked going out on missions. The truth is, she missed the war. She liked being in the action.

"Viktor, do you have what you need?"

"There is no way to know what we might need until we get there to see what we are working on, but I had the team bring as much as we could. We also have the gear to patch holes along the way if we see any in the line."

"I have been thinking about something, Viktor. What if we fix the plant and turn on the water but there are holes in the pipeline? Do we just drive back next to the pipeline and look for water spewing from the ground? And don't you need to turn the water off to fix it?"

"Yes, the easiest way would be to get the plant online and then turn it on. There are shutoff valves every few miles, so if we find a leak, we can just stop and turn the valve off long enough to fix it and then keep going. But much of the pipeline is underground, so we may not actually see the problem just driving by it."

"Okay, that makes sense. Liv, I'll ride with you in the first truck. Do you mind driving, I have not been feeling well this morning?"

"No problem," Liv said and climbed into the driver's seat of the first truck.

One of the soldiers shouted for the team to load the trucks with personnel, and within a minute or so they pulled out of the hangar and headed toward the east gate. Leena smiled as they pulled through it, looking over at Liv who responded with a laugh. They were both thinking the same thing. It had been a little more than two years since they had raided this gate with freedom fighters to end a food shortage. The Aberjay were holding food at a warehouse just on the other side of the gate, using it as a negotiating tactic. They were able to rescue the food that day and distribute it to hungry people inside the wall. That was a good day.

Leena thought about their current task at hand and wondered if it was in the same spirit. Were they still freedom fighters? Were they part of a Resistance? Or were they unwittingly doing the Aberjay's work for them by satiating the people? After some contemplation, she pushed these thoughts away, convinced that providing water to people who are thirsty was a revolutionary act.

The caravan headed southeast and, although it was only about three hundred miles, the many obstacles they faced going through Tullian land slowed them down quite a bit. Rather than the few hours it should have taken to make the journey, it would likely take them a couple of days. And as dangerous as it was to travel at night, they believed it was in their best interest to stop once it became dark and get some rest.

The trucks rolled down the highway at a slow pace as they had to stop and maneuver around stalled vehicles and large trees that had fallen. Some of these obstacles were placed there intentionally by gangs of Tullian who would wait to ambush unsuspecting travelers. Leena felt confident they had enough firepower to withstand any attack, but nonetheless, they wanted to avoid any bloodshed. The big caravan was a threat to small bands, but larger groups out on the plain would certainly see it as an opportunity to increase their stores of guns, ammo, and food.

"What do you think we will find at the plant?" Liv asked, desperate for conversation to break up the long drive.

Leena looked at Liv and then back out the window, developing her thoughts on the matter. "It's most likely empty."

"Yes, that would be ideal. But what are the other options?" Liv asked, trying to get Leena to engage.

"Well, I suppose it could be under Aberjay control. The CPU could have it locked down tight with a massive army outside," Leena said exhibiting her penchant for dark humor.

Liv wrinkled her brow at that prospect. She was a soldier, but she did not care for unwinnable odds.

"Or," Leena continued, "it might be in full working order and immaculately clean. All we'll need to do is hit the power button."

"That does not sound likely," Liv responded.

"You were the one who wanted to speculate. What if the plant is destroyed? We would have to rebuild it. We might be there for years."

"We would not really do that, would we?" Liv said with a tinge of fear that Leena was serious.

"We need the water," Leena said.

"We should just storm the gates into Zone 7 and force them to turn it back on. That would be my vote."

"Then we would be at war with the Aberjay *and* the Chinese," Leena said resolutely.

Liv decided the topic of discussion was too real and went in another direction.

"Tell me about your trip to Zone 7. Did you enjoy roughing it?"

About three hours into the journey, they hit a roadblock. Stacks of crushed cars on the roadway blocked the path. Leena had seen this trap before and had no intention of falling for it again.

"Liv, stop," Leena said. "Do you remember when we were jumped in Tullian territory a few years back?"

"Yes."

"It looked just like this. Let's tread carefully."

Leena exited the truck and ordered all the soldiers off her truck, fully armed. They grabbed their rifles and took a position behind Leena as she walked toward the wall of cars. The cars were stacked about twelve feet high and occupied both sides of the highway. There was no way around. On one side, a slope prevented vehicles from traversing the barrier, and on the other, a sharp decline would certainly send any vehicle plummeting to the bottom of a gully.

It was quiet, and although there was a smell of smoke in the air that reminded Leena of the small stoves in the market near where she grew up, there was no other evidence of anyone present.

"This was set up for an ambush, but there's no one here. Check the other side," Leena ordered as about half her team trudged up the hill on the right side to get around the cars to the other side of the makeshift wall.

Leena walked back to the truck and stepped up on her side to get some elevation. Within a few moments, her team returned from the other side and reported that it was clear.

"So now we just need to get through it. What do you think, Liv?"

"Let's just smash it. The trucks are strong. I think we can bust right through that wall."

Leena turned to Viktor to get the opinion of the engineer, but he only shrugged. She knew he would not say yes without knowing the weight of each vehicle, the dimensions, and all the other details. Engineers were frustrating that way.

"Okay, let's do it." Leena motioned for her troops to stand aside as Liv pressed down on the accelerator, pushing the truck forward until it crunched into the cars. The contact was a jolt to both of them as the wall failed to give. Liv stopped and put the truck in a lower gear then gunned it again, and the wall of cars moved. Inch by inch, she was able to move the wall about ten feet before it split in the center and each set of cars was pushed to the side of the road.

Liv stopped long enough to reload the truck with the soldiers, and they continued their journey. Leena breathed easier. *That was clearly set up to ambush unknowing travelers*, she thought. Either the large caravan scared them away or they did not attend it every day.

About nine hours into their drive, they looked for a spot to rest for the evening. After checking a few exits that didn't seem safe, they found one that had the remains of an old fuel station. The pumps were gone, and the store windows were all broken, but the parking lot was big enough to park the trucks where they wouldn't be seen from the highway. A large grassy area next to the station was a good place to set up some tents. The soldiers went to work setting up camp as Leena walked the perimeter to work out the soreness that had developed in her legs from the long drive. What was once a large parking lot for long-haul truckers was now worn asphalt, with vegetation growing from every crack, struggling for sunshine.

Once the camp was set up, they broke out rations to share. Leena did not care for army food but knew it was all that was available. She hoped they would come upon a market that sold fresh vegetables but knew that was very unlikely. Tullian land had no markets. No stores. Just desperate people fighting to survive.

A soldier handed Leena a box that she tore open to reveal a dehydrated meal of rice, beans, sliced carrots, and a biscuit. The kit was ready within minutes by adding water.

Leena ate as she watched the soldiers set up the remaining tents. The air cooled as the sun went down in sharp contrast to the day, which had been hot. The humidity in the South was enough to choke you in the summer. Some say you get used to it. Your body acclimates. But Leena never felt that way. She did not care to sweat.

The soldiers ate and then began enjoying themselves with some games, stories, and a few bottles of cheap homemade vodka. It was rare they had access to alcohol, but Liv had smuggled the bottles onto the trucks to ensure they had some pleasure in what she predicted would be a challenging journey.

The sound of an approaching vehicle caught everyone's attention. An old muscle car painted black with black tinted windows appeared and with great speed charged into the gas station parking lot. The driving was erratic, as if a pack of squirrels was driving. The car screeched to a stop about fifty feet from Leena as she stood up to arm herself. Many soldiers also moved in front of Leena with rifles in hand to protect her from any threat.

They heard screaming. Muffled screaming. The door opened on the passenger side, and the screaming became louder. A woman of about thirty ran from the car wearing a long gray T-shirt and no pants. Her hair was long and brown, with some strands of gray. She looked as if she had not eaten in some time, her bones almost poking through her skin. Two men dressed in leather jumped out of the car, chasing her as the driver revved the engine and began driving toward her.

The soldiers turned to look for guidance, but Leena put up her hand, gesturing for them to wait before they engaged. Leena didn't want to get involved in a domestic dispute until she knew what was really happening. They watched as the two men caught her and threw her on the hood of the car as it approached. One man struck her across the face and ripped her shirt, exposing her breasts. With that, the soldiers turned again, and Leena signaled to them to proceed with a rescue.

The men had not noticed the large contingent until the men were almost on them. Once they did, they reached for their weapons that were stuck in their jeans. This caused many of the soldiers to fire on their position, killing both within seconds. Leena and Liv ran to the woman, still crying out from the hood of the car.

"Corporal," Leena shouted back to a soldier, "get her a blanket."

"Yes, Lieutenant," a young female soldier said before running to one truck and returning with a blanket to cover her.

The woman was still frantic, not knowing what she was seeing as Leena reached for her. Her eyes were wide, her face bloody; she was in shock.

"It's okay, we've got you now. You're safe," Leena told her.

Her head darted left and right like a frightened bird. They walked her, barefoot, back to the camp and into a large tent that contained eight cots. They sat her down on one, and Leena motioned for the male soldiers to leave. Two female soldiers remained along with Liv and Leena to comfort the woman.

They brought her water and gave her a few minutes to collect herself. Liv handed her a wet cloth and motioned for her to wipe her head with it. The woman complied, and much of the blood, along with plenty of dirt, came off. She then dropped the cloth because she was shaking so much, and Liv picked it up and began wiping her head and face as well as her arms and legs.

"Who are you people?" the woman said.

"You are safe. We're the People's Army," Leena said, but the confusion on the woman's face did not dissipate. "Let's let her rest."

The soldiers left her in the tent, covered by a blanket. Everyone stepped outside of the tent, and Leena ordered them to find her some clothes. Shortly later, they brought some green fatigues that were likely her size. Leena walked back in and placed them next to her, but she was fast asleep.

"Only women in this tent tonight," Leena ordered and then went back to her dinner.

The soldiers created a fire for warmth as the darkness overtook them. Leena ordered them to keep it small so it would not attract any unwanted attention.

After about two hours of sleep, the woman in the tent emerged, dressed in the fatigues that Leena had left by her bed, and walked toward the fire, sitting next to Leena, Liv, and Viktor without a word.

"Are you okay?" Liv asked.

The woman nodded.

"What is your name? I'm Leena."

"Lilian," she said after a brief pause. "Lilian Vargas."

"What are you doing out here with those guys, Lilian?" Liv asked.

"They bought me a few months ago," she said while eyeballing a loaf of bread one soldier was slicing to toast near the fire.

"Would you like some bread, Lilian?" Leena asked, gesturing for the soldier to feed her.

He handed her a sizeable piece of toasted bread with some strawberry jam, and she devoured it as if she had not eaten in weeks. The soldier then smiled and handed her another, which she ate almost as fast.

"You say those guys *bought* you?" Leena asked.

"Yes. I'm from the Graggore Clan. They sold us to them for some guns."

"Us? There were more of you?" Liv asked.

"Yes, about twelve in all. But that's our purpose. They breed us to be traded." Lilian licked her fingers to get every crumb from the toasted bread.

"Wow, that is messed up," Liv said.

"But you're with us now, and we'll take care of you until we get back to town," Leena said.

"So, you are my owners now?" she asked, looking back and forth between Leena and Liv.

"No one owns you; you are free," Leena said.

"I don't understand. You killed my owners, so now you own me."

"No one owns you, Lilian, you are free," Leena repeated.

"No, I must be owned. That is my purpose. How will I eat if I have no owner?" Lilian became agitated.

"No one owns you," Liv chimed in. "You are free to do what you want. We will feed you until we get back home."

"You are taking me back home? To Graggore? No! They will not be happy. My owners are dead. You can't take me back there!"

"Calm down, Lilian, we will not take you back there if you don't want us to. You can stay with us for now. Is that okay? Can you stay with us?"

"Yes," Lilian said, staring at the bread by the fire. "I will stay with you, my new owners."

"Oh boy," Liv said, "she is messed up."

"We'll just have to take care of her. We will figure out what to do with her when we get back," Leena said.

"What about the others?" Liv asked. "Should we attempt a rescue?"

"You know I would like to, but that's not our mission," Leena replied. "Liv, make sure there are guards out tonight in case her other owners decide to come looking for her. And get rid of those bodies."

Leena was up with the sun and slid quietly out of the tent she shared with other female soldiers. The air was crisp, and the birds welcomed her to the day. A light mist hovered just above the trees.

Many soldiers were already up, packing their gear and getting ready to head out. Leena ate some oatmeal one of the other soldiers had made, along with some dried nuts and fruit. They were also kind enough to make her some tea. They knew their commanding officer liked tea.

As the sun moved higher on the horizon, the other soldiers began to wake up and eat their breakfasts. Leena walked toward the truck, which many soldiers noticed, assuming she was rushing them to finish their breakfasts and get packed up. They picked up the pace.

Lilian emerged from the tent, and after eating some oatmeal, began following Leena. Leena was a little creeped out by the shadow, so she asked Lilian to go sit in the truck, which she did without question.

Once the caravan was ready, Leena ordered the drivers to continue east on the highway.

A couple of hours into their journey, the radio squawked. It was Corporal Evans from a couple of trucks back. A tire on one truck had exploded and needed to be replaced. Leena directed Liv to find a pullout off the highway where they could all pull over to the shoulder. Soldiers got to work on the tire as Leena stepped out of the truck to survey the damage and stretch her legs.

She stared down at the busted tire, noticing that a lack of tread must have caused the blowout. Most of the tires on this truck were bald. The People's Army was quite new, but their equipment had seen many years of use in various capacities.

As she walked away from the team changing the tire, something in the distance on the other side of the highway caught her attention. She moved to the front of the first truck to get an unobstructed view, stepping up on her side of the truck and then up on the front fender to get as high as she could. What she saw was large, but dust rising around it hid it from view. She peeked her head into the open door of the truck to address Lilian.

"Lilian, what is that?" she asked as she pointed.

A small piece of metal she was bending forward and backward was distracting Lilian. She looked up at Leena and then slowly her head followed Leena's arm and hand to see where she was pointing.

"Lanthemtown," Lilian said.

"Lanthemtown," Leena repeated.

"It's a trader's village. Great Wizard."

Liv, still seated in the driver's seat, interrupted. "Wizard? Did she say wizard? We have to check that out!"

"I don't think that is a good idea," Leena said.

"Aw, mom, you never let us have any fun," Liv said sarcastically.

Leena could see a dirt road off the highway that likely led to the town. A few vehicles headed toward it were kicking up significant dust and dirt.

"The repair has been completed, Lieutenant," a soldier said to Leena as she stepped down from her perch.

"Okay, let's get moving," Leena ordered.

After another few hours of slow progress, including several stops to push vehicles off the highway or use nature's restroom, they passed a sign that read 'Port Loyal.' The landscape had changed as they entered the city limits, shifting from open fields and pastures to wetlands.

About ten miles past the sign, they saw buildings. First houses, all of which looked abandoned, then some old commercial buildings, also void of activity. The town seemed to be full of ghosts until they reached the city center. A small two-story courthouse marked the spot, and a temporary fence surrounded the building, which was constructed with wood, metal, and apparently whatever the builders could find.

Leena used the radio to tell her troops to stop as they approached the fencing. She saw movement for the first time. A sentry of sorts was peering out from above the gate, holding a rifle. Leena jumped out of the truck and walked toward the fence when the sentry raised her rifle and took a shot, which landed at Leena's feet, blowing asphalt and dust into the air, which quickly dissipated in the high sea winds that permeated the town.

Clearly a warning shot, Leena stopped and put up her hands.

"That is far enough," the sentry said. "Are you CPU?"

Leena looked behind her to ensure her team was not about to take a shot at this lone sentry. "No, we are People's Army soldiers from Zone 6."

Another person's head popped up over the fence next to the sentry peering in their direction. Both exchanged words before the sentry spoke again.

"Send an emissary. One person only. No weapons."

Leena looked at Liv and kept her hands raised as she walked slowly toward her.

"Liv, slowly grab my baton and firearm."

Liv complied with the order. "Are you sure you want to do this? Let me go. We need to keep you safe. Don't be a hero."

"I will be right back. I think if they wanted us dead, they would not have fired a warning shot."

Leena turned and ambled toward the gate, which they pushed open. She stepped into the courtyard as her host pulled the gate closed and locked it behind her.

The man who led her was tall and handsome, with a brown beard. His eyes sparkled blue. He was very thin but had broad shoulders.

"Sorry for the drama," he said. "You can never be too careful. Let's start with who you are and why you are in our sleepy little town."

Leena looked around the small yard in front of the enormous building that had seen little maintenance in years. A garden stretched along the front and sides of the building. Several citizens with hoes worked the dirt, as Leena had done so many times in the past. They seemed to have an abundance of vegetables growing.

"My name is Leena Zhen. I am a lieutenant in the People's Army on a mission to locate something of great importance to my people."

"Something?" the man stopped her.

Leena tried but could not think of a good enough lie that would convince him. "Water. My people need water. There is a pipeline from our town that leads to a desalination plant here on the coast. If we can get it going, we can provide water to millions of people in need."

"My name is Lyon Davis. I am the leader of what remains of Port Loyal. I promise you are in no danger here from us. We stay armed to fight off the CPU as well as other scavengers from the local clans. They come occasionally to take our resources."

Leena lifted her arm to use her radio, signaling the troops to stand down and wait for her.

Lyon escorted Leena to the front porch of what used to be a small courthouse that now looked like a homesteading compound. They sat at a small table as Lyon poured her a glass of water.

"Do you all live here?" Leena asked.

"All that's left of us. About fifty in all." Lyon picked up his glass and took a large swallow of water. After a brief pause, looking up at the sky, he continued. "I grew up playing on these streets. It has all gone to hell now. Many years ago, the CPU started making regular visits. Harassing the people. Taking our grains and fish. We had a pleasant village, but most people moved toward the bigger cities once they realized they were not safe this far out. The CPU is not the only group that comes through taking what they want. We lived in houses all over town for a little while and then the bands of criminals began picking us off one by one. I felt it was safer to group together and fight back. We have been in the courthouse for about ten years. It works well, but we still lack medical care and live on a very plain diet of fish and vegetables we can grow from the garden. You're not a doctor, are you?"

"No, I'm sorry, I am not. You should be happy that you have your freedom," Leena said. "The Aberjay completely control the cities."

"The Aberjay?" Lyon questioned.

"Yes, that is what we call the ruling class. The CPU, the rich—those who control everything. People like them have everything they need. Everyone else struggles to survive. Do you know where the desalination plant is?"

"Yes, it's only a few miles from here down near the beach. But it's guarded by the CPU."

Leena's face turned sullen. "How many?"

"Not sure. They don't even use the plant. It isn't working. They just know it's a target and are keeping it guarded to ensure no one else gets it running. We tried to negotiate with them a few years back. They killed about ten of our people in response."

"Unfortunately," Leena responded, "the CPU presence does not change my orders. I need to get that water flowing for my people. Thank you for the information. We may be in the area for a couple of days getting that plant running, so if you need anything, feel free to reach out and we'll try to accommodate you." Leena then stood to her feet.

"It was a pleasure to meet you, Leena and I wish you the best of luck taking the plant. I will tell you there's an access tunnel that leads away from the plant about half a mile in the direction of the marsh. If you can get into that tunnel, it will lead you right into the plant. They built it as an escape tunnel in case the water rose too high, or they had some other disaster. The entrance might already be underwater though."

"Thank you, Lyon, that is helpful." Leena took a sip from her small glass. "I have one favor to ask."

"What is it?"

"I found a stray along our route. Rescued her from a clan who bought her as a slave. Where we are going isn't safe. I would like to leave her with you."

"We have limited food here. Can she work?" Lyon asked.

"Yes, she is quite capable."

"I guess we can take her in if she can garden or help with other chores. Everyone works here."

"Okay, thank you."

Leena drank the last of her water and then walked toward the gate, hesitating only long enough for a citizen of Port Loyal to open it for her so she could slip out. She walked back to Liv and signaled the others to prepare to leave.

"Liv, they're going to take Lilian."

Liv opened the door and motioned for Lilian to come down from the truck. They both walked Lilian toward the gate while trying to explain the situation.

"Lilian, you are going to stay here where it's safe," Leena said.

Lilian looked back toward the truck as she slowly stepped forward. A look of confusion came over her.

"Lilian, do you understand?" Liv questioned.

"Stay here?"

"Yes, Lilian, you will stay here," Leena said.

"New owners?"

"Yes, new owners."

The gate of the encampment opened slowly as they approached, and Lilian stepped inside. Leena and Liv then turned to walk back to their truck. She conveyed the details of her meeting with Lyon to Liv as the caravan began moving.

They followed the directions Lyon had given to locate the plant but drove slowly. They didn't want to run up to it and sacrifice the element of surprise.

The road they were on became narrow as it turned to the south, and once they reached the ridge, they could see the plant in the distance. It was a large, rectangular metal building covered in rust from the corrosive seawater. It stood more than twenty feet tall, and there was no sign of the tunnel that Lyon mentioned. Leena did not like being on the road leading to the plant because it was out in the open. If the CPU had sentries, they would have already seen them. The first road they came to led inland. She told Liv to take it. Now off the main sea road, they were shrouded in trees. The road turned south again, and Leena could tell they were traveling parallel to the shoreline road they were on before.

It was not long before they came upon a large bridge and a parking area next to a small tributary that led into the sea. They parked the trucks there, well out of sight, and began looking for the escape tunnel. A soldier spotted it on the other side of the river, but it seemed to be floating in a swampy mess of vines and knee-high water. There was no telling what might be in there.

"It looks like we are going swimming," Liv said.

Leena's face turned green. She did not like the water. It was her greatest fear. Even from an early age, the few times she went to the pool instilled a disdain for being in the water. She learned how to swim, but it didn't assuage her fear, and just thinking of wading in that water brought chills to her body and a pain in her stomach. She walked to the edge of the parking area away from everyone to gather herself, but she soon felt worse. Within seconds, she threw up her lunch into the bushes.

Liv ran to her. "Are you okay? What's going on? Is it the water?"

"No, I'm fine. I've had a stomach bug or something for a week or so. It makes me throw up a lot."

"Come, drink some water, and sit for a minute. We can scout out that tunnel for you," Liv said to reassure her.

"What is wrong with her?" Viktor asked.

"She has an upset stomach. She'll be fine," Liv said.

"Good. For a minute there, I thought she might be pregnant," Viktor said as the sound of everything seemed to evaporate.

Leena looked up at Liv, and their eyes grew wide.

"Jumping jackrabbits, you're pregnant, Leena!" Liv said in jubilation.

"I can't be. No, that can't be it." Her mind wandered off as she began thinking about her monthly cycle and the last time she was intimate with her husband. Her face sank as she realized it would explain her recent propensity to vomit as well as the soreness in her breasts. She felt this was the absolute worst time for this to happen, but beyond the initial shock, it thrilled her to be carrying Jordan's child.

Leena sat on the bumper of the large truck to rest for a moment and let her stomach settle. She took a canteen from Liv to wash her mouth out, spitting the tainted water on the ground. For a moment, everything she was doing just faded away as if her soul left her body and elevated hundreds of feet. She thought about her life with Jordan. How they had discussed children several times.

Leena had a good childhood. Despite the poverty, she enjoyed growing up. She spent most days with her mother and Diego, her grandfather. She played in their fabric store every day, helping to fold and roll fabrics while her mom waited on customers. Leena remembered the three of them gardening almost every weekend, playing in the dirt, laughing. They spent a lot of time in the park too as she dashed joyfully between the swings and slides. She enjoyed her childhood very much and wanted her child to have the same.

She could not wait to tell Jordan that he was going to be a father.

Chapter 8

ATTACK

The People's Army soldiers left Viktor and Leena with the engineers while they charged across the bridge on foot and then waded into the waist-high water to investigate the door that seemed out of place in these wetlands. Each of them carried a rifle and sidearm to prepare for conflict.

Leena tried to concentrate on what her team was doing and the task at hand, but she could not get over the thought of being pregnant. She always knew she would have kids, but this was so sudden and unplanned, it made her brain swirl with emotion. She knew it would thrill Jordan as he had talked about having kids even before they were living together.

Feeling slightly better, Leena stepped up on her truck's front bumper to get a better look at the team's progress. It seemed they were nearing the door, rifles above their heads as they waded through the murky swamp water. She wondered if there were alligators this far north and then remembered she would follow the soldiers soon through the desolate waters. A shiver went down her spine. She shook her head as if to throw off the thought, but it was still there, lurking. There were many ways she could die in that water. An alligator was one, but venomous snakes, spiders, and small sharks would be others. *Did sharks swim in swamps?* She didn't know, but it seemed logical.

Once on the concrete platform, one soldier went to work on the door. The hill that housed the door seemed unnatural, sticking up out of the swamp. Based on its construction, what lay behind the door was a staircase that descended into the swamp. It was only the elevation of the platform the door was on that kept water from flooding the entrance.

The soldier successfully picked the lock on the door and swung it wide. Liv stood tall and waved to signal her commanding officer. Leena hopped off the truck and told the engineers to stay put. The plan was to take the plant, then radio back to the engineers to drive around to the front entrance of the plant once they cleared it of threats. Leena left two soldiers to guard the engineers, trucks, and supplies, but she felt she needed the rest of the soldiers to storm the plant.

Leena walked across the bridge, getting nervous with every step. The green muck that floated on the waters below taunted her. At that point, the entire swamp might as well have been acid. She thought she would certainly die if she touched it. She tried to convince herself that it was only water and that a meeting with a shark in a swamp was probably unlikely. It didn't matter. Her whole body resisted, and the shakes she was experiencing felt as if they would never go away. She did not want to show weakness to her team, but they already knew she was afraid of the water, so her attempt to cover her fears was unnecessary.

As she came to the other side of the bridge, several of her troops had found a couple of logs floating in the swamp and tied them together with paracord to create a makeshift float. They walked toward the road with the raft and set it down at Leena's feet. Leena was grateful.

"Thank you. You didn't have to do that. I was more than willing to…"

"It's okay, Lieutenant, just get on the raft. We all support each other in this unit. You know that," one soldier said.

Leena gently stepped onto the raft and then bent down to ensure she didn't lose her balance. The soldiers dragged the tied-up logs over to the door, allowing her to step off onto the concrete and walk down the stairs. She turned one last time before submerging to thank them.

The team regrouped at the bottom of the stairs in a passageway no wider than six feet. More than two dozen soldiers tried to dry off, check their ammunition, and prepare for battle in the small space.

It was at that moment that Leena had a terrible thought. *If she engaged the CPU, would she be violating the treaty? Did it apply here?* Certainly, her incursion would be reported back to their headquarters. She had made a tactical mistake. She should have had the soldiers change their clothes to hide their identities. How could she rectify the situation? Then she had an idea.

"Team, do not fire unless fired upon."

"What?" Liv asked in a hushed tone.

"We can't attack them without violating the treaty, but if they fire on us, it's self-defense."

"It's hard to gain the advantage of surprise without actually attacking, Lieutenant," Liv said sarcastically.

"If possible, let's take prisoners instead of lives," Leena commanded.

The soldiers all nodded, but they knew they were walking into enemy territory with enough firepower to destroy their adversary. It was unlikely this would end any other way.

The team lined up and crept down the long hallway that seemed to stretch for several hundred feet. There was not much light, so the team affixed lights to their rifles to illuminate the tunnel. The walls of the tunnel were stone, like the wall back home that separated the zones. Leena reached her hand out behind her as she walked, dragging her hand across the wall. It had the same feel of stone and mortar that reminded her of her younger days climbing the wall.

After reaching the end of the corridor, the narrow passageway opened to a large room full of pumps and piping. The pumps were not running, and they could hear no sound in the room. There were at least ten large pumps, larger than a truck, all painted in red. The floors and walls of the room were made of the same stone as the hallway. Ahead of them, Leena could see a staircase that climbed three flights to a door at the top where there were many large windows so that engineers could look down on the pump room.

"Split up and clear the room quietly to ensure we are alone," Leena commanded as the team split into four groups of seven each.

Leena walked with Liv toward the stairs and waited at the bottom for her teams to finish their sweep. Once they were reassembled, the first team of seven climbed the stairs to the door. Opening it slowly, they entered another hallway, this one with glass walls that led to a control room on each side. After peering into each one to ensure they were empty, they proceeded to the end of the hallway, finding themselves on a platform with stairs that led down to what looked like a lobby.

Finding no one, the soldiers stopped and motioned for Leena and Liv to come forward. Leena moved past the soldiers and then looked down into the lobby. There didn't seem to be any movement. The plant itself was full of dirt and dust, and remnants of old books and manuals were strewn about the floors. If anyone was here, they didn't spend any time cleaning up.

They made their way down the stairs and into the lobby. The entire front of the building faced the ocean, and the wall of glass revealed a large deck with what looked like remnants of metal seats that were bolted to the ground. Although they probably once sparkled in the sun, every inch of them were now rusted from the salt air.

As they debated their next move, they heard voices and what sounded like a bottle falling on the ground without breaking. The sound emanated from a room at the end of a hallway that led away from the lobby.

Leena directed her troops toward the sound, and they fell in line. Half the team stayed in the lobby to provide backup while Leena, Liv, and the other team stepped slowly down the hallway. Once they reached the door, they could see a light on inside through the cracked door. Leena stuck her head close to the door and could hear three soldiers, likely CPU, talking, laughing, and drinking.

Leena looked to her team and gave the signal to breach the room, quietly counting, "One, two, three." As she finished, several soldiers, led by Liv, burst into the room.

Not a shot was fired as all three soldiers failed to brandish a weapon. They just stared at the intruders while holding their playing cards. The table was set up for a game with bottle caps stacked in the center, obviously being used as chips.

"Freeze!" Liv shouted as the soldiers raised their hands and turned their heads toward the group in astonishment.

Glancing around the room, Leena could see their rifles leaning against a wall, not even within arm's reach. She reasoned these soldiers had been at this post for so long with no action that they believed being at the ready was pointless.

The People's Army troops made the CPU soldiers stand, placing their hands in plastic ties and marching them to another room off the hallway that was a little larger. On Leena's order, they locked them in the room with two guards to monitor them.

Leena walked triumphantly back to the lobby, feeling grateful that she could take the plant without bloodshed. She ordered a few men to sweep the outside of the plant and then directed them to get the engineers and trucks.

Once everyone had reassembled an hour later, Leena communicated the plan.

"Viktor, I need you to find out everything you can about this plant and see if you can get it running. Let me know the moment you have a situation report so we can plan out how long we will be here. I want rotating patrols around this plant and another patrol inside the plant to ensure we aren't surprised by other CPU troops. We don't know how many alarms we might have triggered coming in here."

Viktor went to work with the engineers investigating the plant controls while most of the troops clustered around Liv for specific orders and patrol assignments. Several others created a makeshift bunkhouse in one of the larger rooms and began setting up cots to accommodate a rotating sleep schedule.

Leena handed a handheld radio she had found to a soldier. "Corporal Weiss, see if we can use this to talk to our base. I would like to get a message to Commander Johnson."

The corporal looked at the radio, examining the buttons and knobs. "Yes, it might be possible. Let me work on it a bit."

"Good," Leena said, "but just be careful you don't call the wrong base. We don't want to tip off the CPU that we're here."

Corporal Weiss nodded and took the radio. The People's Army lacked modern equipment. They had no satellite phones or long-range radios that would transmit a message three hundred miles back to their base. The CPU, however, had more advanced communications technology that afforded a greater range.

The first day in the plant was productive. Engineers built a schematic of the plant and even found some operating control manuals that gave them a head start on activating the processes necessary to get it running. There was no further CPU activity, and the prisoners they captured were more concerned about getting back to their poker game than defending the plant. After hearing them complain about it for the entire first day, Leena ordered her people to bring their poker table into the temporary prison cell so they could continue their game.

Leena had her soldiers put tables out on the portico so she could enjoy her lunch while gazing at the ocean. She had never been to the ocean and, although she was terrified of the water, she thoroughly enjoyed watching the waves crash on the beach.

A large pipe, probably six feet in diameter, protruded into the water from the plant. Leena assumed this was how the pumps brought in the seawater. Like everything else, the entire pipe was rusty with remnants of red paint, chipped and peeling.

Lunch was another Meal Ready-to-Eat (MRU), which had the consistency of mush but tasted like a combination of peas and oatmeal. She was not sure what it was supposed to be, but she was sure it failed to mimic it effectively. As she finished her meal and washed it down with distilled water, Viktor came to speak with her.

"I hope this is good news, Viktor," Leena said to greet him.

"I wish it were." Viktor sat in front of Leena, hesitant to continue.

"Well, spit it out."

"We are missing some parts. We figured out how the plant works and, from what we can tell, it's in good shape. I think we can get it to work, but we need to replace some parts that are not functioning because of their age."

"What is it you need?" Leena asked.

Viktor looked at Leena, knowing she would not understand what he might tell her, but continued anyway. "We need a new electrical panel, a three-way control valve, and some eight-inch gaskets."

"And where would we find those?"

"Zone 7 would have them all," Viktor said with a smile.

"Sure, we'll just run back home and pick those up," Leena deadpanned.

"I don't know where we might locate them all the way out here, Leena. Port Royal is barely a town. Even fully functional, I doubt anyone there would have plumbing supplies for a plant this size. Maybe in Charleston."

"What about Lanthemtown?" Leena said.

"What is Lanthemtown?" Viktor asked.

"That trading village we passed on the highway."

Viktor paused for a moment and then his eyes grew bright as he remembered the town they had passed. "That seems high-risk. We know nothing about that town. And how do we know they have those parts?"

"We don't, but Lilian said it was a trading town, so it's likely they'll have plumbing parts, assuming we have something to trade. And if we cannot get it there, we will have to try for Charleston."

"Charleston is entirely Aberjay," Viktor said with a tinge of fear in his voice. "It's not likely they would even let us in the door."

"Yes, I know, but what choice do we have?"

"Okay, Lanthemtown it is. Who do you think should go?"

"You and I can go with a small group of soldiers, maybe five," Leena proposed. "Let's also send a few soldiers to Charleston. Just in case we don't make it back, we need a backup plan."

"Are you sure that's enough security for Lanthemtown? It's a Tullian encampment."

"Too much will spook the locals. We want to get in and out with little attention. It's best we change our clothes as well."

"Okay, let's plan to head out in the morning. My engineers have plenty of work to keep them busy while we go on our adventure."

Liv helped Leena load the truck and selected the five soldiers who would accompany them to Lanthemtown. They decided to take rifles to trade. This would allow them to leave guards on the truck as they walked into the trader village. The other team left for Charleston about an hour earlier.

"I know you want to go, Liv, but I need you to stay here to monitor the prisoners and make sure the work continues," Leena told Liv. "Once we get back, we need to get the parts installed and get back home as soon as we can."

"I understand. You be safe. Don't take shit from Tullian scum," Liv said as she prepared to walk back to the plant.

In the truck, Viktor and Leena sat up front with the driver, the other four riding in the back with the weapons and minimal supplies they needed. The town was only a couple of hours away, but they wanted to be prepared to spend the night if necessary.

They went first to Port Loyal, stopping just long enough to check with Lyon Davis about the parts they needed. He could not provide any help or offer any advice on where she might get the parts other than in Lanthemtown.

About an hour into the drive, they came upon a body of a man facedown on the road and covered in scraps of clothing. The driver slowed, but Leena was suspicious.

"Go around it," she ordered the driver.

"You don't want to stop and investigate?"

"No, it's likely a trap. Don't stop."

The driver slowed enough so he could pull the large truck around the body, but as the front wheels passed it, the man rose from the ground with a small shotgun in hand, firing a shot into the driver's side door. Several pellets from the shot-gun blast broke through the thin metal of the truck and penetrated the driver's leg, causing him to come to an abrupt stop and cry out in pain.

Leena pulled the driver toward her to make space and then jumped over him to get the truck moving again. As she slid into the driver's seat and put the truck in gear, she looked in the mirror to see the attacker reloading his gun and walking toward her door. She dropped her foot on the accelerator just as the man fired another shot.

Checking her mirrors, Leena could see the attacker was not alone, and her troops began firing out the back of the truck. She drove for a mile or so before stopping to check on her troops. She had escaped injury from the last blast of the shotgun, but the driver's leg was still bleeding. She removed a knife from her holster and cut his pants leg before wrapping and binding it to slow the bleeding.

"Viktor, hold this!" she shouted as she jumped down from the truck and drew her sidearm, prepared for anything. She walked to the back. The soldiers were all accounted for and did not appear to have been injured in the ambush.

"You all okay?"

"Yes, Lieutenant. There were several attackers, and they grabbed a bag with some food, but other than that, we're good."

Leena directed them to help the driver to the back of the truck so his wound could be treated. She walked around the truck to ensure there was no further damage and that the tires were still functional. She stood guard as the soldiers properly dressed the driver's wound.

"How is he?" she asked.

"He'll be fine, just a flesh wound," a soldier replied.

"Okay, let's get moving."

Leena holstered her firearm and climbed back into the front seat of the truck. She knew how to drive it but not too well because her feet barely touched the pedals. Within a short time, however, she figured out that she could sit on the edge of the seat and reach the pedals well enough to get them moving. She tried to calm down, but the adrenaline surge prompted by the attack would not subside. Her heart raced and her mind was cloudy. She tried to focus on getting to Lanthemtown without thinking about how she would manage once she arrived.

Many thoughts nagged at her. *Am I doing the right thing? Is this madness walking into a Tullian settlement? Am I putting my unborn child at risk?*

Within an hour, she calmed down a bit and pulled onto the dirt road that led off the highway toward Lanthemtown. A crudely designed sign indicated it was five miles from the highway, along with a message that read 'No weapons.'

As they neared the large settlement, she could see that vehicles were parked all over the open field outside the city. A wall—a hodgepodge of metal sheeting, rocks, and chain-link fencing—surrounded the entire town. It was clear the wall was not a permanent structure. Leena wondered as she came close if the entire town was moved from time to time to another location as it looked more like a collection of tents than an actual settlement.

The town was gated, and the gates were closed. She figured there was an entrance fee of some sort as there were people stationed outside the gates who seemed to be blocking them.

Parking the truck amid many other vehicles, she put two soldiers in charge of guarding it as she and Viktor, along with three others, walked toward the gate.

Outside the gate was a small booth with three rough-looking individuals. All three had multiple tattoos and piercings and wore what looked to be dresses. They were long T-shirts that were filled with holes and extended down to their knees. Two of them were clearly guards as they held guns, one a rifle and the other a shotgun.

As Leena and her fellow soldiers approached, dressed in street clothes to hide their identities, the man behind the booth said, "No guns."

Leena looked at the other soldiers and removed her firearm from its holster, handing it over to the ruffians. The soldiers followed suit. After their guns were placed in a basket, they were handed tickets and pointed toward the entrance.

It was morning, and the streets were mostly empty. The city was like a tent city of homeless people, which Leena had encountered in Zone 6. There did not seem to be many permanent structures. Tent after tent was set up in a long row with wooden signs hand-painted to identify each tent's purpose. Leena tried to read them all, but there were too many. One said, 'Car parts,' while another said, 'Massage.' Another said, 'Girls,' while yet another said, 'Water.'

They felt out of place. The few people they saw scurrying about were not in groups and looked at them strangely if at all. Fires that had burned the night before left traces of smoke and the smell of ash in the air. Leena thought the trip was a mistake. Their street clothes did not allow them to blend in as well as she had hoped.

They walked farther and farther into the depths of the city and found still more tents. After much searching, they located one that said, 'Electric.' The soldiers were posted outside as Viktor and Leena walked inside. In the center of the tent was a long table with two vendors seated at one end in old plastic chairs.

"What do you need?" one of them said as he jumped out of his chair. He was short and exceptionally large, with no hair on his head, his brow, or anywhere else on his body that they could see. Leena had never seen anyone without eyebrows, and it caught her by surprise.

Viktor stepped up to the counter and said, "I need a Giantcore six-hundred-amp electrical panel."

"Wow, are you building a city?" the man asked without actually expecting an answer. He turned to his colleague and quietly had a conversation. Turning back, he said, "We have one, but it isn't here. I have to go get it from our inventory. What are you trading?"

"We have distilled water, the good stuff," Viktor said as he reached into his bag and took out a quart of water, shaking it in the man's face.

"Not good enough. We have water."

"What would you prefer?" Viktor asked, knowing he had extremely limited inventory.

The man looked over the table at Leena, eyeing her up and down. "How about a go with the lady for my friend and I," he said, licking his lips as if Leena were a finely grilled steak.

Viktor looked at Leena briefly in jest, but the look she returned clarified that she was not on the menu.

"That is not an option for us. What else?" Viktor stated.

Looking a bit disappointed, the man looked at his partner and then turned back to look at both of them, noticing their empty holsters.

"Guns? Do you have guns?"

"Yes, we can get you guns. Unfortunately, we are not allowed to bring them in," Viktor said.

Leena stepped up to the counter. "We will give you a nine-millimeter handgun and an M16A2 rifle for the panel we need."

The man put his hand to his chin, rubbing it as he thought about the deal. "Okay, it's a deal. We just need to go to the front gate to exchange your ticket and make the transfer. Let me go get the panel. I will meet you there in about an hour."

"Very well," Leena said as the two of them stepped out of the tent.

As they exited, the three soldiers they had left outside were gone. Standing in their place were four men with multicolored suits of armor holding long antique rifles. Leena and Viktor stopped as they cornered them.

"Come with us. The Wizard wants to see you."

Two of the soldiers fell in behind them while two led the way through the streets of the city. They traveled to the heart of the camp where it appeared that a structure had been constructed. It was two stories high and painted black. It looked unusual as it was the only permanent structure in the entire town as far as they could tell. Everything else seemed to be made of canvas or other light materials.

The soldiers directed them into the building and up the stairs to a large open room filled with sofas, animal skins, and a large desk on one end. Sitting behind the desk was a man in a white button-up shirt with a rawhide vest, black pants, and tall leather boots. He stood with the assistance of a cane that was all black except at the top, which held a glass ball.

"Greetings, my friends, please come in," the man said as he directed them to the waiting couches. "I am so glad you accepted my invitation. Oh, how I enjoy meeting new people."

Leena and her crew stepped cautiously into the room and sat as directed. A tall bald man in black clothes stepped forward to pour some water into small shot glasses set on the table in front of them.

"Please, please, enjoy some water to quench your thirst. I am sure you are thirsty."

Leena went first, picking up the shot glass and drinking the water. It was cold and felt good going down.

The man continued. "My name is Warren Filgotter. And yes, I know the name is atrocious, but you don't get to pick your name, right? Most people just call me The Wizard. Why don't you tell me who you are and what you are doing in my town?"

Leena noticed the man's tone had changed as he began his line of questioning. More insidious. Paranoid. She had not developed a back story because she did not know she would be questioned. She thought the truth might not be the best option as Tullian are rarely pleased to see or do business with city dwellers.

"My name is Leena. We live in a clan south of here. We are just here looking for some parts."

The man picked up a glass and sipped his water. He looked at all of them intently and then sat down wearing a broad smile.

BEYOND THE MINIYAR   159

"Now, you don't expect me to believe that, do you? Do I look uneducated? Do you think I made my fortune and built this place by being gullible?"

Leena paused, unsure of what to do. Within seconds, the man's smile changed to a frown. He turned toward one of his men, standing in the corner of the room, and motioned. Like the attendant, the man was dressed entirely in black. He stepped forward, grabbed one of Leena's guards by the hair, and dragged him over to the balcony of the room. He then threw him onto the floor, inches from the ledge. He pulled out a handgun and pointed at the man's head.

"Wait, wait!" Leena yelled. "I'll tell you the truth."

The Wizard put his hand up to stop his henchman from continuing and waited patiently for Leena to continue. "Well, spit it out, young girl, before I have all of you shot."

"We are from Zone 6. We are on a mission to get the old desalination plant going in Port Loyal to bring water to the zone. We need parts. We are here for parts."

The Wizard walked to the balcony where Leena's soldier was still on the floor with a boot on his neck. He crossed his arms in thought for what seemed like several minutes. Walking back into the room and sitting down, he continued.

"What parts do you need?"

Excited that his tone had changed back to pleasantries, Viktor sat up and rambled off the parts needed. The Wizard thought some more.

"There are two things that the Tullian need to survive out here in this tundra. Two things that make life survivable. Two things that separate those who live from those who die. Do you know what those two things are, Leena?"

"I am not sure. Water? Food?"

"Very close, Leena, you are a smart one. We survive on water and guns. We can go days, even weeks, without food, but we die without water. And if you don't have a gun, you die even sooner. I see you are well-equipped based on what my front-gate guards tell me. Here is what I propose. I will give you the parts you need for your plant. In exchange, you will give me all the water you have with you, as well as all the guns you have in your vehicle outside."

Leena spoke up to begin to protest the deal before she was interrupted. "Wait, if we give you..."

"I am not finished. In addition to the guns and the water that you will generously provide, your engineers will connect this settlement to that pipeline to provide drinking water."

Viktor spoke up. "Mr. Wizard, with all due respect, we don't have the personnel needed to run five miles of pipe from the pipeline to this town and into every dwelling. That would take a year or more."

"Don't be silly," the Wizard responded in a condescending tone. "I don't need you to provide water to all the people. I just need you to provide it to me. I will take care of distributing it to the thirsty people. For a small fee, of course. I bring in water to the town now, but my men must fetch it with a bucket from a well that I own many miles away from here. I have built bigger and bigger buckets, but if you were to provide me a water source that is right next to the highway, it would save me considerable fuel costs and provide a significant convenience."

Viktor thought for a few seconds and nodded to Leena.

"My concern is security," Leena said. "We were ambushed on the way here. If I give you all our guns, we might not even make it back to the plant."

"My sweet girl, you are speaking as if you have leverage, but you do not. I set the terms and you accept; there is no other option." The Wizard motioned toward the door, and his soldiers brought in both of the soldiers Leena had assigned to wait at the truck. They were thrown to the floor in front of the team.

"You see," the Wizard continued, "I already have your truck and your guns, and your supplies. So, I suggest you take my offer without another word and be on your way. I will see that my people load your truck with the supplies you need. And to ensure your compliance, your soldiers will stay here with me until our water station is fully operational. You and the engineer can take the parts to your team to get the water flowing. When you come back and set up my water station, you will get your friends back."

Leena and Viktor stood by their truck just outside the city walls as the Wizard's soldiers loaded the supplies he had promised. The truck was empty, other than those items. Leena's stomach was in knots thinking about making the journey back to the plant with no weapons. She did still have her baton, but that was not much of a match for most Tullian, who always seemed to be well armed.

Viktor volunteered to drive the truck and got them to the highway before Leena broke down and cried.

"I'm sorry, Leena, that was not what we expected, but we got the parts we need," Viktor said to console her.

"It's not just that. I'm in charge of this mission, and everything seems to be going off the rails. There are so many people relying on me. If I don't get the water running, thousands may die at home. If I don't get the water running, the Wizard will kill our people. If I don't get the water running, we go home failures, putting my job and ultimately my life at risk. What else could we pile on to this enormous ball of stress? Not to mention I think I am pregnant! It's like the entire world is resting on my back all at the same time."

"Don't forget that someone is trying to kill you," Viktor said to bring some levity to the situation.

Leena grinned then laughed. "I'm sorry, I didn't mean to dump on you. It isn't your responsibility to listen to me vent."

"I don't mind. Besides, we are all kind of in the same boat. If we don't get water going, my family is at risk as well. I think we all know how important this is. And we are all stressed about it. But we will get it done, just like every large, insurmountable project we take on—one step at a time."

"You're right. Okay, let's get it done then," Leena said as Viktor pulled the truck onto the highway and headed south toward the plant.

Night was falling as Viktor and Leena pulled into the parking lot of the plant. They had managed to get back with no further encounters. They made their way inside to meet up with Liv and break the news. Liv was in the bunkhouse, the room set up for temporary accommodation.

"The heroes return!" Liv said once she saw them enter the room. "Where are the others?"

"Things did not go as planned," Leena started.

"Yeah, let's call it a good news/bad news situation," Viktor added.

"We traded all the weapons we took with us to the Wizard for the parts," Leena began explaining.

"Aw, damn, I missed the Wizard," Liv responded.

"He was not the most pleasant person. He wants us to set up a water station for him on our way back after getting the water going. He is holding our people hostage until then."

"No shit. What a jerk. We better get this thing working then," Liv said as she gently patted the wall.

"Liv, can you get a team to unload the truck and take the parts to the control room? Viktor, get your guys on this. I want them working in shifts through the night if they must so we can get the plant operational as soon as possible."

Viktor and Liv nodded and left the room as Leena walked to a bunk she had been occupying each night. She undressed and slipped into bed to get a few hours of rest. She thought the quiet time in bed would give her time to think through all of her issues and determine the best course of action, but she only ruminated on the problems for about a minute before she was fast asleep.

Chapter 9

INVADERS

Leena slept through the night and woke at about eight a.m., getting about twelve hours of sleep. She climbed out of the bunk, wondering why someone had not woken her sooner. She stood and stretched a bit before putting her uniform on. Leena liked her street clothes, but since becoming a soldier, the green fatigues just felt like a better fit.

She grabbed a few ration bars out of her pack before walking out toward the lobby and then up to the control room to check on the progress. Viktor was in the room, studying gauges, along with several other engineers.

"How goes the battle, Viktor?" Leena asked cheerfully.

"Well, look who finally woke up. We were going to wake you earlier, but there was no point. We figured we would let you get some rest."

"Thank you for that. Where are we with this gigantic pile of pipe and bolts?"

Viktor turned without a word and walked to the farthest wall where a small tap handle was positioned on a pipe that ran through the room. He put a clear glass under the tap and turned the knob, filling the glass. He walked back to Leena, holding it to the light.

"Pure salt-free water," Viktor said, handing her the glass with pride.

"Is it safe to drink?"

"Ok yes. Drink, bathe, cook. Whatever you want to do with it."

Leena drank from the glass he gave her. "I don't believe I have ever tasted anything so good. This is amazing!"

"Yeah, well, most of what you drink now is rainwater or runs through miles of rusty pipes before you drink it. This is pure and from the source."

"Are you sending it home yet?"

"No, we have some tests we need to do on water quality, and we have to pressure-test the lines first, but we should get there today or tomorrow."

"That's fantastic. So, I guess we should plan to move out tomorrow."

"We will need to leave a contingent here to guard this place," Viktor said.

"Okay, I will leave one team of ten. The rest can accompany us back to Lanthemtown to get the water station up and running. How long will that take?"

"It should only take a few hours to tap into a pipe and provide him with a way to fill jugs. Let's hope he holds up his end of the bargain." Viktor finished and went back to his panel.

Leena walked from the control room to the platform that stood high above the lobby. Seeing many soldiers in the lobby, including Liv, she shouted, "We have water!"

The small group shouted in celebration as she descended the stairs. Leena filled Liv in on the plan and asked if they could eat lunch together out on the patio later that day, facing the ocean one last time before they had to leave.

Leena entered the small room on the main floor that had been set up as a base of operations for the mission. Corporal Weiss was using the handheld radio they had taken from the CPU guards.

"Did you call me, Corporal?" Leena asked the soldier.

"Yes, I got the radio working. It goes in and out as we are right at the far end of its range, but we can talk to headquarters. I had them a little while ago but then lost them again. If you want to take it outside to try it you may get a better result."

Leena took the radio and stepped onto the patio. She pressed the button on the radio to try to reach headquarters.

"CQ, CQ, come in, this is Loyal Eight."

"CQ, CQ come in, this is Loyal Eight."

Loyal Eight, we read you broken, this is CQ.

"CQ, I need Actual."

Loyal Eight, stand by for Actual.

After a few minutes of waiting, Leena received the response from headquarters indicating that Commander Johnson was on the line. The codes used were common to mask the conversation from those who might be listening on the unsecured channel.

Loyal Eight, this is CQ Actual, go ahead.

"CQ Actual, flow rate is a go. Flow rate is a go. Will return partial, 0600. Over."

Loyal Eight, received. Be advised, Charlie is hostile. Over.

"CQ, received. Charlie is hostile. Over and out."

Leena returned the radio to Corporal Weiss. Liv was standing nearby.

"Did you get through? What's going on?" Liv asked.

"Gather the troops in the lobby in thirty. I need to address them," Leena said.

Liv gathered the troops who were at the plant in the lobby. Leena climbed the stairs to address them. She looked at their faces, mostly young people. She felt the burden of their loyalty. She felt the expectation in their hearts. They believed in what they were doing. They counted on her to ensure their work had an impact. This frightened her a great deal.

"Team, I have received confirmation that we are at war with China," Leena said in a commanding voice.

The soldiers grumbled among themselves at the news.

Leena continued, "I don't have any further information. I know this is something we expected, and being far from the front lines, we don't expect an immediate impact, but it is likely our leaders will ask some of us to fight. Try not to overthink this. We are soldiers, and this is what we do. Some days, the enemy is on the other side of the wall, and some days, the enemy is on the other side of the world. It doesn't make a difference. We go where we are told and fight who we are told to fight. That makes us soldiers. Do not speculate on anything else until we have more information. Thank you."

Leena stepped down from her spot above them and made her way outside. She could hear the questions beginning to be asked by the soldiers and knew she had no answers to give them.

Leena walked to the beach after lunch. She had removed her boots so she could feel the sand between her toes. She didn't go near the water as that still gave her anxiety, but she paced up and down the beach, enjoying the wind and the salt spray from the crashing waves. She felt like a child picking up seashells and exploring all types of sea creatures that she occasionally found. Hermit crabs were plentiful, and she could see them scurry along the beach, hiding deep in their holes when she came near.

Liv approached her, also without boots on. She ran at Leena as though she was going to drag her into the waves. Leena ran from Liv's grasp.

"C'mon, you chicken," Liv yelled. "It won't hurt you to get a little wet."

"No thank you, I am fine just how I am," Leena responded.

After a few minutes of horseplay, they sat on the beach, looking out at the waves.

"It's amazing there is such beauty in this world, and we rarely get a chance to see it," Leena said.

"Yeah, this is pretty cool. I could probably live here. I just need a little shack on the beach, right down there," Liv said as she pointed down the beach near a grove of live oak trees. "We could build a tree house or small bungalow and never go home."

"I wish it were that simple. We have too many people depending on us."

"I guess we have to enjoy it while we're here. It all ends tomorrow," Liv said.

The two young women enjoyed the sun and the sand for another hour before something on the horizon caught Leena's attention. She sat up and shielded her eyes from the sun to get a better look. Dots. There were dots on the horizon. She then stood and walked toward the water.

"What is it, Leena?" Liv asked.

"I see something. Go get me a set of binoculars, Liv."

Liv ran from the beach to the plant above and returned with a small pair of binoculars. Leena put them to her eyes and was transfixed by what she saw.

"Well, what do you see? What is it?" Liv asked.

"Ships. I see ships."

"What kind of ships?"

"Chinese ships. Lots of Chinese ships."

Leena handed the binoculars to Liv to get confirmation as she began racing back to the plant. She shouted for a corporal to round up all the soldiers as they had done earlier, but Leena stayed on the balcony staring out to sea. Liv returned shortly and handed the binoculars back to Leena.

"If I didn't know any better, I would say this is an invasion force," Liv said.

"Yes, it certainly looks like it. But why on the East Coast? How did they even get over here? Our forces will never be ready for this. We expected the battle to be in the west. Corporal Weiss, get CQ back on the radio."

"Leena, what do we do? We can't abandon this station. We need to ensure the water flows," Liv said.

"We will defend it with our lives," Leena said.

"Against the entire Chinese army?" Liv asked, trying to apply reason.

Leena just looked at Liv, thinking through the situation.

"The smart thing to do would be to abandon the station and head back after turning on the water. But my fear is that the Chinese will turn it off immediately. Our work would have been for nothing. We'll be lucky if they don't blow the whole plant to hell from the water."

"We must fight then. Hold out as long as we can," Liv said.

"We have little ammunition. And we gave a bunch of rifles to the Wizard," Leena said.

"Well, it's a good day to die," Liv said with no hint of humor.

"It very well may be, Liv. But let's hope it doesn't come to that."

The soldiers gathered again in the lobby for the second time that day.

"Earlier, I told you we were at war with China," Leena began. "Unfortunately, we are closer to that war than we thought. I just saw dozens of ships flying the Chinese flag headed toward these shores. Their destination is likely Charleston, but they may come ashore in different places, and we have to be prepared for whatever comes. Master Sergeant Zolenski is going to give you your orders. We need to stockpile as much ammo as we have and prepare for the fight of our lives."

Leena then walked back out to the patio to gauge how long they had until the ships arrived. She reasoned they were about an hour or two from arriving, assuming they were not going to just sail by and on to Charleston.

Within an hour, Leena could count more than sixty ships about a mile off the coast. They were troop transport ships. As they watched, troops from these large vessels boarded landing crafts and began their voyage toward the coast. Leena wondered why they would land here. There would be no strategic value in this section of the coast other than the desalination plant, and it had not been in operation for years.

Her team took tactical positions on the roof of the plant as well as on the patio. They had time to stack some sandbags to create a few small, fortified nests. They had no major weaponry, only handheld pistols, about twenty rifles, and a few explosives. It was not much against the approaching forces.

The first two troop landing crafts hit the beach and dropped their bow as more than fifty soldiers ran out of each one, all dressed for battle and carrying rifles. Leena ordered her troops to fire on their positions as they came off the ships, and many of them fell from the gunfire. Those who made it to the beach quickly found protection behind some small dunes and returned fire.

"Target the carriers!" Liv cried out as each member of the team turned their fire on the soldiers exiting the arriving landing crafts that had stalled near the beach.

The two forces fired on each other for more than an hour as more and more soldiers hit the beach and took cover. Before she knew it, they were outnumbered by at least fifty to one. Leena knew this was a losing battle. Nine members of her team had already been killed, while the Chinese were down about forty. It made no difference. They had the numbers, and they knew it.

Leena waited until her team signaled that they were out of ammunition. Both sides sat silent for what seemed like ten minutes before the Chinese stood and began slowly making their way up the hill, through the dunes, to the platform.

Leena gave the order to surrender, and all members of the team dropped their spent weapons and stood in unison with hands held high. The Chinese swarmed the platform and took all of them into custody, binding their arms behind them and marching them into the plant. Once blindfolds and earmuffs rendered them unable to see or hear, they were placed side by side on the lobby floor.

Leena lost track of Liv but knew she was there somewhere. She had no choice but to await her fate. After about an hour, she was pulled to her feet, pushed into a room, and shoved into a chair.

Once again, she waited, unaware of her fate or the fate of her soldiers. She used her feet to kick around the chair, hoping to determine if others were tied up near her. But there was no one. She struggled to get her earmuffs off but couldn't position her body in the right way to do so. As she wiggled, she could feel someone wrap a strap around her waist and tie her to the chair.

A while later, her earmuffs were briefly removed, and a Chinese soldier shouted at her.

"What is your name?" the soldier asked with a thick accent.

"My name is Lieutenant Leena Zhen."

With that answer, the soldier put muffs back on her ears and moved on. She heard voices but could not make them out. She occasionally saw the light in the room increase or decrease but could not see well enough through the blindfold to determine if it was a light going on and off or sunlight intermittently streaming through a window.

The fear of not being able to see or hear was paralyzing. They could have shot them in the head at any moment and they wouldn't even see it coming. Her mind raced. She thought about her unborn child, her husband Jordan, her soldiers trapped in

Lanthemtown, and the soldiers in the room. All of them were counting on her. *Were these the images of her life passing before her eyes? Would she soon see her end?*

Minutes turned into more than an hour. As a soldier removed her blindfold, Leena could see she was in a small room with Liv and a few other soldiers, likely segregated because of their rank. Liv and the others were freed of their blindfolds and earmuffs as well. Any attempt at speech, however, was met with shouting by those who guarded them. The others could not understand the language, but Leena knew Chinese. She heard them say "shut up" repeatedly. She felt they were waiting for something—or maybe someone.

Minutes later, a Chinese officer entered the room. A chair was placed in front of the group, and the officer sat down in front of them. His soldiers handed him a water bottle, and he drank from it slowly.

"My name is Captain Guo Huang. You are now my prisoners and will do as I say. Your imperialist country has impeded the spread of goodness and charity throughout the world by propagating greed and materialism. Today, that ends. China will no longer allow the world to be controlled by the hypocritical patriarchs of America."

As the captain continued his speech, an aide walked in and whispered in his ear. The captain looked around the room.

"Zhen, Leena. Who is Zhen, Leena?!" he shouted, even though it was a small room.

"I am," Leena said through nervous lips.

"Let her go," the captain said in English to his soldier. "She is one of us."

The soldier stood Leena up and cut the ties that bound her hands.

"I don't understand," Leena said.

"Yes, you do. We ran the names of all prisoners through our database. It seems you are especially important to our ambassador and are favorable to our cause."

"What?!" Liv screamed. "What the hell is going on, Leena?! You betrayed us?!"

"No," Leena said, "it isn't like that."

"You played us? You scammed us all? You traitor!" Liv shouted, tugging at her restraints. She jumped up out of her chair and threw her body against Leena, knocking her against the wall. Liv then ran past the captain to the small gap in the door behind him. Her hands somehow came free as she burst through the door and sprinted to freedom.

"Get her back!" the captain ordered in Chinese.

"Liv, stop!" Leena shouted to no avail. "Captain, I don't know what you have heard, but I am not a friend of communist China."

"You must be, dear child, because our database does not lie. We keep immaculate records."

A soldier ran into the room and explained to the captain that Liv had stolen a radio and escaped to the north side of the plant. The captain reiterated to his troops to find her.

"I can assure you she will not get far. I have more than fifty thousand troops scattered on these shores and many more to follow. We will have her back shortly. Please escort Mrs. Zhen to a private area where we may talk as friends. As for the others, let's see what they know."

The Chinese soldiers escorted Leena out of the room. She could see the disappointment in the eyes of her soldiers as she was directed through the door. Her heart sank, knowing they had the wrong impression of her loyalties. She got the sense that the captain knew it would set her against her soldiers and placed her in that room for that purpose.

She was now free of her cuffs in a small room with a table that had been set up with a tiny hotpot and travel tea kit. She was directed to sit across from the captain as tea was poured for the two of them.

"I really don't understand this," Leena said in protest.

"I see you prefer English. That is fine. I am sorry about that display in there. It was important that your friends know you are a traitor for the plan to work."

"What plan? I am no traitor," Leena said.

"Yes, but your friends don't know that, do they?"

The captain quickly downed his small cup of tea and motioned for a nearby soldier, who poured some more.

"Did you not meet with Ambassador Feng Lao in Zone 7? I believe you had a pleasant conversation with him on two occasions when you agreed to stand down your soldiers during our invasion in exchange for leniency."

"No, that is not what happened," Leena protested.

"So, you did not meet with the ambassador?"

"Yes, I met with the ambassador, but..."

"Then we have the correct information," the captain said with finality. "You had your soldiers stand down during this fight, and you will do so again when we attack your city. You are indeed a friend of China."

"I ordered my soldiers to stand down because we ran out of ammunition. Continuing the fight would have led to more bloodshed."

"You are a good leader, Lieutenant. That is why we picked you. We knew you would do the right thing when confronted with an impossible choice."

"I will not help you destroy my people," Leena said.

"Destroy? My sweet girl, this is what we are trying to avoid. Your country has been around the world, forcing your imperialist values on others and destroying those who get in the way. We are not like your stars and stripes. We want peace. For all of us to live in harmony. Won't you help me complete this transition so that we can avoid bloodshed?"

"I won't."

"Yes, you will, Leena Zhen. Do you know why?"

"Why?"

"Because your people need water. And we are now in control of this water plant. And because your people are outnumbered by my force, ten to one. And because you are smart and don't like to see the loss of life. I am like you. I don't like to see my men shot full of holes. We can make this transition very peaceful, you and me. We can save the world, Leena Zhen. We can do it together."

"I can't give you the city. I don't control the entire army."

"No, but you are a lieutenant, meaning that you control thousands. When we invade your city, they will put you in charge of guarding against our attack, most likely on one of your many walls. We will expect your people to throw down their arms and surrender to avoid destruction. If they do, I will give you a prominent place in the new Federated States of China. If they do not, we will destroy this water facility, so your people will never get the water they need to survive. And then we will kill the soldiers here who you are going to leave behind. And then we will invade your city and take control anyway. The only difference is how many of your people must die. We are not brutal like the people in your government. What do you call them? The Aberjay? We don't want anyone to die needlessly. We can all live in peace once we have liberated your cities from the fascists."

Leena sipped her tea, her mind racing as to her next move. She knew she could not overpower even the guards in that room. She had to outwit them somehow. She was worried about her soldiers' lives, not just those at the plant but those who were left behind in Lanthemtown. She could think of no outcome that would free them all. She was caught in a situation with no good outcome.

"What must I do?" Leena asked.

"Excellent, I am glad to have you on the team. I will give you a truck to make it back to your people. I will turn on your water so you can arrive as a hero. They will praise your name in the streets. We will then march on your city within days and will expect your cooperation. If we have an easy entrance and quick surrender, we will radio back to our comrades here to release your people and keep the water flowing. If not, we will kill your people and turn off the water. Then we will destroy this station to ensure it never flows again."

"Can I take my lead engineer Viktor with me? He's the only one who knows the way back, and my people will be suspicious if he does not return. Also, my master sergeant. I need her for security on the way home."

"You can have your engineer, but I can tell your master sergeant is important to you. She stays here. I will let you take a loaded pistol with you for protection. I wouldn't want you being murdered on the way home."

"I will also need some supplies to fix any holes in the line that we find as we make our way home," Leena added, knowing she had to build a water station at Lanthemtown.

"Very well. You will have what you need. You better get going. And to ensure there is honesty between us, we will ask that you wear this GPS device." The captain took a small device shaped like a flower and painted gold from his pocket and pinned it to her lapel.

Leena knew the device would make her travel much harder. She tried to be positive and set that worry aside until she had to consider it once again.

Chapter 10

RACE

Leena and Viktor stood by the truck, surrounded by the Chinese army, waiting for them to finish loading the truck. They slowly walked to the edge of the parking area to look down at the beach.

The beaches were full of soldiers, as Captain Huang had said. Landing crafts full of equipment were taking turns unloading tanks, trucks, stacks of ammunition, and more soldiers. After each carrier was empty, the crew would return it to the anchored warships to load more cargo.

"Wow, that's a lot of gear," Leena whispered to Viktor as they waited to be released.

"Without a doubt. I hope Commander Johnson knows about this or this could be a short battle."

"It's not likely they know unless Charleston has radioed ahead." Leena paused, staring out at the thousands of troops and equipment that lined the beach. "No, this was a surprise. No one expected them to come from the east. My guess is the federal troops are headed to Utah or Arizona, thinking the battle will be there."

"Did you tell the captain about Lanthemtown?" Viktor asked.

"No, I didn't figure he needed to know. I am hoping we can stop there quickly and set up a water station."

"It isn't that easy, Leena, It will take some time."

Leena pointed to the GPS device on her lapel. "I am not sure we have it. One thing at a time, I guess. Let's see if we can get there in one piece first."

They walked back to the truck and climbed in the front. Viktor sat in the driver's seat because his legs were a little longer and Leena wanted to be free to fire on any enemies they met along the way. A Chinese soldier handed a handgun to Leena along with a separate magazine full of bullets.

As they pulled out of the parking lot, Leena looked back, hoping to get a glimpse of Liv to somehow communicate that she was not a traitor. She wondered if they had caught her yet. Was she bound in a temporary cell? She felt responsible for her. She felt responsible for all of it.

Viktor drove the truck out of the parking lot and up the hill. The truck howled as it climbed, loudly displaying its power. Both of the occupants had made this trip before.

"Uh-oh," Viktor said in an ominous tone.

"Uh-oh what? Don't say uh-oh. I don't like uh-oh," Leena responded.

"We need fuel," Viktor said as he looked over to Leena for direction.

The two had not made it more than a few miles from the beach.

"Did they load fuel into the back?" Leena asked.

"Do you want to stop to find out?"

"No, let's just stop in Port Loyal. If there isn't any in the back, we can ask Lyon."

"Who is Lyon?" Viktor said.

"The guy who runs Port Loyal. I guess you didn't meet him."

"And we are on a first-name basis with Lyon?"

"Well, I wouldn't say friends but definitely acquaintances," Leena said with a grin.

"Let's hope you made a good impression on him," Viktor said as they pulled into what looked like the only fuel station in town, about a hundred yards past the judicial building where the town's residents lived.

Leena stepped out of the truck and walked to the back, then climbed the few ladder steps to access the supplies. She saw plumbing supplies, electrical wire, and some pumps but didn't see any gas cans.

"Nothing here!" she shouted to Viktor.

"Let me try the pumps," Viktor replied.

Lifting the front hood of the truck, Viktor pulled the handle from one of the gas pumps from its resting place and inserted it into the tank. He pressed the start button on the pump but couldn't get it to start.

"There's probably a cutoff inside," Leena said as she walked toward the door to the station. It was locked. She shook it, hoping it might come free easily. When it didn't, she took out the baton that the captain had graciously allowed her to keep and, with a flick of her wrist, extended it fully. Right before smashing the glass with her baton, she heard a shout from behind her.

"Stop!"

Leena turned quickly, prepared to fight, but the voice was Lyon Davis, backed by five men and two women who were armed with rifles.

"Hi, Lyon. I hope you don't mind. We're out of fuel and need to get back home."

"I do mind, Lieutenant. Just because we don't seem to be very mobile does not mean we don't need our fuel just as much as you do."

"Well, you made an impression, didn't you?" Viktor said under his breath.

"I meant no disrespect, Lyon; we just need fuel."

Lyon motioned to his people to lower their weapons.

"We need compensation, Lieutenant. That is how it works now, no?"

"Lyon, I would love to oblige, but I don't have much to give. Are you aware of what is going on at the beach?"

"The Chinese? Yes, I am hoping they can clean this place up a bit. I have never been fond of communists, but they can't do much worse at this point."

"We need to get home to warn my superiors, Lyon. The fate of thousands hang in the balance."

"That may be true for you, but that don't make it true for me."

"I can give you a full tank of gas for that handgun," Lyon offered.

Leena sighed loudly. She knew how important it was that they have some sort of weapon for their trip home. She thought for a moment and reasoned that maybe she could get a rifle out of the Wizard.

"Okay, deal." Leena slowly reached for her pistol and held it out to Lyon. He took the gun from her hands, inspected it to ensure it was functional, and then dropped it into a small canvas bag.

"I like your bag," Leena said. "I once had one just like it."

"Thank you. Let me get that door for you," Lyon responded.

Lyon took out a large metal ring that held more than one hundred keys. He searched for a particular key for about a minute and then unlocked the door to the station. Walking inside, he reached behind the counter and then shouted to Viktor, "Try it now!"

Viktor put his thumbs up once the fuel flowed into the tank. The truck had a large tank that held close to a hundred gallons. Lyon walked back outside and took a seat on a bench next to Leena. Joining him, Leena was the first to break the tension.

"You really don't care about the Chinese invading?"

"No, we have nothing they want. They will probably blow right by us. And if they stay, they can only make things better. I used to care about things like that. Politics. Who's right? Who's wrong? It just doesn't mean much when you don't know where you will get your next meal." Lyon looked toward his people, holding rifles. "These folks just want to live. At this point, it doesn't matter how. Or whose banner is flying on the flagpole. Survival takes precedence over civility. Maslow had it right, I guess."

"Maslow?" Leena asked.

"Yeah, Maslow's hierarchy of needs. Didn't you study it in school?" Lyon asked.

"I don't think so."

"Every human has a hierarchy of needs. The need for food and water is paramount. If that need is met, humans are concerned about security. Their safety. If that one is met, it's love, and so on. If food and water are scarce, we don't care about much else."

"Yeah, that sounds about right," Leena mused.

"That's it," Viktor shouted as he put the pump handle back in place.

"Thanks again, Lyon. I know you consider it just barter, but you didn't have to make the trade. Maybe we do care about more than food and water."

"Maybe so, Lieutenant, maybe so."

Lyon waved goodbye as they pulled the truck back onto the road out of town and headed toward their next stop—Lanthemtown.

Viktor pulled the truck onto the dirt road that led to Lanthemtown and immediately stopped. He jumped out of the truck before Leena could ask him why he stopped. She joined him and watched as he walked up and down the highway, frantically looking for something.

"What is it?" Leena asked.

"Water pipes. They must come through here somewhere. Help me find them."

Leena began walking along the highway, not even sure what she was looking for but certain she did not want to run into any Tullian without a firearm. As she walked south, she noticed a mound of dirt about a hundred feet from the dirt road. It rose up in an unusual way that made her think it was not natural. It was just a mound but a mound with a particular shape. It reminded her of the mound sticking up out of the swamp they used to access the plant.

"Viktor!" she shouted. "Is this something?" Leena pointed at the mound as Viktor ran her way.

Viktor climbed to the top of the mound and began digging with his hands. He pulled and pulled at the dirt until it came free as if it had been piled there. Before long, he reached some concrete and began following the edges. As he extracted more and more dirt from the mound, it revealed a cage and, after the front of it was also excavated, they found a padlock, old and rusty, and likely buried there for decades.

"Bring me a hammer!" Viktor shouted as he continued to remove dirt from the mound. Leena ran to the truck and returned with a small sledgehammer.

"It's all I could find," she said.

"Stand back," Viktor said as he raised it high above his head and landed the enormous head of metal on the lock. A spark leaped from the old lock, and he struck it again and again. On the fourth attempt, the lock finally broke, falling from the cage. Stepping up on top of the cage, he grabbed it with both hands and pulled until it came free. The inside of the wire cage was also filled with dirt, so he began digging again.

"Ha!" Viktor cried out. "We found it!"

"What did we find?" Leena asked.

"This is the pipe. Well, it's a small pipe that leads to the pipeline, but it's good enough. We can attach it here and give the old Wizard a pumping station from which he can draw water."

"I know it might not make much sense, but I have a thought," Leena said cautiously.

"Well, spit it out, lady."

"The Wizard is going to use this to take advantage of people. He isn't going to give the water away for free."

"Well, duh, I thought that was a given," Viktor said.

"What if we don't give it to him?"

"I'm sorry. What do you mean by that?"

"Well, what if we just set it up for the people and let them all have at it?"

Viktor raked his hands through his hair in frustration and then began walking toward the truck. As he reached the supplies, he climbed into the back and began throwing the parts needed onto the ground.

"Viktor?"

"Viktor?" she repeated.

"How on earth are we going to get back home if we don't give him the water? How will we rescue our people if we don't give him the water? Leena, how will we escape with our lives if we don't give him the water?"

"I don't know. I have not really thought that far ahead. But do you think it's a good idea?"

Viktor stopped and walked right up to Leena and put his face only inches from hers. "I think it's lunacy."

Viktor began collecting the supplies on the ground and dragging them toward the pipe they had found. Leena walked to the truck and sat down on the dirt in the shadow, shielding herself from the sun. She had to figure out a way to do the right thing. There must be a way.

Constructing the connections necessary to connect the pipes took about two hours. Once the proper pieces were in place and the valve was turned, the water flowed freely. Viktor cheered when it did but then noticed he was alone as Leena was sulking by the truck.

Viktor returned to her to deliver the good news.

"The water station is live. Water is flowing."

"Great, now Mr. Wizard can trade it for the souls of the people who live here."

"Leena, you don't know any of these people."

"That doesn't mean I don't care. Are we not an army that fights for those who are oppressed?"

"I'm an engineer, not a soldier. And as much as I like to do the right thing, there are limits. There are boundaries."

"What are the boundaries?"

"Getting your head cut off is a boundary for me. And it should be for you. If you die here, you can't help Liv and the others. Please get in the truck."

Leena could tell Viktor was losing patience with her. She knew he was a good man. A reasonable man. Maybe he was right.

They pulled the truck near the water station Viktor had engineered so they could fill all the containers they had on board with fresh water. Then they drove to Lanthemtown.

The same men were out in front of the main gate.

"Guns," they said as Leena and Viktor approached.

"We don't have any," Leena said.

One guard motioned, and a tall one walked toward them, slowly running his hands up and down their legs and torsos to ensure they were not carrying any firearms.

"You must be insane to walk around out here without a gun," the small one said.

"Well, you must be crazy to just sit here while there is a fully functional water station just five miles from here, out by the highway," Leena said in response.

"What are you doing?" Viktor said with disdain.

"Nothing. Just letting them know where they might get fresh water if they need it." Leena stared at the three men, expecting them to take off running toward the water, but they just stood there.

Viktor pulled Leena toward the front door. With a knock, it opened for them, and they walked down the familiar street lined with tents. As it was late afternoon, there were many more people on the streets than before. They huddled in groups, drinking and playing cards. Fire barrels were lit to provide warmth.

The two walked toward the Wizard's residence, trying to avoid contact with drunks and pushy vendors. They walked past the first tent they had entered on their first visit when Leena stepped away from Viktor and slipped inside. Without waiting for them to ask, she addressed the people inside.

"We just built a water station out by the highway," Leena announced. "The water is free. Help yourself."

The two shopkeepers just looked at each other, befuddled.

"Go, get the water. It's free!" Leena shouted.

"C'mon, Leena, they're not interested." Viktor took her by the arm to walk her out.

"Why won't anyone go get it?" Leena asked.

"They don't believe you. No one gives away free water."

"That is just silly. We must make them go get it."

"Free water! Free water!" Leena shouted as they walked through the streets. "There's a water station out by the highway. Free water!"

As they approached the Wizard's residence, guards surrounded them.

"Hands up," one of them said.

"We need to see the Wizard. We are expected," Leena said as one of them dashed inside to get approval.

Leena examined her surroundings as they waited. The city that had been a sleepy little trading post during their morning visit before was now a wild party. Drunks were stumbling about. Women, clearly women of the night, giggled and shouted as they cavorted about in skimpy outfits. People gathered around barrel fires just as they did in Zone 6, but it was more social, more jovial. It wasn't just the warmth they were after. They laughed and drank and told stories. The debauchery was obvious, but something about the environment spoke to a desire in Leena to be free. These people she watched were obviously the derelicts and dregs of society. Those who live on the fringes. But they were free. Freer than she had ever felt. These thoughts flooded her mind, but she knew she had no time to unpack them.

"This way," the guard said when he returned.

They walked the familiar stairs up to the second level and were directed to the couch where they sat before. The Wizard was not present in the room. The heat was overpowering as there was no air conditioning in this building, just a squeaky ceiling fan that turned slowly. They counted off the minutes as they waited. Sweat beaded on Leena's neck and drizzled down her back. She squirmed, feeling uncomfortable in the heat and humidity but unable to do anything about it.

An hour later, the Wizard came up the stairs.

"My friends from the west, it is so good to see you again," he said as he opened his arms wide and walked into the room to face them.

Leena and Viktor stood. "We have set up your water station as directed. Let my people go," Leena said with confidence.

"In time, young lady, in time. First, let's toast to your success!"

The Wizard motioned for an attendant, who brought a large bottle of water, pouring a small glass for each of them.

Leena grabbed her glass as soon as it was full and downed it. Viktor drank with more caution, suspicious of the Wizard.

"Okay, can we go now?" Leena asked.

"It is late and beginning to get dark out. There is no way for me to verify the work you have done to provide water. Stay the night and we will go in the morning to confirm, then you can be on your way."

Leena protested but then realized it would be a wasted effort. They were at the Wizard's mercy. He had the power, the weapons, the guards. They had no leverage and no bargaining chips to barter with this time.

The Wizard's guards escorted Leena and Viktor to the ground floor of the building, then down a dark hallway with doors on each side, all painted black. They opened a door and pointed inside. Leena and Viktor stepped inside the room, and the guards shut the door before they could turn around. The sound of a lock turning from the outside broke the silence in the room. They were prisoners, not guests, as the Wizard had suggested.

The room had three small beds, an oversized chest of drawers, a painted cement floor, and a tiny light hanging from a string in the center of the room. It was hot, and there was minimal ventilation, which came from a small slit above the door that looked as if it were meant for a window, but the builder never finished installing it. The heat in the room was overpowering, almost insidious in the way it lay on them, sapping them of their energy. It was likely not intentional, just the result of poor construction and the lack of air conditioning.

"I guess we're here for the night," Viktor said.

"Lovely," Leena replied as she sat on the bed and removed her button-up shirt, revealing an undershirt soaked in sweat.

The sounds outside grew louder as the hours ticked by. Shouting, screaming, laughing. They rose like an ocean wave and then subsided, only to come again a few minutes later. They had no way to determine the time, but the roar subsided after many hours, likely well past midnight. They both tried to lie on the small beds and sleep, but it was way too hot. Leena had no idea when the guards would come for them and felt powerless.

"Viktor," Leena said deep into the night. "Are you awake?"

"Yes, who can sleep in hell?"

"The Chinese have asked me to help them storm the city."

"That does not surprise me. They are a slippery lot," Viktor responded.

"I am not sure what to do."

"About what? We cannot surrender to the Chinese."

"If I don't do what they're asking me to do, they will kill Liv and all the soldiers at the water plant. And they will shut down the water. Is it so bad to just let them have the city? They vastly outnumber us anyway, and standing down our forces will save lives."

Viktor sat up in his bed and turned to Leena.

"We give up our lives because we fight for an ideal that is worth fighting for, Leena. We fight to stay free. That is what it means to be an American."

"Are we really Americans when we are slaves to the Aberjay? We may think we have won our freedom, but we have won nothing. They still control our lives. They control our food supplies. They determine what they will allow us to do. It isn't freedom, Viktor."

"Americans have always struggled to find their identity. The Irish, the Blacks, the Jews. Each group must find their own way, and while they may start out subservient to some other group, it gets better. Little by little, it gets better. The Irish suffered in this way when we came to this country. Besides, the Chinese don't have a recipe for a perfect society. They have their own issues. The only question is this: Who is in power? War is about power."

"I'm very confused. I'm new to all the politics," Leena said with resignation.

"Even if there are challenges to our society, imbalances that need fixing, and inequalities that should be addressed—we fight for the right to address them. We are Americans because we believe we can always change what is not working, and the people should have a voice. China won't give you a voice. They will tell you how to believe and live and exist. You may not have freedom, but America allows you to fight for it. Do you think China will listen to cries of inequality if things don't stack up in our favor?"

"I guess you're right. But that does not fix my problem."

"Leena, Liv and the others are casualties of war. You need to do what is right for your country. If people die because of it, then people die. The Chinese are at fault here, not you."

"Well, that's cold," Leena said.

"No, that is reality. Try to get some sleep if you can; I envision another long day ahead of us."

During the early morning hours, Leena finally fell asleep. The rattle of the door being unlocked woke her, and she could tell by how she felt that she had not slept for long. Her eyes hurt, her muscles were sore, and the bed she was lying in was soaked with sweat.

"You two, let's go!" a guard announced from the door.

Leena and Viktor followed a guard upstairs to the Wizard's office once more and then out onto the balcony where a round table with five seats awaited. On the tables were pastries, eggs, and salted pork strips.

The breeze they felt was liberating. It blew fiercely, quickly drying up the sweat that had accumulated on their bodies. It was still hot, but the slight deviation in temperature produced by the wind was noticeable.

"Please," the Wizard began, "have a seat and dine with me."

The two sat and began eating, enjoying the meal as if they had not eaten in days. It was a welcome change from meal rations. The coffee was hot and paired well with the cool breeze blowing over the tent tops. It was early morning, and the sun was just peeking over the horizon.

"Eat up, and we will go see your water station," the Wizard said. "I sent men to secure it this morning."

If he sent men to secure it, why were they still being detained? Leena wondered. *And where are my soldiers?*

"Where are my people?" Leena asked.

"They're around." The Wizard smiled and looked at Leena intently. "You're always worried about others, aren't you?"

"Yes, she is," Viktor said as he pried a pastry into his already full mouth. "It's exhausting!"

"You two are quite resourceful. You should stay with us for a while. I could use a couple of good minds."

"You would have to upgrade our accommodations," Leena said haughtily.

"Mr. Wizard, are you aware that thousands of Chinese soldiers are marching on your city?" Viktor asked.

Leena looked at Viktor. Her eyes clearly communicated that she was unsure if it was smart to tell the Wizard about the invading army.

"Excuse me? Chinese, you say?" the Wizard responded. "I am not worried about the Chinese. They don't care about Lanthemtown. They will probably just blow right by. And if they want to fight, we will fight."

"You cannot match their army with this tawdry band of soldiers," Viktor said.

"No, maybe not, but we don't need to beat them. We just need to distract them long enough for us to run and hide in the hills. They won't pursue. They are not after us." A few minutes later he continued. "I like war. War is good for business. Don't you agree? In every war ever fought there were opportunist making money on the conflict."

"How do you sleep at night," Leena asked.

"Surrounded by women most nights," the Wizard replied accompanied by laughter.

Upon finishing breakfast, the guards directed Leena and Viktor to wait downstairs. Within moments, an open-air electric cart pulled up. Both took a seat as the Wizard, clothed in black robes and carrying his cane, stepped onto the cart to sit up front. He waved his cane in the air, and the driver took off toward the gate. Leena could hear a truck following them as they pulled through the gate entrance and, turning around to check, saw that it was their truck.

"That is positive," she said to Viktor, pointing to the truck following close behind.

The drive was bumpy, and the dust it produced seemed to engulf them, making it hard to breathe. Leena pulled the side of her shirt that was unbuttoned because of the heat and covered her mouth with the material, providing a rudimentary filter for the dust.

As they approached the water station, Leena could see that the Wizard's team had already built a chain-link fence, more than eight feet tall, around the perimeter. Several guards in their eclectic armor stood guard. Leena spotted her unit's own rifles in their hands, obviously an upgrade from the antiques they were using before. She reasoned the Wizard truly had little power. He ruled by fear and a ragtag band of people he called soldiers. Her weapons had only made him stronger.

The guard inside the fence unlocked the bulky sheet-metal door and pulled it back to allow entry. The Wizard walked into the small, fenced area with Leena and Viktor trailing behind. Sauntering to the spigot, he produced a glass from his long robes. He handed the glass to an attendant who filled it with water. The Wizard held the glass high in the morning sun and looked through the glass.

"Looks clear. I half-expected it to be dirty water."

"The plant filters the water more than sixteen times, removing sediment and other minerals. It's part of the desalination process," Viktor said.

The Wizard drank from the glass and nodded.

"Taste good. This will do. Yes, this will do just fine."

Leena spotted something in the distance. On the highway to the south, she could see trucks. She could tell they were Chinese. They didn't seem to come closer though. She wondered if that was the front moving toward the city or possibly a police force sent to ensure she got to where she was going.

"You have fulfilled your part of the bargain, Mrs. Zhen. You are free to go, although I wish you would consider staying."

"No thank you, we have had enough of Lanthemtown," Leena replied. "And what of our soldiers?"

"I'm afraid I cannot accommodate that request. Your soldiers were put to use in the city and cannot be returned."

"That was not the deal. You will return my soldiers immediately," Leena demanded.

Viktor stepped close to her and put his hand on hers, gently pulling her back while evaluating how the Wizard would respond to her demands.

"Things change, Lieutenant. I suggest you adapt. And, technically, I have already returned your soldiers."

"What do you mean?" Leena asked as she looked around, hoping that they were standing nearby. "I don't see them."

"Did you enjoy your breakfast, Mrs. Zhen?"

"What? What does breakfast have to do with…"

Then she understood what the Wizard meant. The salty pork she had for breakfast was not pork. She turned and ran back to where her truck had been parked, stopping about halfway to throw up. She forced herself to continue throwing up to remove the vile meat from her stomach.

Viktor came up behind her and grabbed her by both shoulders, pushing her toward the truck. They could hear the laughter of the Wizard in the distance as they climbed into the truck and drove away.

Chapter 11

HOMECOMING

The ride toward home was rough. It seemed the news of the impending invasion had brought out many travelers seeking to avoid being in the path of the eastern interlopers. The Tullian were scrappy and vile but no match for an army of Chinese and their weapons of destruction.

Leena and Viktor spent most of the day avoiding trouble. When they spotted activity, they attempted to pull over and wait for it to clear or, in some cases, took an exit and hid among the large fallen trees and abandoned buildings that littered the highway.

Leena was tired. She had been going nonstop for weeks now, and the demands of her schedule had set in. She thought about her unborn child as Viktor drove slowly through the aftermath of a battle scattered over a mile of highway. The smoking vehicles and bloody bodies offered evidence that it was recent—likely a clash between two clans.

Will my child survive this world? Does it even make sense to bring a child into this unnatural societal structure of Aberjay versus Miniyar? And what if the Chinese upend that structure, replacing it with something worse? Is there any hope of a normal upbringing?

She was convinced after much thought that it had to be her primary mission to ensure her child was reared in a safe place, free of all the fighting that had consumed her world for the last few years. She wanted something better for her child.

The truck rattled and bumped along as they crossed parts of the highway that had been blown up by explosives. She wondered if all the jostling was a threat to the health of her baby and made a mental note to see a doctor as soon as possible. She did not know the first thing about having a baby.

They were within twenty miles of the zone when they spotted the fire. The sun had gone down, infusing the sky with a pink tone that lit up the clouds. The fire was miles ahead of them but burned brightly as if an entire town was ablaze. As they drew closer, they saw it covered the entire highway and was obviously not natural, as evidenced by the piles and piles of wood and paper products that had been dumped in the center of the highway to keep it going. Large fallen trees lay on top of the kindling to extend the height and life of the fire, feeding it into a fury. Behind the fire were stacks of crushed cars that had become a staple on this highway.

"What is that?" Leena asked as they drew closer.

"It's a wall of fire meant to stop travelers. We better get off the road."

Viktor turned off onto the shoulder and crossed a shallow ditch to pull the truck into a field. The truck kicked up dirt and dust from the land that bordered the roadway, creating a flurry of particles that obscured their view.

As they began driving further toward the edge of a forest, headlights appeared near the massive fire—two pairs, then three—heading toward them.

"Viktor," Leena said.

"Yes, I see them."

"We need to get out of here!" Leena shouted as they reached the trees and couldn't continue because of the density of the forest.

"We need to go on foot," Viktor said.

"No, we have no weapons. Turn the truck around," Leena ordered.

Viktor put the truck in reverse with a loud scraping noise as the gear engaged. After pulling back about twenty feet, he turned away to escape the oncoming threat.

"No, turn the other way, Viktor!" Leena shouted.

"What?"

"Just do it!"

Viktor turned toward the three vehicles that were headed in their direction and accelerated. They could see that two compact cars and a pickup truck were headed straight for them from about a quarter mile away. The truck was white or used to be white. Two armed men stood in the truck bed with rifles and faces covered by masks of some sort. The two smaller vehicles were two-seaters, both fully occupied.

"We're headed straight for them, Leena," Viktor said in desperation.

"I know. The truck is the only weapon we have. We need to ram them!"

"What?"

"Aim for the truck. If we can disable them, we may stand a chance."

Viktor clung tightly to the steering wheel and put the truck in a higher gear, picking up speed as they rambled across the open plain toward their enemies. Leena reached down for the strap that would serve as a seatbelt and pulled it tight, then reached over to grab Viktor's, securing it for him. She then reached to her side and removed her baton, her only weapon, and braced for the impact.

The pickup truck driver tried to turn as it became clear that they were the target—but it was too late. The large army truck smashed into the driver's side of the vehicle, sending the men in the bed flying and showering the front of the truck with glass and metal. The seatbelts held fast on impact, allowing Viktor and Leena to escape injury, but steam poured from the front of their vehicle as Viktor turned the steering wheel to make another pass.

Leena could see the result of their attack as the truck turned. They nearly cut the pickup truck in half, smashing it beyond recognition. The two men inside were dead, and the two thrown from the pickup could not be seen. A fire engulfed both pieces of the truck.

The other two small vehicles had turned after passing the wreckage but began racing back to the scene.

"Hit that one," Leena said, pointing to a small hatchback painted in many shades of gray.

Viktor pressed the gas pedal, but the truck slowed. Steam still poured from the front.

"The radiator blew; the truck is overheating!"

"Hit that car, Viktor!" Leena said.

As the truck lost momentum, it slowed but not before hitting its target, pulverizing the small vehicle while also stopping their truck in its tracks.

Leena and Viktor looked at each other.

"Now we run," Leena said as they unbuckled their seatbelts and jumped out of the truck.

The other car had stopped nearby, and two men with clubs jumped out with their weapons in hand. Leena ran toward both of them, sliding under the first one to knock him to the ground then she stood face to face with the other.

He swung first, but Leena easily blocked the attempted blow before delivering a quick kick to the groin. With her enemy bent over, she struck his head several times with her baton, ending his life before turning to face the other attacker, who got up off the ground, lunging for her.

Sidestepping her attacker, she struck his side with her baton and delivered a kick to the face, knocking him unconscious. She sprinted toward Viktor while surveying the field for other attackers. There were two in the distance, the two that had been thrown from the truck, who were regaining their strength as they slowly rose from the ground. A shot rang out as one of them fired at them. They took cover behind their truck to discuss their next move.

"Toward the forest," Viktor said as they ran as fast as they could, putting the truck between the attackers and their escape path to cover their exit.

Reaching the woods, two more shots rang out, penetrating the trunk of a nearby tree but not accurately enough to be dangerous. They continued running until their strength gave out and they stopped to rest beside a boulder in a small clearing. Darkness had fallen, and the moonlight seemed to spotlight the area around the boulder.

"Did we lose them?" Leena asked once she caught her breath.

"I don't know. I doubt it. I think I can hear their footsteps in the woods."

"We need to change direction," Leena said as she stood and surveyed their location. The enemy was to the south. Heading west would take them parallel to the highway while north would lead them into deeper woods. "Let's go north into the dense part of the woods and then we'll head west when we feel we've lost them."

Viktor nodded, and they pushed off the boulder, still huffing. They walked into the darkness of the wood, barely lit by the half-moon above them.

The forest was thick but free of brush. The tall pine trees provided a canopy that blocked sunlight during the day, holding the brush at bay. This wooded area was natural, not planted, as all the trees were of different sizes. While most were tall pines, an occasional oak or poplar would stand wide, creating a natural clearing around them where the pines could not grow.

They walked for what seemed like miles before stopping again near a ridge that opened onto an extensive field. They saw no homes or signs of life—just tall grass, about three feet in height.

"This is a good spot to turn because the grass will give us cover if we need it," Leena said as she turned and followed the row of trees, winding downhill with thick forest on one side and the open field of grass on the other.

Leena led the way down the ridge. The smell of honeysuckle was prevalent; it grew wild in this part of the country. As they made their way to the end of the field, a shot rang out in the darkness.

Leena dropped to the ground on her belly, having no time to think of how it might endanger her unborn child, and turned to find out where the bullet had come from.

"That seemed really close. Did you see where it came from, Viktor?"

"Viktor," she repeated, noticing she could not see him behind her any longer.

Leena crawled on her belly about twenty feet until his fallen body came into focus. She reached for him as she grew close and, once she had a hand on him, shook him.

"Aaahh," Viktor responded.

"Good, you aren't dead," Leena said. "Did you get hit?"

"Yeah, they got me in the back," Viktor said through gritted teeth.

"Is it bad?"

"Getting shot in the back is not good, so I would gather it is bad," Viktor said.

"Well, you haven't lost your sense of humor. Do you think you can walk? Let me see the wound," Leena said as she looked him over, lifting his shirt to locate the wound in the dark of night. "Oh, I see. It isn't bleeding too badly. The bullet went straight through. Maybe it missed vital organs."

"Missed or not, it still hurts like someone is pouring gas in my belly!" Viktor said.

Leena looked around to make sure the enemy was not close and stopped for a moment to listen for footsteps in the forest. She took her outer shirt off, revealing her gray sleeveless T-shirt, ripped a sleeve off, and folded it, then placed it over Viktor's wound.

"Hold this here," she said as she tried to tie the rest of her shirt around him to keep the bandage in place. Then she heard footsteps cracking sticks and rustling leaves in the nearby woods.

She stopped long enough to pinpoint a position. "It sounds like they're about a hundred yards away. We need to move. Can you stand?"

"Yes, I think so," Viktor said, still pursing his lips.

Viktor rolled onto his side to stand and bit his lip to keep from crying out. He got to a crouched position but then stopped.

"This hurts like hell."

"Yeah, I'm sure it does. Let's go," Leena whispered as they made their way down the ridge.

They moved slowly, Viktor holding his hand over the exit wound and wincing at every step. Leena knew they could not outrun their pursuers. As they reached the bottom of the small ridge where the field ended and more forestlands arose, she spotted a small barn. It was about twenty feet by twenty feet, just big enough for a tractor or haystacks. It was old, in disrepair, and had begun to lean. She grabbed hold of Viktor's arm and, still crouching, slowly led him toward the barn about a hundred feet away.

As they reached the structure, they went around to the other side of it to shield themselves from their attackers, who they assumed were behind them on the edge of the forest.

Leena helped Viktor to the ground so he could lean his back against the barn.

"Stay here," she commanded.

"Where are you going? You can't take them by yourself. They have guns."

"Just stay here. We have to do something. We can't run anymore."

Leena ran into the dark forest and, using the trees as cover, began making her way back to where she believed her enemy was waiting. As she got near, she raised her foot and then carefully placed it on the ground, shaking it before finding her footing to ensure it didn't rustle the forest floor. She did this over and over, one foot at a time. She needed to be stealthy. She needed to surprise them.

As she ambled, she monitored the ridge. The moonlight lit up the field, but the darkness of the trees edged it. As she eased back to where they had come from, she caught a glimpse of a rifle. The person holding it was on one knee, looking through a scope. No wonder they hit Viktor despite the darkness. The scope helped them target their prey.

She continued to move toward the sniper's position in the black of night until she was only about twenty feet away. As she slowed her movements even more to hide her position, the enemy lay flat on the ground, still looking through the scope, pointed toward the barn.

Leena was ten feet away and still didn't see or hear anyone else. She had no choice but to risk being seen so she could take this sniper out. As she moved in right behind him, she removed her baton from its holster. In one smooth motion, she kicked the gun from his hands while extending her baton with her right hand, then came down hard on his head, splattering blood on the moonlit ground around them. While one hit was probably sufficient, she hit him three times to ensure he was out.

Leena then turned swiftly, thinking that her victim's partner might be nearby, but nothing in the forest moved. She listened intently, waiting for someone to charge out of the darkness or for a sound to give away their position, but nothing materialized. *What happened to the other one? There were at least two.*

After waiting for what seemed like many minutes, she reached down and pulled the rifle from the dead man's hands. Turning one last time to look and listen and finding nothing, she began the walk down the ridge toward the barn.

As she approached the old leaning barn, she called out to Viktor. "I got him. I think we're safe." She rounded the corner to find a stranger standing in a shaft of moonlight next to Viktor and pointing a gun at him.

He was just a boy, about sixteen. Frightened. Shaking. Sweating profusely. The gun he held was small, almost toy-like in size. Snot ran down his face as he shook and bared his teeth.

"Stay back or I'll kill him!" the young attacker demanded.

"Calm down. Take it easy," Leena said in a calm voice as she slowly raised the rifle to a prominent position about waist high. She did not know if there was a shell in the chamber. *Will the rifle even fire if I pull the trigger?*

"I'll kill him!" the young boy repeated.

"What do you want?" Leena asked him.

"We just want your food, your weapons," the boy said as he used his sleeve to wipe the snot from his face.

"Your friend is dead, and you have nowhere to go. Why don't you put down the gun?" Leena said calmly.

Viktor was wide-eyed. He looked at the young man with a disposition of innocence. He said nothing, but his face cried out, *Please don't do this!*

The boy looked back and forth between them, clearly agitated and desperate. Leena heard him sniffle as he began to cry, obviously fighting to hold back his emotions.

"Just set the gun down. No one else has to die today," Leena said to calm him.

"I can't... I don't... I'm a soldier... My brother said..."

Leena's rifle released a blast of fury as it fired, hitting the young man in the chest. The gun he held fired as he fell but only penetrated the ground next to Viktor. His body fell hard on the ground and convulsed five times before going still. His eyes were wide open, looking at the sky as Leena walked to him and stood over his lifeless body.

"Viktor, are you okay?" she said as she turned to attend to him.

"No worse off than I was a few minutes ago, although I may need a new pair of underwear."

"I would be shocked if you didn't."

"Thank you, Leena," Viktor said as he looked at her with gratitude. "I really thought that was it."

Leena reached over to the young villain and closed his eyes. She felt bad about the kill but knew she had little choice. She couldn't risk Viktor's life.

"You're still alive. Let's see what is in this barn," Leena said to Viktor.

She walked to the front of the barn and removed a board that was keeping the doors from swinging open. Looking inside, she could see it was mostly empty except for a few bales of hay that someone had strewn about on the dirt floor.

She helped Viktor move into the barn and positioned him more comfortably next to a pile of hay. He leaned back and took several shallow breaths.

"I think we need to rest here for the night. We can't see out there, and we need to get our bearings. I know you need someone to stitch you up, but I think if we stumble around in the dark, we'll just get lost."

Viktor just nodded. He was in no position to move, much less walk long distances.

"Maybe you should go get help," Viktor stuttered as the cold of night overtook him.

"I would if I knew where we were. Or who I could get to help. At this point, I think we just need to rest and find our way in the morning."

"Okay, Leena."

"Try and get some rest," Leena said as she lay back against a haystack, closing her eyes.

The sound of fighter jets woke Leena from her slumber. Their wake crackled across the sky above. She could not tell how many from the noise, but they were clearly heading east.

The light shone in through the boards of the dilapidated barn, signaling it was far past morning. Leena turned from her makeshift bed of hay to look over at Viktor. He was still alive, but his breathing seemed raspy.

"Viktor, are you awake?"

She moved to his side and gave him a shake.

"Viktor?" she repeated.

"I'm awake," he mumbled as he turned to lie on his back. Then he winced, placing his hands on his wound, still covered by the makeshift dressing applied the night before. "Am I alive?"

"It would seem so. We need to get moving. I think we slept late," Leena said.

They exited the barn a few minutes later. Viktor was stumbling badly and could only take small steps. Leena tried to help, but her height made it difficult. Viktor was not a large man, but he was quite stocky, as the Irish often are.

Before them was a dense forest, tall trees growing close together. They saw no roads or paths, nothing that would help them understand where they were. Fortunately, Leena's brief basic training kicked in. She could determine the direction they were going based on the sun. She knew if they headed west, they would likely run into one of the zones.

With only a sliver of hope of getting Viktor to a doctor in time, they trudged on through the forest. Little by little, step by step, they put miles beneath them. After walking for most of the day, broken up by multiple breaks for rest, they crested a hill and could see the wall that surrounded the zones in the distance.

Although other walls separated the zones from each other, this one extended the length of the two zones on the east side, giving the appearance of a fortress. If you were to view it from the air, it made an 'H' of sorts. The south and north ends of the structure were mostly chain-link fence, with some remnants of brick and stone from earlier versions of the wall.

The site reminded Leena of their vulnerability. She knew the Chinese would have no issues rolling their tanks across those chain-link fences and lighting their neighborhoods on fire. It seemed only a matter of time. Provisions could have likely been made to extend the wall around the entire city, at least around Zone 7, but no one ever thought the Chinese would invade from the east. It was just not considered a possibility.

As they walked down the ridge, looking across the plain, Leena could see a significant presence of soldiers outside the wall. There were thirty or so tanks she didn't recognize as well as a few helicopters that neither the People's Army nor the CPU had in their arsenals. These must be federal, she thought.

The remnants of old neighborhoods stood between them and the gate. Only a few desperate squatters lived in the old neighborhoods now, but many of the structures, including rows of dilapidated houses and some empty storefronts, were still there. Leena did not recognize the gate, so she assumed it was Aberjay—the east gate of Zone 7.

As they reached level ground, they walked on old asphalt that was cracked or, in some places, completely broken. Large weeds grew between the cracks, and a faint image of the painted lines remained.

Leena wondered as she walked why they had never renovated this area outside the gate. She reasoned they likely considered it unsafe because of the risk of a Tullian attack. Many of the houses looked almost livable. But then she reminded herself that what she considered livable in her zone was likely not up to the standards of Zone 7.

As they stumbled closer to the city gates, they saw a temporary guard post. Two men with rifles stood guard while many others around them seemed to be unpacking, setting up the site.

"Contact!" one soldier shouted as both stood rigid and pointed their rifles toward Leena and Viktor.

"Wait, wait!" Leena shouted, putting up her hand while slowly lowering her rifle while trying to keep hold of Viktor.

"Don't come any closer!" the men shouted.

"I have a wounded man! I need help!" Leena shouted across the one-hundred-foot divide.

One of the two soldiers used a radio to talk to someone. Leena and Viktor just stood there, waiting. After a minute went by and feeling impatient, Leena let go of Viktor and took a few steps toward the guards with her hands out, palms extended.

"Let me come talk to you. I can explain," she said.

"Stop! Do not move! We will shoot!" they shouted again.

"Ugh," Leena heard behind her as Viktor fell to the ground. Leena ran to him. "Viktor, talk to me. Stay with me. We're almost there."

"I think I am done," he whispered. "I feel it."

"No, stay with me. I got you. Dammit, I need help here!" she shouted back at the soldiers.

"We did it, didn't we?" Viktor said, losing clarity.

"We did," Leena replied.

"We got the water. They needed the water, and we got the water," he said, sounding like a child.

"You did it, Viktor. It was all you. You are a hero."

Tears welled up in her eyes as she realized she was losing him. The soldiers from the gate began running toward them.

"I was wrong," he said, struggling to stay conscious.

"What?" Leena replied. "What were you wrong about?"

"The Aberjay. It isn't American what they do to us. They need to be stopped."

Leena began weeping. "Hold on, Viktor, help is coming."

"Show them, Leena. You show them," Viktor said as his breath gave out and his eyes closed. His body slumped.

Leena held his head and stroked his red hair. "I love you, Viktor. I am sorry. I am sorry I couldn't save you. You are the hero. You did it. You brought the water."

A soldier grabbed Leena from behind, pulling her to her feet while clasping her hands behind her back and putting them in handcuffs. The others attended to Viktor and, within a few seconds, said what Leena already knew.

"He's dead."

Leena cried out. The emotion was too much. Her body felt like it had been hit hard, and fire raced through her veins. She felt mad. She felt betrayed. She wanted to hurt someone. She shouted and pulled away as the soldier attempted to hold her, pulling her away from Viktor's body.

Leena cried for what seemed like twenty minutes or more. She felt like a failure. She had trudged through the forest with Viktor with every intent to save him, only to have him die on the doorstep of salvation. The weight of her guilt was overwhelming.

CPU guards drove up in a Jeep as she lay in the dust, cuffed and weeping. The guards placed her in the back seat, her rifle and baton confiscated. She lost consciousness as they drove through the east gate, overwhelmed by grief, and spent by her journey.

Chapter 12

SECRETS

Leena woke with a massive headache. Even as she lifted her head from her cot, she felt pressure in her head, a pounding ache that signaled a head injury or a severe lack of sleep. She sat up to see she was in a prison cell. The walls were concrete, and the cell was small, almost small enough to touch both sides at the same time. This was not new for her; she had been in prison before. But this was not like the holding cells she had been in at the CPU detainment complex. That one had bars while this one was much smaller, and the walls were made of cinder blocks. A small door with a tiny window at the top allowed her captors to look in on her.

She pulled herself up off the bed and walked to the small metal sink, drinking some water and then using it to splash on her face to wake up completely. Her body hurt. She was still dressed in her camo pants and armless T-shirt—and covered in Viktor's blood. She didn't know why she was in a cell.

Leena sat there for another hour before the door to her cell opened. Two CPU soldiers entered and placed her in handcuffs.

"I demand to know why I am being held," Leena said, exhibiting disdain for her captors.

A CPU guard directed her down the hallway without responding. She concluded that superiors had ordered the guards not to speak to her, so she didn't bother to protest further.

She was led to a small interrogation room with one metal table and a chair on each side, then handcuffed to the table. Leena was familiar with rooms like this as she had interrogated many from the other side of the table.

The soldiers left her alone in the chair. She was chained to the table for several minutes before the door opened and a tall blonde woman entered. She was wearing a business suit and a holster, but no gun. Leena knew the rules forbade guns in the interrogation room in her zone, so this zone probably had similar guidelines.

"I am Captain Tina Smith of the Citizens Protection Unit. I am going to need you to answer a few questions."

"Am I being charged with a crime?" Leena asked.

"Not yet. First, we have to figure out who you are. What is your name?"

"My name is Lieutenant Leena Zhen. I am People's Army."

"Is that so, Lieutenant? You are not Tullian?"

"No. Do I look Tullian?" Leena knew when she said it that it probably didn't help her case. At that moment, she probably did look Tullian.

"Well, yes. You look quite Tullian," Captain Smith said.

"Okay, well, I know I look bad right now, but I am a lieutenant in the People's Army. You can call my commanding officer, Commander Johnson, to confirm."

"What were you doing out there by the east gate? Who is the man who was with you?"

"I have been on a mission for my commander. The man with me was our engineer, Viktor Brommel, Chief of Community Services."

"Why did you shoot him?" the captain asked.

"I didn't shoot him. A Tullian raider did about ten miles outside of town."

"We checked the rifle and the bullet. He was shot with the rifle you were carrying."

"Yes, I realize that looks bad, but I took the rifle from the person who shot him."

The captain paused as she shuffled papers and studied the one on top. Leena could not tell if this was an intimidation tactic or if she was really reading.

"Can you tell me why you were out there? What was your mission?"

"I'm sorry, but I cannot tell you that. It's classified," Leena responded.

"I see." The captain stood up and put her hands on the back of the chair. "There isn't much I can do if you won't talk to me. We cannot release you because you are a murder suspect."

"Murder suspect? What murder, I just told you I didn't do it?" Leena retorted.

"If I had a credit for every time a suspect said they didn't do it," the captain said with a stone face.

"I told you; I didn't kill him. I took the rifle from the Tullian I kill...the Tullian who attacked us."

"So let me get this straight. You were traveling with this Viktor Brommel in Tullian land on a secret mission with no weapon other than a baton? You were attacked by armed Tullian raiders, and you killed them, stole their weapons, and walked home?"

"I had weapons when I left. I really need to speak to my commander. There is vital information I need to pass on as a matter of national security."

"The Chinese? Yes, we already know about that."

"It's more than that."

"Why don't you tell me, and I will pass it along?"

"You know I can't do that."

"Right, it's classified. I get it."

"Ms. Zhen, if you do not come up with a better story really fast, you are going to be charged with murder."

"Call Commander Johnson. He will vouch for me."

"I am sure he will. Unfortunately, with what is going on with China, we are radio silent with Zone 6. I couldn't call him if I wanted to. Do you have anyone here who will vouch for you?"

Leena thought long and hard about who might be on this side of the wall who could not only vouch for her but might even fight for her release.

The captain turned toward the door with her paperwork in hand. "Good day, Ms. Zhen."

"Vincent Ryder. Call Vincent Ryder."

"Vincent Ryder?" the captain repeated as she turned toward Leena. "Why does that name sound familiar?"

Leena swallowed slowly, wondering if telling her would help or hurt the situation. "He works in Senator Rollins' office."

The captain's eyes grew wide at the mention of the senator's name.

"You know someone in the senator's office?"

"Yes, just ask him. He will tell you I'm legit."

"Okay, let me see if I can get hold of him amid all this chaos with the Chinese. For your sake, you better hope he really knows you."

The captain turned and walked out of the room, and moments later, soldiers escorted Leena back to her cell.

Nothing ever seems to happen fast when you're behind bars. There was no clock on the wall, but Leena could feel the time slowly tick away, moment by moment, minute by minute, hour by hour. The small cell had no windows, so it was difficult to determine the time of day. Based on the degree of her exhaustion, she reasoned it was after dark. The body has an internal clock that reminds you when it's time to sleep and eat. She could feel her body ache for sleep.

She tried to assess her situation to prioritize what she must do. She informed the commander of the invasion from the east, so that was not news. What he didn't know was that the Chinese had taken the water treatment facility. *Wouldn't he assume that?* she wondered. Leena also needed to inform him about Liv and the soldiers who were now prisoners. She knew it was not likely he would let her stand down an entire division of the army during the Chinese assault, but maybe they could figure out a way to take the water treatment facility and save her team.

The senators were another story. She had to break the news to them about Viktor. They had grown close over the last year, working together during the election and then in the Capitol. Her heart hurt for Viktor. He was good. His death was so meaningless. As she lay there, she could hear his voice saying,

"It's all part of the greater good," and "You don't know how one action might affect another." He was very positive like that. While Leena always seemed to face things with an explosion of emotion, he was the opposite. He dealt rationally and positively with adversity and always seemed to come out on top. Until now. Leena wept.

And then there was Jordan. She needed to talk to him about the baby. Amid war and chaos, they needed to plan for a son or daughter. She wished her mother was alive to meet her grandchild. To teach the child how to play checkers and take the child for walks in the park. She hated that she would miss that. She could feel her allegiance shifting. For years, she had been on the side of the needy, fighting for what was fair and equitable. Now those things had become less important. Only her child was important. She knew that wasn't true, and that she would always fight for her people, but at that moment, in that cold cell, holding her belly, she knew her life was changing. Her efforts would certainly have to be split to care for her child.

As she thought about everything a baby needs, she became afraid. More afraid than she had been in years. *How will I get everything ready in time? Where will the baby sleep?* The baby will need a crib or bassinet. A nursery. Diapers, powders, clothes. *What do babies eat?* Most of her food came from her garden when she wasn't eating military meal rations. *Can babies eat vegetables?* That's silly—of course they can. *How do you make baby food?*

The questions swirled in her mind before landing on the most important one. Would she be a good mother? Would she be able to teach the child right from wrong? Be there for all of the child's needs. Would she be able to put aside her world for the sake of her child? It seemed an insurmountable task at that moment.

Sleep came once her mind yielded to the complete exhaustion of her worn-out body.

The rattle of the cell door opening startled Leena from her slumber. She had not remembered falling asleep.

"Leena Zhen," the guard called out.

Leena's eyes opened. She was still in the cell.

"Leena Zhen, on your feet," the guard called out again.

She turned to put her feet on the floor and then stood to go through the same drill as the day before. Within minutes, she was back in the same interrogation room as the day before. A few minutes later, Vincent Ryder entered the room with a teacup and a small pot in his hand.

Leena could not stand to hug him, but she was grateful for that. She was still angry about his betrayal and did not want him to think she had forgiven him. A friendly face was a welcome sight, however, despite her longstanding grudge.

"I brought you tea," Vincent said as he set the teacup on the table and poured the tea from the pitcher. It was hot and steamy. Vincent had remembered that Leena preferred tea to coffee.

Leena wondered if accepting this peace offering relinquished her ability to hate him, but then the fragrance of the hot tea filled the room, and she had no choice. She had to have it. She brought the glass to her lips and sipped the heavenly beverage. Leena had not had a cup of tea in some time. The hot liquid filled her insides, making her feel whole again.

"I also brought you some scones. Apple, I think." Vincent reached into a bag, pulled out a large fluffy pastry, and handed it to Leena, who took it as if she had not eaten in days. She took hefty bites from the scone and sipped the tea, holding out the cup for a refill once it was empty.

"What are you doing here, Leena? And murder? That does not sound like you."

Leena took a moment to swallow, clearing her throat. "I didn't kill him, Vincent. Viktor was my friend. Tullian ambushed us, and they shot him. I carried him here hoping they would help, but he didn't make it."

Vincent gave her a strange look as if he was processing the story he had just heard.

"What?" Leena asked.

"I have no reason to doubt your story, but he was shot with your rifle. And you carried him? You are way too small to carry a full-sized man."

"Like I told the captain, the rifle was the Tullian's. I took it from them after they shot him. I had it with me for protection. We had lost our other weapons. As for carrying him, I'm stronger than you realize."

"What were you even doing out there? It's so dangerous."

"Don't talk to me like I'm twelve, Vincent. I was on a mission."

"A mission for your little army."

"You condescend…"

"Okay, sorry," Vincent said, putting up his hands as if to block her verbal assault.

A quiet moment passed as Leena finished a second scone and another cup of tea.

"Vincent, on the day I last saw you…"

Vincent moved uncomfortably in his chair.

"Did you spend time with me to distract me?"

"I only did what I was asked to do. I did not know what he was planning," Vincent said suspiciously.

"Who? Senator Rollins?"

"He said they just needed to talk to the senators without you present. Something secret. How was I to know?"

"I was fifty feet from the explosion, Vincent. I still have scars from the shrapnel."

"You were not the target."

"What? Who was the target?"

"Senator Chin," Vincent admitted.

"Why? Who would want to hurt him?"

"It had something to do with a land deal. He didn't vote the way the senator asked him to, and that was the deal."

"What deal?" Leena pushed.

"I've said enough about that. Let's talk about your situation," Vincent said.

"I need to get back to Zone 6, Vincent. Can you get me out of here?"

"Maybe. Let me talk to the captain. She had a lot going on and does not need an investigation like this right now. I can probably get your case transferred to your people. Let me see what I can do, and I'll get back to you."

Vincent stood and turned toward the door, looking back briefly. "But come up with a better story."

"It's not a story! It's the truth!"

The door to the room closed momentarily then opened again to allow guards to return her to her cell. Leena knew the outcome was out of her control. She could only hope that the sliver of feelings that Vincent had for her would drive him to do the right thing and get her transfer moving quickly.

Another day passed in her cell. Food was delivered three times. That was the only way she knew to keep track of the time. The provisions were better than MRUs, but she longed for something healthy. Her diet was mostly vegan when she had a choice. Collards she loved the most. She craved them. It could have been a response to pregnancy as she had heard cravings are a part of it, but it would not be new. She had always loved collards and any type of green veggie. She ate them with salt and hot sauce.

As she finished her breakfast, her cell door opened once more. Captain Smith stood in the doorway, holding a file folder.

"Zhen, I sent an emissary to your government to inform them of your capture. They have agreed to take you along with the evidence we have against you in the case. Get ready to move."

The captain closed the door as Leena smirked. *Get ready to move,* she thought, *as if I have a large suitcase of things to pack or correspondence I need to write before my departure.*

A few minutes later, the door opened, and she was escorted to an exit. She was cuffed, her hands in front. As she walked from the building, the sun shone brightly, and it took a few seconds for her eyes to adjust. She could see she had been a guest in a government building of some sort. It was all red brick with dark windows. She could see the giant wall to her left, so she knew she was near their east gate. A guard helped her into a waiting van, which was black and had several rows of seats. She was the only passenger.

They drove for about twenty minutes. Leena could tell where they were headed, for the north gate, as the wall to her left remained in sight throughout most of the trip. The two soldiers driving the van were in CPU uniforms. She could see out the window as she drove that a significant CPU presence was gathered on the streets near the wall. There were tents set up, soldiers standing in line, groups of soldiers socializing, as well as lines of soldiers marching about. They were preparing for an assault, likely the defense of the city.

The van stopped at the north gate, and the soldiers motioned for her to exit. She stepped onto the asphalt and looked through the tunnel to the other side where she could see several People's Army soldiers waiting. One CPU soldier guided her as she walked toward them. The other soldier retrieved a rifle wrapped in plastic, along with a file folder full of papers, from the van and walked behind them.

Leena was ready to be free. She never cared for handcuffs or the feeling of prison, and she felt she had experienced way too much of it for her age. She knew her people would throw out these silly claims of murder and welcome her as a hero for getting the water turned on.

Leena smiled as they stopped in front of her soldiers. She knew all of them. Not intimately, but she knew their names. They were all under her command. The CPU guard handed the rifle and the paperwork to one of her people as the other one uncuffed her and put the handcuffs in his holster.

"She's all yours," one of the CPU soldiers said as they turned and walked back to the van.

"Lieutenant Zhen," a People's Army soldier said. "Please hold out your hands."

"What?" Leena said, shocked. "You can't be serious."

The soldier grabbed her hand and put a new set of handcuffs on her wrists.

"Soldier, you're out of line. What is the meaning of this?" Leena demanded.

"You are being arrested for the murder of Viktor Brommel and treason."

"Treason? Are you kidding me? I brought the water! I finished my mission."

Leena's mind was a swirl as they guided her to a Jeep to take her to the base where she would likely be placed in another holding cell. She could not understand why she would be accused of treason or why those in charge would even believe it. For a lieutenant to be arrested, it had to come from a commander. Commander Johnson would never approve such an order.

"I demand to speak to Commander Johnson," she ordered, but the soldiers had stopped talking. It was protocol not to talk to prisoners during transfers, so Leena decided not to waste her breath.

As they drove south through the streets, passing the old neighborhood where Leena grew up, she noticed several large pieces of equipment that were already clearing land and pouring a foundation for new construction. She wondered what would replace her old home. Homes? Businesses? Maybe a factory?

As they passed a water station, Leena was shocked to see it in ruin. The glass surrounding the station had been destroyed, and the rigid steel and aluminum frame had been torn down. Nothing remained but the pressure tank and spigot used to dispense the water. It drew from a well system, not the city water supply, so it was likely abandoned once the water came back on. The citizens had obviously grown restless waiting for the city's response to the water crisis and took matters into their own hands.

Driving farther toward the base, it was obvious the People's Army was mobilizing for war. They didn't have tents and tanks like the east gate of Zone 7, but there were more trucks and groups of soldiers gathered than Leena had seen in some time. They obviously knew the Chinese were coming. Leena knew their force would not be enough on its own. The force headed toward them was more than four times the size of their army, and they lacked heavy weaponry, such as tanks and anti-aircraft guns. Without help from the CPU or the Federal Government's forces, the battle would be over within hours. Leena imagined the Chinese war machine rolling over the chain-link fence on the Zone 6 southern border—reaping destruction, leaving bloody bodies in their path. She hoped the commander had a plan that would stop the inevitability of the slaughter.

The soldiers led Leena to a room that was familiar. She had been in this room many times interrogating criminals, terrorists, and violent protestors. Her last visit to this very cell was to question Nolan Redmont about his activities on the day the governor was shot. Now she sat on the other side of the table, her hands, once again, chained to the metal table.

She sat for more than an hour before the door opened and Commander Johnson entered. He looked red, flushed, and was wearing a belt with an empty holster, his firearm likely surrendered before his entry.

"Lieutenant," he began in a formal tone.

Leena could tell by his tone that this would not be the homecoming she expected.

"Can you please provide the details of your trip east to the water plant?"

"Commander, what is this all about? I did what you and the governor asked me to do," Leena said, pleading her case.

"I understand you believe that, but we must get the facts straight. Please provide the details so we can get on with this."

Leena did not want to know what 'this' meant. She felt on trial but could not understand why. She reasoned that playing the game and embracing an attitude of obedience would likely be the best strategy.

"We traveled east and overnighted the first night in a parking lot off the highway..." Leena began.

She told him about Lilian, her visit to Port Loyal, and her interactions with Lyon as well as their assault on the water desalination plant. Leena reported the trip to Lanthemtown to retrieve supplies, her meeting the Wizard, and the trades that were made. She told the commander about the Chinese coming ashore and the brief battle that ensued until her troops ran out of ammunition. She continued with her report (leaving out the part about her being considered 'one of them'), telling him about the second visit to Lanthemtown and their success in escaping the madman. And finally, she told the story of the highway fire, the chase, Viktor being shot, and their long walk back to town.

The commander typed into a tablet as she spoke, feverishly recording her testimony. When she stopped, he took a minute to finish typing and then seemed to read the text back in his mind while she waited in silence.

"I appreciate the story, Leena. We have known each other for a while and have fought with one another on the battlefield more times than I can remember. You are a good soldier, so I have no reason to believe you would lie."

"I feel a *but* coming," Leena said with a smirk.

"But...we received a message that you had betrayed the People's Army and your country and joined with the Chinese to help them with their invasion."

"What message? What are you talking about?" Leena demanded.

"You met with the Chinese ambassador without permission."

"I told you about that when I returned. I could not help taking that meeting. He cornered me in a café and just sat down."

"Yes, I know what you reported, but you also said you did not commit to any assistance, and yet we have a message that contradicts that story." The commander waited for a reply.

Leena gathered her thoughts and brainstormed in her mind what message he might be talking about. And then it hit her. Liv ran from the room when she broke free of the Chinese and stole a radio. She must have used it to send a message to the base station.

"Commander, if you are talking about a message from Liv—I mean Master Sergeant Zolenski—I can explain."

"I sure wish you would, Lieutenant."

"We were being held captive. The Chinese captain came in and told them to release me, saying that I was one of them. I don't know why. They seemed to have a record of my conversation with the ambassador and figured it meant I was willing to be compliant—but it didn't. They had their facts wrong or were trying to put enmity between me and my soldiers. Liv believed what they said without thinking about it and ran off with a radio before I could explain. I'm sure she didn't get far, but they never let me see her again to explain."

"And what about this?" the commander said as he placed a small golden flower pendant on the table. "It's a Chinese-made GPS we found on your clothing."

"They made me wear that!"

Leena examined the commander's face to see if she was getting through, but he had a poker face that was a challenge to read.

"Lieutenant, you are in a lot of trouble here. I really want to believe you, but the evidence of your treachery is overwhelming. It could be your story is correct and Liv got the wrong impression, but it could also be that you're a spy, and we've caught you. The message we got from Liv was cryptic and did not last long before it ended. But having this GPS in your possession shows us you intended to lead the Chinese right to us."

"You must believe me, Commander; I have been nothing but loyal to this army," Leena pleaded.

"I want to believe that, but for now, because I don't know what is true, I need to keep you in custody until we can figure it out. I have enough on my plate right now fending off the Chinese. We don't have time for a trial. You will remain in custody until a formal court-martial can be convened."

"Commander, please don't do this. You know me. You know I would never betray my country."

"We will see, Lieutenant, we will see," the commander concluded ominously before turning for the door.

"Numbers," Leena said. "The Chinese force is enormous, maybe one hundred thousand. With tanks and troop carriers. We are no match for them."

The commander reached the door as a soldier on the other side opened it for him. He turned in the doorway and looked back at Leena. "We have our own intel. This is no longer your fight, Leena. I am terribly sorry about Viktor, but if evidence proves you murdered him, you will spend the rest of your life in prison."

A few minutes after the commander left the room, a guard came to escort Leena to a cell. It was in the same building but on the other end of the hangar. As they walked down the long hallway, Leena could see about twenty rooms set up as holding cells for inmates. Because this was not really a prison, the rooms were not cemented but created with movable partitions. They were meant for the temporary incarceration of suspects and those awaiting military tribunals, not long-term habitation. The room she entered had a solid door with no window and a simple lock on the doorknob that could be easily broken with a swift kick. The armed guards in the hallway were the real deterrents to escape, not the room itself.

In the room was a small bed with a thin mattress, a portable composting toilet, and a portable sink with a hand pump for hand-washing. A roll of toilet paper, a towel, a toothbrush, and a small bar of soap were on her bed along with olive-green pants and a T-shirt of the same color.

Leena sat for a few minutes on the bed, stunned by what had just happened. Jailed for treason. She just could not believe it. She cursed the day that stupid ambassador had happened by her breakfast spot and interrupted her life. Leena was upset but too tired to process it all at that moment. She eventually stood and changed her clothes. She was still in the clothes she wore in Tullian land, and it had begun to wreak.

234 JOSEPH MICHAEL LAMB

Once naked, she used a small towel and the tiny bar of soap to clean her face. Next, she washed the rest of her body. The towel was brown when she was finished, revealing how truly dirty she had become on her journey. She wrung out the towel and wet it again to try to bring back its gray color before hanging it over a hook to dry.

Exhausted, she lay on her bed, shocked at how uncomfortable it was as she could feel the hard bars of the bed frame through the light fluff of the overused mattress. She tried to think of her next step, but all she could come up with was that she was in prison again.

"Does it make sense yet?" The voice came from the other side of the wall, obviously another inmate.

"What?" she asked, trying to determine if the voice was meant for her.

"Does it make sense yet? Why you are here?"

"Who are you? Why does your voice sound familiar?"

"Well, because you put me here."

"Nolan?" Leena said as she turned her head toward the wall next to her bed to determine the location of the voice on the other side.

"Indeed."

"What are you still doing here? I thought they would have let you go by now," Leena said.

"I can go when I'm ready. They only think they're holding me."

"Yes, the security is light, but they would shoot you before you left the hallway."

"Have you figured it out yet?" Nolan asked, changing the subject.

"What is there to figure out?" Leena asked in a subtler and more defeated tone, realizing she was now just a prisoner like Nolan.

"Things are not always as they seem. My guess is that there are things that have gotten by you."

"Do you know something I'm supposed to know?" Leena asked.

"As true as that might be, these are not things that I know but things that you know. You just haven't processed them yet."

"Now you are speaking in riddles."

"Try to think about all the major events that have taken place since the election. How are they connected?" Nolan said, leading her into thought.

"I'm not sure it will matter as I can't get out of here. But okay, I'll humor you. The election took place. The governor was elected. They assigned me a new role. There was a bomb in the van. You shot the governor."

"You know I didn't but continue. You missed one."

"We went to Zone 7 for the week of meetings."

"And the ambassador?" Nolan said.

"How do you know about that?" Leena asked.

"I know many things, but please continue. How are they related?"

Leena sat up and crossed her legs, leaning her back against the wall. Deep in thought, she tried to connect the dots. In her mind, they were separate events. The only commonality was that they happened to her. What was Nolan getting at, and how could he possibly know how the events connected?

"I don't get it. What am I looking for?" Leena said after several minutes of thinking on the topic.

"How did you meet the ambassador?"

"He just walked by my table while I was having breakfast," Leena replied.

"You think the Ambassador of China, who lives and works in Washington, D.C., just happened to walk by your table and randomly chose to sit with you?"

"Well, I guess not. He must have known about me. I had never met him, but he seemed to know a lot about me."

"So, then, the meeting was not random. You could say you were targeted. Please continue."

"Then we met again later that week. He must have been looking for me...or was he having me followed?"

"Now you're catching on," Nolan said.

"The ambassador targeted me. And the captain at the desalination plant said something about a plan. What was the plan? To get me to stand down the army? And what does that have to do with the bomb? The day that happened, I spent time with Vincent under that tree. He said Governor Hamrick was a plant for Senator Rollins. I didn't believe him then."

"How about now?"

"Vincent said yesterday that his boss wanted Senator Chin dead. I was not the target. Something about a land deal."

"And what do you know about land deals?" Nolan pushed further.

"Land deals. I don't know anything about a land deal, except the...wait a minute. Giant Core."

"What is Giant Core?" Nolan said, obviously leading her.

"The company that bought the land where my home used to stand. We were trying to get it back, but they voted against us during the congressional session. Senator Lansom said we were going to try again."

"And who owns Giant Core?"

"I don't know who owns it, but Senator Rollins is the CEO. Viktor told me that under the tree."

"And you believe he is responsible for the bomb to kill Senator Chin?"

"Yes, that's what Vincent said. Well, he didn't say it, but he implied it."

"And who was in the van?"

"The driver, me, Senator Lansom, and Senator Chin."

"If he clearly stated you were not the target, and that Senator Chin was the target..."

"Wait, why would he say that?" Leena asked, interrupting him.

"Say what?"

"Why would Vincent say Senator Chin was the target? If they both voted against Senator Rollins, why wouldn't both senators be targets?"

"And who sent you to the desalination plant to get you out of town as they began construction on the land?"

"Senator Hamrick sent me there."

"Did he?"

"Well, yes, I mean no. He had been shot. Senator Lansom took over after that and sent me. She even sped up the timeframe."

"Are you seeing clearly now?"

"Senator Lansom is working with Senator Rollins!"

"There you go," Nolan said.

"But why? That makes no sense?"

"What piece of information are you missing?"

Leena thought for a few minutes, running the pieces through her brain, desperately trying to remember anything she might have missed.

"I need to know who owns Giant Core. This was a conspiracy to gain the land rights. It's about money. It always is with the Aberjay."

"And how would you find that information?" Nolan asked.

"It's in the public records at the courthouse in Zone 7. I will never get back in there."

"Where else might you find it?"

"Whatever they are building, the construction requires a building permit. It would have to include the name of the company and the owners. I need to get to the Capitol building. It will be in our records. But I will never be able to walk into that building without being arrested."

Leena took a deep breath, feeling like she had just discovered buried treasure. Now she just had to figure out how to get out of this improvised prison cell.

Chapter 13

ESCAPE

T he sound of jet planes passing overhead startled Leena out of deep thought. It was a common sound in the last twenty-four hours, but the rumble still startled her every time. She had spent several hours the day before talking to Nolan and trying to figure out why she was in prison. What events led to it? Was it someone's plan to get rid of her? She was not merely a victim of unfortunate circumstances; there was a collective attempt to put her in prison.

Leena had to get out of this temporary prison cell. She could not face court-marshal. She was certain the city would not repel the Chinese onslaught and, as a prisoner of war, she would likely be executed along with any other prisoners. But how could she stop a war? How could she help the army when she had been stripped of rank and power? How could she convince an entire division to stand down when the Chinese arrive so that they would set Liv and her soldiers free? She knew she probably shouldn't even attempt it, but she also knew it didn't matter. The Chinese army was so large and well-armed that resistance was futile. She might as well save lives by getting them to stand down. This would also keep the water flowing.

First things first, she thought. She needed to escape. It was obvious the room was not meant as a maximum-security facility, and a swift kick to the door would probably open it. But she wondered how she would get past the guards.

"Nolan, are you awake?" Leena asked as she tapped on the wall.

"Yes, I've been awake for some time. How about you? Are you awake?"

Leena shook her head. So many riddles. *Why does he talk that way?*

"I need to get out of here. Can you help me?"

"Do you know what you must do? Are you ready to lead the Resistance again?" Nolan asked.

"I think so. What can we do?"

Leena did not fully understand the talk of the Resistance. She was a part of the Resistance many years before when they demanded equality with the Aberjay and won their independence through the treaty. The Resistance became the People's Army. As far as she understood, there was no Resistance.

Nolan grew silent, and a few minutes later, returned to the wall. Leena could not see him, but the walls were so thin she could see the wall move next to her bed when Nolan was on the other side. She reasoned his bed must be in the same spot on the other side of the wall and his weight on the bed pushed against the wall.

"I sent up a flare," Nolan said.

"A flare?!" Leena replied.

"Figure of speech. Help is on the way."

Leena was not sure whether to trust Nolan, but her impression of him had changed since her earlier encounters. He was no terrorist. He seemed to genuinely care for the people of the zone. He talked of his solitude after losing his own family to the CPU a few years before in one of the eviction campaigns. Leena could not tell if they might have died on the day she visited the CPU camp and saw them shooting the citizens many years before, but the idea of it, just thinking that she might have witnessed the death of this poor man's parents, was enough to bring tears to her eyes.

She would have to trust him. She didn't really have a choice. Being in this prison made her more connected to Nolan and his situation than her army or her duty. She decided she would trust him until she had a reason not to do so. If he could indeed help her get out of prison, she had to let him.

The consequences of escaping her detainment were not lost on her. She thought about it but reasoned the Chinese would soon come over the walls, making their current system of justice irrelevant. And if by some miracle they fended off the Chinese, she would be seen as fighting for their cause and would certainly drop any charges against her. It was a stretch, but she figured she had to save as many of her people as she could, even if it ended badly for her. Prison is not the ideal place to have a baby, but it might be better than living under Chinese rule. Despite the picture the ambassador painted, Leena had seen how their soldiers operated. If they were truly fair and believed in equality for all, it was not evident in the actions of Captain Huang or his soldiers.

Hours after Leena requested help from Nolan, she heard her door unlock. The People's Army guard entered and gave her instructions to stand, snapping handcuffs on her wrists. With one guard in front and one behind her, she walked the long hallway to the front of the building. She didn't know if she had a visitor or if they were planning more interrogations. The expectation made her slow her steps until the guard behind her gave her a little push and said to keep moving.

As she entered the front of the building where the two guards normally sat to monitor things and check in unknown visitors, she saw two other People's Army soldiers. The first one—a small Hispanic man, a corporal—she did not recognize. The other one had her back turned and bright red hair under her Sergeant's cap. As she turned, Leena recognized her immediately. It was Tina Redmont.

Leena tried not to look too surprised, but because Nolan had told her just weeks before that Tina was dead, it was difficult to contain herself.

The guard in front of her turned and removed the handcuffs.

"Leena Zhen, you are being transferred to a high-security facility by order of the commander. These soldiers will escort you." The guard motioned for Tina to take Leena. "I will get the other prisoner."

Leena looked at Tina and could not help but smile. She had been a soldier under her charge many years before, and they had fought many battles side by side. Tina had her hair pinned up under her cap, but Leena would recognize that hair from a block away. It was so bright red that it looked artificial, but Tina had always insisted it was her natural color. Tina was tall and strong, with an athletic body suitable for soldiering.

Within a few minutes, the guard returned with Nolan and followed the same procedure as they uncuffed him. Tina and her partner pulled out their own cuffs and placed them on Leena and

Nolan before escorting them outside to the waiting Jeep. The vehicle was old, not unlike the one Leena drove. As they drew closer, they realized it was not only like Leena's Jeep, it *was* her Jeep.

As Leena sat in the back seat with Nolan, the two soldiers sat in the front and began the drive off the base.

"How did you get my Jeep?" Leena asked Tina.

"They repossessed it after they charged you with treason. Some mindless private left the keys in it when they parked it in the impound lot. We borrowed it."

"Stay quiet. We are not out of the woods yet. We need to get off the base before we're home free," the second soldier said.

Leena playfully punched Nolan in the arm and whispered, "Why did you tell me she was dead?"

"I never said dead. I said she was not with us, and at the time of our conversation, she was not with us," Nolan replied stone faced.

Leena leaned forward and wrapped an arm around Tina who was driving as a tear fell down one side of her own cheek. "It is good to see you."

"I missed you too, now sit back before you get us caught."

They drove with purpose toward the entrance gate and Tina gave a quick salute to the officer at the gate as they exited. Fortunately, they didn't inspect vehicles leaving the base, only those entering. Leena figured that because they had made it onto the base, their forged paperwork would likely stand up to any further scrutiny.

"Okay, we're clear," Tina said as they turned onto the main road, heading north. "This is Hector Rodriguez, but we just call him Roddy."

"Nice to meet you," Leena said.

Nolan just nodded.

They drove mostly in silence. Leena could see a city in turmoil. People's Army trucks were everywhere, transporting people and supplies. Barricades were being constructed. Citizens were boarding up their houses and placing sandbags around them to catch stray bullets. Leena knew it would make no difference. Anyone who stayed would likely die. Between the tanks and the mortar brigades, the city would take a beating.

They drove for about thirty minutes and then turned into a mall parking lot. The people of Zone 6 had not used the mall for more than fifty years, and most of the roof had long since caved in because of its age. They drove into an underground garage beneath the facility and parked by a set of double doors. There were many vehicles there: cars, trucks, and motorbikes. While some were stolen People's Army vehicles, most were civilian-owned.

Tina and Roddy helped the prisoners out of the Jeep before removing their handcuffs. Nolan gave Tina a big hug after having his cuffs removed.

"Thanks, sis," he said to her.

"Not a problem—according to plan, right?" Tina responded.

"Plan?" Leena said.

"Yes," Tina replied. "Nolan got himself arrested the moment he heard you were charged with treason. He knew they would take you there."

Leena was still bewildered over why they thought she was so important. Nor did she have a clue where they were taking her.

Roddy took the lead and walked through the double doors leading to a long hallway that used to be white. Now it was darkened with dust and dirt and had very few lights that still worked, making it almost completely dark in stretches while other sections of the hallway were lit by a fading or flickering bulb that glowed yellow.

As they reached the end of the hall, they opened a door to reveal a wide-open atrium that used to be part of the mall. The glass ceilings had long since been demolished by weather and vandalism. Plants and shrubbery grew from the tiles beneath their feet and out of the walls. Long vines hung down from the open roof. Leena could see two escalators that many years before moved shoppers from level to level, now just stationary stairs damaged by rust and corrosion.

The room was full of soldiers, although they were not dressed alike. Some wore People's Army uniforms while many were dressed in street clothes. Some were sitting cross-legged around a fire while others ate from small metal bowls.

As the four entered, the entire place erupted in shouts and applause. They shouted and clapped for several minutes before the roar subsided. Leena was still confused. What was this rabble? Another army? A militia?

Nolan climbed the stairs of one escalator and stopped about halfway up, turning to the crowd.

"We did it! The Crow rises!" he said as another round of applause and shouts began.

"This is a momentous occasion in our movement. We have shown the establishment that we are not taking 'no' for an answer!" he continued as the crowd continued to roar.

"We will not sit idly by while they pad their own pockets and tell us the war is over! We will not go quietly when injustice is at our door! We will not lay down in resignation when our future and our children's futures are at stake!"

Leena was impressed. Nolan was a good speaker. He seemed to have control of the crowd, ebbing and flowing with their cheers. He displayed signs of a great orator. But the content confused her slightly. And then it hit her. They were not talking about the Aberjay. They were talking about her, about Governor Hamrick and the government she helped build. *Have we really become the enemy of the people? Or were these antagonists just overzealous terrorists looking to stir the pot?*

Nolan continued.

"And now, with great pleasure, I give you your leader. A woman who led the last great Resistance against the Aberjay. A soldier who saved our people from genocide and eliminated CPU leadership. She has killed hundreds if not thousands of those bastards and is here to lead us to victory again! Please welcome your commander, Leena Zhen!"

Leena was shocked as the crowd shouted louder than before. Hundreds roared in admiration, and she had no idea who they were. They all looked at her with big smiles on their faces, crowding in around her as Nolan motioned for her to climb the stairs. She looked up at Nolan and then back at the crowd, then over to Tina, who was also smiling ear to ear and clapping. The pressure was too much. Instinct took over, and she turned and ran through the dilapidated mall and ducked into the first store she saw that had enough light to see where she was going.

Tina ran in after her.

"What's wrong, Leena? These are your people."

Leena tried to compose herself as she paced back and forth, waving her hands as if to shake off the responsibility that was being thrown at her once again.

"I don't know these people, Tina. I am the People's Army liaison to the governor. I'm not a rebel anymore."

Tina went over to Leena and leaned on an old counter. She stayed quiet for a minute to let Leena cry.

"Think about where you are, Leena. You have been attacked, conned, captured, imprisoned, and judged. All by your own government. Are you still ready to fight for them? You are not one of them. Certainly not anymore. You are a criminal. We just broke you out of jail. If you stayed there, you would have been tried for treason and likely imprisoned for life. Is that what you want?"

"No, but it is just a mistake...I just thought..." Leena started. "I just thought we could fix it. That we were making a difference. We were helping people to be free."

"But we are not free," Tina said. "I know you think the treaty helped people, and maybe it did a little, but what they offered is exactly how totalitarianism works. They want you to take the few crumbs from the table and go on with your life. They want you to have an image of freedom when in fact their boot is still on your neck. You have to take them down to dust, crush their institutions, and establish new leadership. I fought with you before. I know you know this. Why did you let them convince you that their concessions would give you freedom?"

"I guess we were all just tired of fighting," Leena said as Tina handed her a small cloth for her runny nose. "I don't really want this. I was happy with my job and my husband. I just wanted to build an ordinary life."

"You can't do that," Tina said.

"Why not?"

"Because you're a patriot. And patriots don't have the luxury of ordinary lives when freedom is at stake."

Tina's words hit Leena hard. She did care about her people. She cared about true freedom, but it was becoming clear to her that she never really had it. She didn't even know what it looked like.

"These people here want to fight with you, Leena. They want to set things right and find our true freedom. Freedom from the Aberjay. Freedom from false governments. Freedom from the Chinese. Will you help them do that? Will you lead them?"

"And when we topple this government and put a new one in place, how do we ensure that corruption doesn't take hold again? How do we make sure their power is limited to the will of the people?" Leena asked earnestly.

"We can't be sure, Leena, but what is the alternative? Live in fear? Live in prison? Live without hope? We have to believe that people are good and that among us there must be those who can govern honestly and without concern for themselves. That is what America is. It's hoping and trusting in the righteousness of those who govern. It's faith that the leadership will truly represent the needs of the people—that they will put their constituents above their own needs or desires. It's called public service, isn't it?"

Leena thought about her situation as Tina waited for an answer. She knew she had several things to accomplish that would be easier with an army. She had to figure out how to make a path for the Chinese to keep water flowing and save Liv. She needed to find her husband and make sure he was safe. She needed to get to the Capitol building and find records of that land deal to confirm who owned Giant Core. And then she had to continue the fight against the Aberjay by removing the wall that separated them.

"They will fight for me?"

"Yes," Tina said with a growing smile.

"And we can do things my way?"

"As you wish."

"Okay, I'm in. Gather the troops."

"Excellent! You will not regret this, Commander. Welcome to the murder," Tina said as she ran from the room.

"Murder?"

Leena ate some corn and peppers from a steel bowl as she studied the maps. Nolan educated her as she studied.

The group of fighters called themselves the Crow. Their symbol, a crow with a small dot of red on its beak, was painted on walls all over the headquarters building—the old mall—including the room where she now found herself. They considered it to be their command center. It was a large meeting room at the top of an old tower that had been built to accommodate executives. It had wood floors and glass on three sides with a view of the parking lot. They were the only windows in the mall that were not broken.

Tina and Nolan brought her up to speed on the position of the Chinese army. Drones had been deployed by the Aberjay to pinpoint troop movements, and the Crow had a friend inside the Aberjay communications office who relayed the information. The Chinese were moving toward the city, but slowly. They were camping about ten miles outside the city to begin preparations for their assault.

Nolan became Leena's senior advisor as it was well-known that he was a high-level thinker but not much for detail. Tina was born to be a soldier and was considered captain of the Crow, relaying information to the soldiers who numbered more than three hundred.

"They will probably attack the city tomorrow or the next day. Based on this data, they are building a camp from which to launch their siege. Nolan, what is the news in the West?" Leena asked.

"According to the news we're getting, the Chinese took Phoenix and Salt Lake City in one day. Our federal troops have kept them from moving further east for now, but they are likely just regrouping and shoring up their resources for the next push. The attack on the East was intended to divert resources away from the West. It didn't work as they expected. Although we need them, the Federal Government has sent us only about thirty thousand troops, all of which are in Zone 7 at the moment."

"The entire People's Army numbers fifty thousand," Leena interjected. "We are no match for their numbers or their strength. We need more troops or more firepower. Any ideas?"

"It's over fifty now with the draft, probably closer to seventy thousand," Tina said.

"What draft?" Leena inquired.

"Senator Lansom announced a draft the day you left for the east. She figured she would shore up resources for the People's Army before the Aberjay took all their young people for their CPU," Nolan said.

"I don't know if that was wise or incredibly selfish," Leena commented as she leaned down to stare at the map.

"Can we ask the CPU for help?" Tina asked.

"If we can't get the Federal Government to send troops into the zone, I'm certain we won't get the CPU here. They have little interest in protecting Zone 6."

"But they could use our numbers, no?" Tina asked.

"I'm sure they would be happy to have our seventy thousand on their front line as we would be the first to die in that battle."

"Then let's give it to them," Tina suggested.

Tina walked toward the table piled high with maps. "Where is the likely entry point for their forces?"

The team gathered around the table and spread out a map of the zones.

"They won't attempt an attack on our east side as that wall is the strongest. It's stone and mortar and fifty feet high. They will attack here," Leena said, pointing to the part of the map that showed the southern portion of Zone 6. "This is where the 'walls' are mostly chain-link fences. Their tanks can roll right over them."

"So, if we meet their troops with the People's Army on the south side, we'll be fighting out in the open. There is no cover and nothing to restrain them." Tina paused momentarily as she pondered multiple options. "What if we aren't there at all?"

"What do you mean?" Nolan asked.

"We can't face them head-on in that spot, and it's the likely attack point. What if we instead wait for them behind the homes and buildings inside the zone? We hide our numbers and make them wander the streets looking for us while we attack small squads. We have the advantage of knowing the city." Tina waited to see how the group responded.

"That's good, Tina, but I'm afraid we would put our people in too much danger," Leena said. "Too many civilians would be caught in the crossfire. What if we abandon the whole zone?"

"What?" Nolan asked.

"Let's take the entire army and all of the citizens into Zone 7. The Chinese will walk right into an empty city. And because their entire army will be on the south end of Zone 6, they will have little choice but to march north and attack Zone 7 where the defense is the strongest. Plus, the battle will take place in Zone 7 and not in our neighborhoods. Assuming we are victorious and drive them away, the damage will be done to their neighborhoods, not ours." Leena smiled, stepping away from the table and sitting in a nearby chair.

"That is a brilliant plan, Leena, but how do we get them to let us in? And how do we tell the citizens? Not to mention you don't really command that army anymore," Tina reasoned.

"Yes, that is quite the challenge." Leena looked around the boxes, debris, and trash that littered the room. She found a ball of paper that she unwadded and tore off a small piece. Using a pen from the table, she scrawled an address. "Tina, can you get a couple of soldiers to go to this address and bring me the resident?"

"Yes, of course. Who is it?"

"A friend named Maggie Cho. I have a job for her."

Leena sat at a small table in what the Crows called the mess hall, finishing her breakfast of lukewarm oatmeal with sliced bananas and almonds. She had eaten better meals, but it was gourmet compared to the rations she had been living on recently. The mess hall was the mall's food court in happier days. The Crow had cleared the area of debris and added tables and chairs. A long table was set up with trays of food for the troops to enjoy twice a day. It was not luxurious, and the lights in the room were unreliable, causing them to flicker, but it served its purpose and kept the soldiers fed.

Sleep eluded her the night before. After being thrown into leadership of this ragtag bunch of freedom fighters, and now facing the additional pressure of knowing that her team was still being held at the desalination plant, rest did not come easy. She felt responsible for Liv's fate and had not determined how she would rectify the situation. Liv's life depended on her compliance with the Chinese, but she was not sure how to stand down her army which she no longer commanded. Even if she could get the army to comply with their plans and move into Zone 7, would that be enough to meet the criteria set by the Chinese captain? If the Chinese felt no resistance marching into Zone 6, would that be enough, causing them to radio the plant and let her people go? Or was she being foolishly optimistic that the Chinese army during a time of war would be so generous as to let enemy troops walk free?

Late on the previous evening, Leena had dispatched a few soldiers to find Jordan. She knew he would want to know she was safe, though she was not sure if the army would question him, or worse, take him into custody as a collaborator. Leena knew he could take care of himself, but without the right information, she feared he might get the wrong idea. She was certain he would never think of her as a traitor, but given the accusations against her of murder and conspiring with the Chinese, she felt he deserved an explanation.

"Commander," a soldier said as he entered the mess hall, "the resident you wished to speak to is in room seventeen."

"Thank you, Wallace." Leena stood and moved toward the door before realizing she didn't know where room seventeen was located. She turned back toward the soldier with a questioning look.

"The room that smells like candles," the soldier said.

"Okay, got it. Thank you."

Leena walked from the mess hall into the main hallway. Rain dropped from the broken panes of glass on the ceiling high above her head. She assumed the Crows had not been here long or they might have done some renovations to at least keep the weather out. She guessed it was a temporary space or they didn't want to make any updates that might signal their position to the enemy. Either way, the state of this old mall was frightful. It reminded Leena of the building where she grew up with its soft floors and caution tape where balconies or stairs used to be. The weather had bored holes into floors and walls in some places, revealing metal studs.

While the large mall walkway was brightly lit by the broken skylights, the rooms in use off the main corridor were dark and required artificial light. Room seventeen used to be a candle store based on the scent. Although very few candles remained, years of burning them had seeped into the walls and ceiling tiles, providing a lingering fragrance. It smelled nice, mostly of flowers.

Leena stepped into room seventeen, lit only by one working light in the center of the store. Under the light, a chair had been brought in for interrogations. Her friend Maggie was in the chair looking terribly frightened. She was not restrained but, based on her disposition, she felt like a prisoner.

"Maggie," Leena said as she walked into the room.

"Leena!" Maggie cried out slowly, rising out of the chair and looking left and right at the guards who surrounded her to ensure her movement was allowed.

Leena gave her a big hug before motioning for her to be seated. She walked to the side of the room and dragged an additional chair to sit in front of Maggie.

"Sorry about all this. This is just how they operate," Leena said, reassuring Maggie that she was not in any sort of trouble.

"Okay," Maggie said nervously, still looking around the room at the soldiers standing like statues, holding their rifles close to their chests.

"I need you to do something for me, Maggie. I know you probably heard that I'm a traitor and working with the Chinese, but I can assure you none of that is true."

"I didn't believe it for a second when they told me," Maggie said.

"I need you to poke around in the building permit office and find me the application used for the construction that is taking place in the north end of the zone. It should list the contractor company and the owner of the land."

"Okay, I can do that. I work in that office all the time," Maggie said confidently.

"The company on the application that owns the land will probably be Giant Core or some subsidiary. Then I need you to cross-reference that in the business license office to see who owns the company listed on the construction permit. I need names."

"I should be able to do that. I don't work in that office as much, but I have a friend I have lunch with sometimes who would have access."

"Great, I really appreciate your help. Let's try not to share that this is for me, though, or it may raise alarms."

"Leena, what is this all about? Who are these people you're with?"

Leena stood and looked around at the soldiers in the room, still motionless.

"They're patriots, Maggie. True American patriots."

The soldiers escorted Maggie back to her home as ordered. Once at home, she would make her way to work as she normally did and hopefully retrieve the information Leena requested. Leena's next meeting was with the war council, as they called it. It included Nolan, Tina, Robert Bruce (a former People's Army captain), and several other soldiers who were trained in wartime strategies.

"Good morning, everyone," Leena said as she walked into the room in the tower before pouring herself a cup of coffee. "Let's get to it."

Everyone sat around the large table, maps still covering most of it.

"We need to figure out how we're going to get the army on board with our plan. Let's hear some ideas," Nolan said.

"We still have a few high-ranking officers who would listen if we wanted to try to convince them," Tina offered.

"No," Leena replied, "that would only get a fraction of the army. We need everyone to be on board or it won't work."

"Don't forget the civilians," Robert said. "We need them to know as well. And we need a plan to give them. It's hard to sneak a million people into Zone 7."

"First things first. We need to get the army on board, then we need to convince the Aberjay to let us in," Leena said. "I'm not sure which will be harder."

"If you can get to Commander Johnson, Leena, could you convince him to help us?" Nolan asked.

"It would be a long shot. He already thinks I'm a traitor. He would certainly think it's a trick."

"I don't see another way of getting the entire army to follow the plan," Nolan said.

"How do we get to Commander Johnson? He's on the base, surrounded by an army, and lives out of the command center. We can't fight our way in there without taking heavy losses," Tina commented.

Leena's eyes grew wide as she jumped up out of her chair. "Not at night."

"What do you mean?" Tina said.

"He does live in the command center, but at night, he goes to a private barracks. A building with multiple private rooms where senior staff can sleep during times of war or when they work overnight on the base. I know where Commander Johnson's room is. It's easily accessible on the edge of the base and not very well guarded."

"We have a map of the base here," Tina said as she sorted through the maps on the table. "Just point it out, and we will do some surveillance and get a plan together."

Leena pointed to the map to show where the building was located. "It's here."

Tina motioned for a soldier who was standing guard at the edge of the room and whispered some instructions into her ear. She disappeared through the door to carry out her surveillance orders.

"Tina, no casualties. These are our people; I don't want anyone hurt."

Tina looked at Leena slightly surprised by the edict. "I can promise to use nonlethal means to secure the facility, but the stakes are too high to..."

"No casualties," Leena repeated.

"Yes, Commander," Tina relented.

"We go tonight assuming your team returns with good surveillance data. Once we have the commander on board, we will talk about getting Zone 7 to comply. I have an idea that might work."

Chapter 14

PERSUASION

The air was chilly as Leena finished her shower. She stepped out and ran a comb through her hair. The bathroom was enormous and once had about twenty stalls with toilets, but the walls had long since rotted or been torn out entirely. The shower she was using was more of a camping shower. The water was lukewarm, and instead of a showerhead, a hose had been rigged to drip into a bucket with holes about eight feet off the ground, providing an experience similar to walking in the rain. Leena was happy to just get some water on her body to wash away the stink. The mall was hot during the day and cool at night as there were no windows to stop the wind in the evenings from whipping through the empty halls.

Leena stared into the only mirror left on the wall. Though it was cracked and broken, there was enough reflection to be useful. Drying off with a towel and quickly dressing in another outfit of army-green pants and a T-shirt, she ruminated on how her face had changed. She was only twenty-three but felt she had aged a decade or more in the last year. She tried to understand how she got to this place—the head of a rebellion! Did she know what she was rebelling against? Was she in the right? It was hard to tell. The lines between right and wrong were blurry.

She tried to outline in her head her goals. *What am I trying to accomplish? What is the best-case scenario?* She figured surviving the Chinese attack was paramount, along with clearing her name of treason and Viktor's death. She also had to free Liv and her soldiers from their detainment at the desalination plant. If she could accomplish those things—no easy task—removing those from power who were corrupt would be her next priority.

She knew Senator Lansom was involved but couldn't prove it. She knew Senator Rollins tried to have Senator Chin killed and that Vincent Ryder helped him do it. Somehow it was related to the land deal. It did not seem right that they were still fighting for basic freedoms while behind the scenes their current representatives were buying property that the Aberjay had taken. It was certainly possible that it was altruistic. Were they coordinating with the wealthy to develop the land as a benefit to the Miniyar? Not likely. Although Leena wanted to give them the benefit of the doubt, something inside her screamed that they were up to no good. Leena had to figure out what they were planning.

"Commander," a soldier called out to her from the doorway of the enormous bathroom. It still felt strange to Leena to be addressed that way.

"Yes?"

"Your husband is here; we have him in the candle room."

The soldiers had begun using the term 'candle room' instead of the room number to accommodate Leena, who couldn't keep the numbers straight. There were more than two hundred rooms in the mall on two levels, although this ragtag group of crows used only about thirty of them.

"Okay, thanks. I'll be right there," Leena replied as she finished putting on her boots.

She was excited to see Jordan but nervous about telling him she was pregnant. She knew logically that he would be excited, but she felt a hesitation to tell him in case she had misread the signals. They had talked about having children but had not planned to do it so soon. They were both so young. She hoped that if the news was disappointing to him, he would not show it well or it might crush her.

Leena started the long walk down the mall walkway and couldn't contain her excitement at finally seeing her husband. With each step, she moved faster until she was in a full run. Reaching the candle room out of breath, she ran into her husband's arms, who was standing in the room next to the chair where Maggie had sat earlier that day.

"Hello, darling," Leena said as she squeezed him hard.

"I'm so glad you are safe," Jordan replied. "I have been bugging the shit out of Commander Johnson and his staff trying to find you, but they wouldn't tell me anything. I heard rumors."

"Don't worry about that. Let me look at you."

Leena stepped back, still holding his hands. He was dressed in a People's Army uniform with fatigues, a belt, black boots, and a cap. His brass showed he was a private.

"You look quite stunning," Leena said as she gave him a little wink. "What are you doing in this uniform?"

"They drafted me right when you left."

"Drafted by who?"

"Governor Lansom implemented a draft for anyone in their twenties. She figured if she didn't, the CPU or Federal Army would do it and take our people out west. It seems that was a good idea now that we have a threat from the east."

Leena tried to shake off the shock of his attire. Jordan had fought with her as a Resistance fighter, but she was not used to seeing him in a uniform. Not in the last couple of years anyway.

"What are you doing here? Who are these people?" Jordan asked.

"It's hard to explain, but they arrested me for treason and murder when I got back from the desalination plant."

"Treason? Murder? You must be joking."

"It's a long story, but they think I am working with the Chinese," Leena explained.

"And the murder?"

"Viktor," Leena said quietly as a tear formed in one eye.

"I'm sorry, Leena. I know he was a good friend. But you didn't kill him?"

"No, of course not," Leena said, wiping the tear.

"Where are you stationed? What is your post?"

"I'm on the base right now, but I am being moved tomorrow morning to the east gate. The Chinese are camped just outside of town. We could be under attack at any moment."

"Come with me; I want to catch you up on things," Leena said as she took him by the hand and led him to an area of the mall used as sleeping quarters. She motioned for Jordan to have a seat.

They talked about her journey and what she went through in the Tullian lands, as well as Lanthemtown, Port Loyal, and the drama at the desalination plant. She trusted her husband and left nothing out of her story. Once finished with the briefing, her face grew serious as she took his hands and looked him in the eye.

"Jordan, I need to tell you something else."

"Uh-oh, that does not sound good," Jordan replied.

"It is good, it is good. Well, it may not be timely, but it is certainly good."

Leena took a moment to run her hands through her hair, still wet from her lukewarm shower. She stood and began pacing the floor in anticipation of the conversation. Leena didn't know what Jordan would say or if he would be excited. She knew he wanted a baby, but that was before all of this had happened. Before the Chinese were at the gates. Before the accusations of treason and murder. Her trepidation was obvious to him.

"Well, spit it out," Jordan said.

Leena sat down in front of him again and took a deep breath. "I'm pregnant."

Jordan's eyes grew wide. His face was stoic. Leena held her breath, waiting for his reaction. Then he smiled, first with a slight grin and then showing teeth. He stood and pulled his wife to him, picking her up off the ground and spinning her around.

"This is fantastic! How long have you known? When did this happen?"

Jordan set her back on the ground, and she smiled along with him, glad that he had the reaction he did.

"I assume the night we downed that bottle of wine."

"Yes, that must have been it. Wait, are you okay? Do you need to sit down?"

"I'm fine, Jordan. I had some morning sickness and threw up for a few days, but it seems to have subsided."

"Is it a boy or a girl? I bet it's a girl. This is great! We're going to have a family!"

"A little early to tell the sex, honey. I haven't even seen a doctor to confirm it yet."

"We need to get you to the base to see the doctor. Why are you waiting?" Jordan asked, still excited from the rush of adrenaline.

"I can't do that, Jordan. I am wanted. They would imprison me the moment I step foot on the base."

"I don't understand. What are you doing here in this dirty place?" Jordan said as he looked around the room. "This is no place for my child to be born."

"Slow down, Jordan. I know the timing is bad, but we're at war. I'm on the run. I can't just pop back up on the base and ask forgiveness."

They both sat silently for a brief spell.

"Let's leave."

"Leave what?" Leena replied.

"Let's get out of the zone. We can go to a different city, somewhere up north. I heard Richmond has jobs. It's a Minyar City—well, most of it. We could get jobs there and start again."

"I can't leave, Jordan. This army is depending on me."

"For what? Who are these people? Are you their leader?"

"Yes. They are just like us, Jordan. Resistance fighters. People who want a more equal world, a more egalitarian society."

"We have been through this before, Leena. You know that is idealistic nonsense. All we can do is get what we can for ourselves and try to find some peace in it. You can't change the world." Jordan stood, now using his arms to talk as much as his mouth. "We have to get out of here and find a safe place for our baby."

"I know you don't really believe that. Freedom is worth fighting for. I don't think running to another city will change anything. The Chinese are coming whether we like it or not, and they won't stop here. They will move north."

"This isn't our fight, Leena! There is no reason to risk our lives and the life of our child!"

"We must do this, Jordan. We must help these people. Our people."

"Why?" Jordan asked, tears forming.

"Because we're patriots like them. Because we're Americans. Because we believe in freedom. Something has gone terribly wrong in our country. And if good people don't stand up to fix it, nothing will get better. We must fight. Not only for these people but for us and our future family. Everything depends on what we do here right now."

Leena turned her back on Jordan and began pacing again. She had too many emotions to make sense of them. She tried to breathe deeply and calm down.

"Jordan, if we don't do this, many years from now, living in chains, how do we look our children in the eye? Knowing we had a chance to make a difference but fled instead?"

Jordan looked at her with tears in his eyes. Slowly, his face turned to resignation as he knew he would not win the argument. He never did.

"I don't agree with this decision, but I know I won't talk you out of it. How can I help?"

"I need you to go back to your post. We're going to try to get in to talk to Commander Johnson tonight. We want to convince him to make a deal with the CPU."

"A deal with the CPU? Wow, you *are* desperate."

"We only stand a chance against the Chinese together; we must get them to see that. We are going to assault his living quarters on the base. Tonight, around midnight. I need you to do what you can to lead any guards away from that building before we strike. I want to limit any casualties."

"Okay, I can do that," Jordan replied.

Jordan and Leena spent another hour together attempting to talk about their future. They stayed away from the burdens of their current situation and talked whimsically about what life would be like once they put everything right. They talked about children, planting another garden that would be larger than their current one, and a move to another city. They enjoyed their time together before Jordan needed to leave. This was not the first time they had been embroiled in conflict with major repercussions for their family and their people, but as they lay there in the bunk's dark room, talking about their future, the stakes were higher.

Rain poured down on the runway of the base where fifty or more years before, planes had taken off and touched down almost one per minute. Now it was dark, desolate, and saw little activity. The People's Army had replaced airline terminals with bunkers for ammunition storage and barracks for soldiers. Leena's team crouched in the small, wooded area just outside the base, hiding in the brush, waiting for the opportune moment to begin their assault.

Within thirty feet of them was a chain-link fence topped by razor wire. Just on the other side was a Quonset hut, about two hundred feet long. Small portholes lined the building. Most were dark, but a few at the end of the building, where Commander Johnson's room was located, were still lit.

A patrol of two men walked the fence line about every fifteen minutes. It was quiet except for the sounds of the rain pounding the metal building and gurgling through long drainpipes that emptied on the ground nearby.

In the distance, Leena could see a Jeep with a soft top that sheltered the driver from the rain. The vehicle drove slowly with headlights illuminating the fence. She thought for a moment that this might pose a problem, but then the lights of the Jeep went off, then on again. That had to be Jordan. He had promised to help draw the sentries away from the building for their assault.

She saw the Jeep driver follow the fence line in the direction of the sentries. After about three hundred yards, it stopped, and the driver turned off the lights. The two sentries walked to the window and, within a few minutes, ran to the other side of the Jeep to get in the passenger side, avoiding the rain.

"This is our chance. Let's go," Leena whispered to her team.

Two men with a long collapsible ladder ran to the tall fence and extended it, then set it against the fence. One man scurried to the top of the fence and lay a large blanket across the barbed wire. With a tool that was difficult to make out in the rain, the soldier leaned over and snapped the razor wire in a few places to clear it from the path. He then climbed down and, using a flashlight, signaled twice.

The rest of the Crow that were present, about thirty men and women, emerged from their hiding spots to climb the ladder and drop to the other side. One by one, like a pack of rats, they climbed the aluminum stairs and fell to the other side, congregating beside the Quonset hut.

Leena went last, along with Tina, and climbed the ladder with ease. The rain made the rungs slippery, but her boots held fast, and she was over the fence in seconds. Once Tina was over, the two soldiers left behind secured the ladder and walked back to the wooded area to stay out of sight to await their colleagues' return.

The team, armed with batons per Leena's orders, crept next to the building in single file. Their rifles were slung on their backs and easily accessible, but Leena commanded that they try to avoid casualties. They faced no resistance as they turned the corner to the back door of the building. A soldier bent down at the door with a lock pick to attempt entry. After about thirty seconds, the door sprung free of its lock, and the band of wet Crow ran inside.

The hallway was well-lit and ran the length of the building with doors on each side. Its appearance was almost identical to the makeshift prison cells that held Nolan and Leena on the same base. The only sound was that of a fan and the dripping of water from the soaked soldiers.

Leena pointed to a door labeled as the commander's residence, and the troops gathered around the door. Tina moved forward and tried the handle, but it was locked. The locksmith moved into position and once more began working on the door. Within seconds, the doorknob turned.

Opening the door, Tina entered the room with Leena on her heels. The Commander was at his desk with his back to them. Once they came a few steps closer, he noticed the intrusion and reached for a desk drawer that presumably contained a weapon. Tina rushed in and, using her baton, brought it down on his arm, causing him to wince in pain and pull it to his chest while several soldiers restrained him. As they swung him around, he recognized the ladies of mayhem.

"Tina? Leena? What is the meaning of this?"

"Keep your cool, Commander," Tina said as she pulled him in his wheeled chair away from his desk. "We're just here to talk."

The officer composed himself and gave little resistance as he knew he was greatly outnumbered. A third of the Crow filed into the room and closed his door while the remaining troops went back to the exterior of the building to guard their exit.

"Commander," Leena started, "I know you think I'm a traitor, but I am not. Contrary to what it might look like right now, I am just as committed to this army and our people as you. I did not kill Viktor, and I did not betray Liv. I have a plan for dealing with the Chinese, and I think it will work, but I need your help to make it happen."

The commander took a deep breath and, looking around the room, realized he had little choice but to listen.

"I'll listen, but I cannot promise my help. I still don't know which side you are on, despite your persuasive words."

"I understand. What is the status of our army?"

"You know I can't answer that."

"My concern is that the Chinese are right outside our gates, and I don't see battlements, tanks, federal troops, or anything that would indicate we are getting help." Leena said this as a statement more than a question.

The commander took another deep breath, hoping to avoid answering any of her questions, but realized she was not leaving without some answers.

"There is no help, Leena. The Federal Army is mostly out west, and the few troops that were sent are holding up in Zone 7. They said it was because they have more accommodations for them, but you know as well as I do they don't care about saving this zone. The Chinese would do them a favor if they wiped us out."

"And the CPU?" Leena asked.

"They're in the same place. No one is coming. We have to do the best we can with what we have. We were told the British and the French are sympathetic and may get involved, but we haven't seen any movement from them yet. We put together a plan with the small number of troops we have, but there is not much hope in it seeing that we are so vastly outnumbered."

"I think I can help with that. Here is what we propose. Convince the Aberjay that we are stronger together—that we cannot beat the Chinese without working together. Their own numbers do not guarantee them victory. They know they need more soldiers. We volunteer to be their front line, but they have to let us into Zone 7 so we can defend from behind the wall."

"How do you know the Chinese will attack from the south?" the commander asked.

"Because they will think we're still here. They will assess our walls and realize a southern attack is the most workable. Once they roll right in with little resistance, they will have no choice but to head north to complete the march. We have a better shot of defeating them if we do it from the wall."

"They have heavy artillery; they will bust right through that wall..." The commander stopped as he saw Leena grin. "That is what you want, isn't it? To destroy their wall? To annihilate their zone?"

"I don't know about annihilation, but I would not mind the destruction of that damn wall. It overshadows who we are as a people. It is a symbol of their dominance over us, a stalwart separation between those who have opportunities in life and those who are destined for poverty. Yes, I will cheer the day that wall comes down, and they will rue the day they underestimated us. But, despite my desire for their destruction, this plan is about survival. I just don't see a way we can save our lives otherwise."

The commander put up his hands in surrender to Leena's speech. "Okay, let me think a minute." He rubbed his face with his hands and then bent over, dropping his head. His face seemed to twitch involuntarily as he thought about Leena's plan.

"Okay, I guess it's worth a try. It's better than just waiting to be slaughtered. I can make a call to Commander Lawrence, head of the CPU, and have a conversation. But what about the citizens, Leena? How do we protect our people from the attack if we're in Zone 7?"

"We take them with us," Leena said matter-of-factly.

"What? How do we march a million people into Zone 7? I know they won't go for that in a million years."

"We won't tell them."

"Oh, Leena, I'm afraid you have really lost your mind."

"Maybe," Leena said with a grin, "but they will never expect it. Are the tunnels still in use?"

The commander looked at the ground. His lips were pursed, and it was clear his tolerance level for these invasive questions was being tested.

"Commander," Leena asked again, "are the tunnels still in operation?"

"Yes, we have about thirty of them, but the Aberjay sealed up a few."

"Tunnels?" Tina questioned. "What tunnels?"

"The ones we used during the last conflict to sneak into Zone 7," Leena answered. "We can use them to move citizens into the zone."

"Leena, there is no guarantee that they won't be waiting on the other side," the commander reasoned. "They're on high alert because of the Chinese. They will have every street covered with CPU."

"We put them in uniforms," Tina said. "We must have thousands of People's Army uniforms. We get as many citizens as possible in uniform and blend them in with our troops when we walk them through their gates. We can load the trucks with citizens and march our troops on foot. It will look like normal troop movement. And the ones who don't get in that way can use the tunnels."

"That actually might work, but you won't get them all." the commander commented as Tina responded with a knowing smirk.

"We don't need to get them all. Those left behind can stay in their homes. If we move enough of them out, it will look like the zone is empty," Leena said.

"How do you know I won't have you arrested the moment I walk out of here, Leena?"

Leena stepped forward and looked the commander in the eye. "Because you are a good person, and you know in your heart that I didn't betray our nation or our people. And I certainly didn't kill Viktor."

The commander nodded, and Leena motioned for the soldiers to unhand him and step away. Sounds from outside indicated they were at risk of being discovered. *Jordan likely kept the sentries busy as long as he could then released them back to their patrol,* Leena thought.

A knock at the door caused the occupants to stir. Leena looked to the commander and made clear she wanted him to invite the visitor inside. The soldiers moved away from the door to allow it to open as the commander shouted, "Come in."

A young People's Army private walked in with a note in her hand and instantly was grabbed from behind by two Crow, causing her to scream momentarily until they put a hand over her mouth.

The commander put up his hand to calm her as Leena stepped forward and grabbed the note. After reading it, she turned to the commander, still in his chair.

"We need to get you to the command center. There's a call on the long-range radio," Leena said.

The commander noticed the angst on Leena's face. She was obviously stressed over the idea of moving thirty freedom fighters across the base with the commander in tow.

"It's okay, Leena, get your people off the base, and you and Tina can escort me to the command center. I will make sure no one takes you into custody."

"And how am I supposed to believe that?" Leena questioned.

"I guess you will just have to trust me."

Leena thought for a moment, confused over whether it was wise to give up her advantage. She knew the commander was not her enemy, but she was unsure how persuasive she had been. She looked at Tina, who just shrugged. Leena felt the weight of leadership and relented.

"Okay, we'll just have to trust you," she said to the commander as Leena and Tina pulled him up out of his chair and motioned for the soldiers to open the door.

"What about her?" Tina asked, pointing casually at the messenger.

"Bring her with us," Leena said.

The Crow went back to the fence, waited for a sentry to pass and, after climbing it, carefully slid over to the other side. They took positions in the wooded area so they could remain out of sight and wait for further instructions.

Leena followed the commander, who was now without any restraints. He walked into the command center slowly, as if he were waiting to be pulled or directed by his escorts. Leena and Tina were behind him, hoping that the other soldiers would not notice them Both of them were armed with handguns, which was not unusual in the building, and while their uniforms were the same as People's Army uniforms, they lacked the brass and silver insignias indicating rank, which would stand out to anyone paying attention.

The commander had given orders to the messenger not to reveal their ruse and motioned for her to have a seat in the command center. The three walked past many soldiers at their stations and then into a room that contained communications equipment. The room was mostly empty of personnel because it was after one a.m. Inside was an array of equipment covered with knobs and screens as well as video monitors mounted on the wall that seemed to be displaying images and data from multiple locations around the city. The room had a scent of burned rubber and electricity as if the heat of the equipment was melting the wiring.

A soldier seated at a console rose as the commander walked in and recognized Leena immediately. He reached for a sidearm while Tina and Leena did the same. The commander put up his hands and ordered the man to stand down, forcing him to return his sidearm to its holster.

"It's okay, soldier. Stand down. I was told there was a call for me."

"No sir," the soldier said.

"There isn't a call for me?" the commander pressed.

"Yes sir, I mean, no sir. There is a call, but it isn't for you."

"Then why was I summoned to answer it?" the commander demanded.

"Because it's a call for her," the soldier said as he pointed to Leena. They all turned to look at Leena with confusion in their eyes.

"Who is on the radio, soldier? Do they have clearance codes?" the commander asked.

"Yes, sir, they had the proper codes."

The soldier looked at the commander, and he nodded his approval as they directed Leena to the chair to use the radio. Leena had never been on this side of a radio and had only used it in the field. She didn't know how to address the anonymous caller.

She pressed the button on the microphone and with a click said, "Hello, this is Leena." A moment later, she tried again. "Hello, this is Leena. Go ahead."

Leena looked up at the soldier and then at the commander. The radio then squawked, fuzzy and unable to connect. Then there was a voice.

"Leena. Leena. I...here."

The voice was male and broken. Familiar but unrecognizable.

"Who is this?" Leena inquired.

"Leena? It's...Davis."

"It's Lyon Davis," Leena said to the others.

"Lyon, are you there? We hear you, but you're breaking up."

"Who the hell is Lyon Davis?" the commander interjected.

"...wanted...you...explosion...plant." The transmission was so broken up that it was difficult to decipher.

"Say again, Lyon, what explosion?"

"...the plant...Chinese."

"Say again, Lyon, we are not reading you," Leena pleaded.

"What does that mean?" Tina asked.

"Does he mean the desalination plant?" the commander suggested.

The transmission stopped.

Leena turned in her chair, noticing a small bathroom with a frosted glass door near the communications room.

"Soldier, go turn on that water."

The soldier looked to the commander for approval and then rushed to the restroom and turned the silver handle on the sink. Nothing came out.

"It's the plant," Leena continued. "The Chinese blew it up."

Leena leaned forward and put her head between her knees. Tears formed, but she choked back the urge to weep.

"Leena, what is it?" the commander asked.

"Liv was there, along with a team of soldiers, captured by the Chinese."

"You don't know what they did or didn't do," Tina reasoned, attempting to reduce the tension and the impact of the pain Leena felt. "They could have moved the troops with their army. They could have sent them to prison camps. You just don't know."

"The Chinese don't take prisoners, do they, Commander?" Leena asked as she looked to Commander Johnson, who kept his composure but was clearly bothered by the loss.

"Let's not speculate, Leena. We just don't know."

"Commander, it's time you made that call to Commander Lawrence," Leena said. She raised her head and looked him in the eye as tears rolled down her face, which was now filled with vitriol. "If they hurt our people, we need to make them pay."

Chapter 15

ASSAULT

L eena drove through town at a snail's pace, dodging citizens who were packing their vehicles to leave or just desperately looking for direction, as well as debris—remnants of the water wars that had taken place and were erupting again. The work they had done to clean up the streets in the previous months had been undone. And the sound of fighter jets every few minutes overhead signaled that the conflict between nations had begun.

Tina sat next to Leena in the small Jeep while trucks followed behind, full of uniforms. It was everything they could scrounge up on the base and in the surrounding storage units. People's Army soldiers walked by the trucks, handing out uniforms and issuing instructions. Leena knew they could not save everyone, but she was resolved to save as many as possible. She hoped that if she could partially empty the city, those who remained would hunker down inside their homes and be safe from the war.

Leena had tuned her radio to the frequency provided by Commander Johnson. He said he would contact her once he had spoken to Commander Lawrence. She was confident he could convince him, but an uneasy feeling in her stomach reminded her that many things could go wrong with the plan.

A buzzing sound above drew her attention. She looked up to see a small drone hovering above. She could tell by the markings that it was not a CPU drone, and based on the colors, she deduced it was Chinese.

"Tina, look. That drone. We can't let the Chinese know what we are up to. Shoot it down!"

Tina grabbed her rifle and stepped out of the Jeep, firing on the drone several times before succeeding, sending it to the ground in pieces. Leena walked over to where the drone fell and picked up the remaining pieces. It was black with some red markings and Chinese characters that divulged its origin. She ripped the camera from the drone and smashed it under her boot to ensure it had no power.

Leena used her radio to communicate the existence of these drones and requested the commander put out a bulletin ordering soldiers to shoot them down if they were seen over the city.

"Let's keep moving," Leena said as they stepped back into the Jeep.

They continued through the city for hours, handing out uniforms and instructions. The plan was to get citizens to stand on a particular street that led all the way to the north gate so they could mingle with the troops once they made a push toward Zone 7. Conducted correctly, they could take their troops and a small portion of citizens into Zone 7, where they would be safe from the initial attack of their enemy. Those who didn't have uniforms could hide in trucks or go to designated safe houses around the city where tunnels under the wall could be taken to enter the zone. The tunnels had been dug and used during the last great Resistance that ended only a couple of years before.

According to Commander Johnson, most of them were still functional.

"CQ Actual to Loyal Eight," the radio rang out.

"CQ Actual, this is Loyal Eight," Leena replied.

"Loyal Eight, CQ Actual target was reached. Return to base."

"Ten-four," Leena replied, indicating her willingness to travel back to base for a conference. Even though they spoke in codes, they wanted to keep any hint of their plan off the airwaves as the enemy was likely listening on every channel.

A couple of titanic explosions that shook the ground beneath them made all of them stop and gaze at one another. The explosion was distant but powerful.

"What the hell was that?" Tina asked.

"Sounds like our fighters are bombing their camp. This will certainly cause them to march. We'd better hurry."

Leena informed the truck driver that they were heading back to base and to continue with their mission of handing out uniforms until they ran out. The two women climbed into the Jeep and headed toward the base as quickly as the messy streets would allow.

Leena and Tina walked into the command room to meet Commander Johnson. He was standing over a table examining a map of Zone 7. Leena noticed his sidearm, which was unusual to see in the command center. His thick black belt and holster were tight around his waist, holding what was likely a .45-caliber pistol.

"Did you reach Commander Lawrence?" Leena began.

"Yes, I spoke to their commander, but I could not discuss the plan with him on the radio. He committed to having a conversation about it though. We need to go see him right now."

"What are you studying?" Leena asked, pointing toward the maps.

"If he says yes, I am curious where our troops should be during the attack. They have set up lines of mortar stations beyond the wall to drop fire down on them once they get near the wall. Many of them are on rooftops, according to our scouts. There are not a lot of open fields, so this will be an urban assault. Small groups of soldiers will fight one another street to street rather than engaging in open combat on battle lines."

"That benefits us, doesn't it?" Leena said. "We know the city, and they don't."

"It might, but at these odds, I'm not sure it will matter. They outnumber us ten to one. We'd better get moving. Commander Lawrence expects us shortly, and the sounds of war indicate things are in motion. They will be knocking on our door in hours."

The three of them left the command center along with two other soldiers to assist with security. They climbed into a waiting sedan that was Commander Johnson's private car. Pulling out of the base, they heard another enormous explosion in the distance and felt the ground rumble. No one commented. But each explosion prompted them to look at one another. Their eyes held fear, knowing that the sounds of battle they could hear in the distance were on their way, and the size of the threat was likely to swallow them like a wave.

The location for the meeting was a temporary command center about a mile inside the gate. The CPU had set up a park with large tents to house soldiers, communications, and the command center for their troops. Leena, Tina, and the commander headed into the large tent while the two soldiers who accompanied them stayed with the car.

Commander Lawrence was a short bald man. Physically fit but stocky, he wore army fatigues similar to their own. The room was full of tables, and the grass beneath them had been beaten down by so many feet that it was mostly dirt. In the center of the tent was a makeshift conference room table made up of multiple small tables stacked with maps. There were a few chairs. Another table in a corner of the tent featured a spread of pastries, bagels, other snacks, and several large coffeepots.

"Commander Lawrence," Commander Johnson said as he came up to his colleague, extending his hand.

"Johnson," Commander Lawrence replied, shaking his hand but with less enthusiasm than one might expect.

Commander Johnson turned toward his group and introduced them. "This is Tina Redmont and Lieutenant Leena Zhen."

The reference to her last name without a rank clearly bothered Tina. Leena looked in her direction and signaled with her hand for her to let it go.

"Leena Zhen?" Commander Lawrence questioned.

"Yes?" Leena replied.

"I have heard many things about you. I thought you were in prison."

Leena didn't know how to respond or how much the commander might know. She hesitated, and the commander rescued her.

"Lieutenant Zhen is more than willing to deal with the accusations against her, but right now, we have different priorities," the commander said.

"It is not surprising you released her. Your zone is weak. If you would take a stronger stand against criminals, you would not have so many traitors in your midst," Commander Lawrence said snidely as he cut his eyes at Leena.

Commander Johnson put up his arm to restrain Leena as she lunged forward to respond to the commander's crass comment.

"Commander, please. Can we put aside differences and have a conversation? I believe we have a common enemy."

Without another word, Commander Lawrence turned and walked toward the back of the tent, where multiple folding chairs were set up in a circle.

"Have a seat and tell me why you're here. And it better not be to ask for our help in your zone because we have enough problems of our own."

Commander Johnson began to explain. "We are not here to ask for help. We are here to offer it. It's our belief that the Chinese will attack our southern border."

"That chain-link fence is not much of a border," Commander Lawrence noted.

"True. And we believe they will roll right over it. We are no match for their troop count or their weaponry. And neither are you." Commander Lawrence smirked, showing he did not agree with that statement. "The only way we stand a chance is if we work together."

"I told you we are not deploying troops to that cesspool you call home. We would leave our own zone defenseless."

"I am suggesting we join you here, in this zone, to help you fend off the invaders," Commander Johnson finished, and the room grew quiet before Commander Lawrence replied.

"You want to join us here and help? And leave your own zone undefended? You're just going to give up? Are you *all* traitors?" Commander Lawrence asked as he looked toward Leena.

Leena interrupted. "We are not being traitors, you smug son of a bitch! We are saying we want the best chance of survival. The Chinese won't stop in Zone 6. They will head north, and your southern border is the best place to defend against them. If we fight them in Zone 6, they may flank us on our west side, which is your weakest side. If we are not there when they roll into the zone, they will have little choice but to move their troops north and attack the wall rather than backtracking to make the long trip around to our west. And when they get here, and we are here to help your troops defend the wall, we believe we can hold them."

The commander rubbed his face with his hands, thinking about the repercussions of the plan.

"We have areas where we could use soldiers to fill in. But don't think for a minute that your defense of this zone entitles you to anything in it. When this is all done, your soldiers all go home. Is that understood?"

"Yes, Commander," Leena agreed.

"Okay then, let's look at the map and make a plan. Our scouts say the Chinese are already making preparations to move. We hit their camp this morning with a couple of federal fighter jets, but they brought in several of their own from their aircraft carrier in the Atlantic to drive us out."

The commander led them to the stack of maps to put together a plan. The map of the city was color-coded in reds, blues, greens, yellows, and oranges. Leena tried to figure out what the colors might indicate, but there was no key, and it seemed quite random.

The conversation was less collaborative and more of a list of orders the commander instructed the People's Army to follow. As Leena had predicted, the commander ordered the People's Army troops on the front line of the zone's southern wall while their troops would fall back behind them and fill in gaps on the north and east sides.

After the planning was complete, the team went back to their vehicle to journey back to their zone to mobilize the army. The sounds of war grew more regular as they drove back. Fighter jets passed over regularly, and for the first time, they saw the darker-colored jets of the enemy. The battle for the skies had begun.

Leena requested the commander allow her and Tina to be dropped off at the Capitol building. She needed to talk to Maggie before escalations rose further. She also wanted to see where she stood with the governor.

Leena and Tina entered the Capitol building together. It was now full of People's Army soldiers in full combat gear. Bureaucrats and their staffs scurried about, obviously securing the building's assets to ensure that if the Chinese took the building, they would have to dig deep for any records that might help them. There was a vault in the basement. Leena had helped to write the procedures and knew that at that moment, they were stacking filing cabinets and other items in the vault, preparing for an evacuation.

Leena went to her office and found her door draped with police tape. She stripped the tape off the doorway and entered her office. It was in shambles. The floor was littered with paper, the bookshelves were bare, and someone had emptied all of her desk drawers on the floor.

"What a mess," Tina exclaimed.

"This is what they do when they suspect you're a traitor," Leena replied with an acerbic grin.

A few minutes later, Maggie poked her head in the door.

"Leena!" she said excitedly.

"Come in, Maggie, it's good to see you. Shut the door."

Maggie walked in, holding a stack of papers close to her chest. Tina startled her when she entered the room as she had not expected her to be standing behind the door.

"This is Tina Redmont. Tina, this is Maggie Cho. She's a friend." Tina nodded to her.

"Did you find what I need, Maggie?" Leena asked.

"Yes, here are the records you requested."

"Tell me what you found."

"The Aberjay sold the land to Giant Land Development, a holding company. There are many companies within that one. As we traced each one to the owners, it got interesting."

"You found Senator Lansom on the list, right?" Leena asked, assuming she already knew the answer.

"Well, *Governor* Lansom," Maggie said, correcting Leena, who had forgotten that the governor died from his gunshot wounds.

"Governor Lansom is indeed the owner of one company, but Tao Fen, a Chinese company, holds most of the shares."

"A Chinese company? Why would they own land here?" Tina asked.

"I wondered that myself, so I did some digging. Tao Fen has purchased more than twenty percent of the property in the zone that was for sale in the last few years. And not just here. I called over to Zone 7 and talked to a friend I have there. She found that they own a lot of land in Zone 7 as well."

Leena sat down and turned toward the window. She leaned back in her chair, thinking deeply about this new information as the sound of fighter jets shook the window.

"And the owner of Tao Fen?" Leena asked once the roar had subsided.

Maggie opened a folder and began scanning documents to locate the answer. "Feng Lao."

"Feng Lao? Ambassador Feng Lao?" Leena asked loudly.

"Yes, it seems so," Maggie said.

"That son of a bitch. No wonder he wanted us to stand down. He doesn't want the army destroying his assets. He bought those properties because he knew once the Chinese had control of the zone, he could get rich building businesses under the new government."

Leena stood to her feet as an explosion shook the entire building, sending all of them to the floor. Glass rained down from the windows that had shattered instantly from the blast. Smoke filled the room from the outside as screams and sirens began blaring from somewhere in or around the building.

Leena pulled herself up, coughing the smoke from her lungs and picking glass particles from her hair. The taste of blood filled her mouth. "Tina? Maggie?" she called out through the smoke as she regained her footing and pivoted to the other side of her desk to find her friends. She reached around in the gradually dissipating smoke and found Tina on the floor. She felt her body move as she touched her leg. "Tina?" she said again.

"Yes, I'm okay," Tina replied as she tried to pull herself up from the floor, grabbing the desk to steady herself. "What the hell was that?"

Leena looked to the left and reached for Maggie, finding her on the floor, her arm covered in blood. She followed the arm to Maggie's head and torso and found her motionless. She grabbed her head and turned it toward her, shouting her name. "Maggie! Maggie!"

She felt warm blood cover her hands as she cupped Maggie's face. A shard of glass had ripped through her neck and severed vital blood vessels. Maggie was dead. Leena struggled to accept what she was seeing as she called her friend's name again. "Maggie! Stay with me! Stay with me!"

Tina, now on her feet, reached down to pull Leena up. "She's gone, Leena. There's nothing you can do."

"No! She's my friend! We must save her!"

"She's gone. We need to go," Tina said gently, trying to be sensitive to her commander's fragile state.

Leena held her friend, soaking her fatigues in blood and weeping powerfully. Within minutes, her despair turned to anger. She composed herself and stopped crying. Her face grew stern as if she had identified the culprit of this traumatic event and prepared to deliver a heavy response.

"We need to go, Commander," Tina said with a little more force, reaching down to take her arm and help her to her feet.

Leena let her friend go as she stood, wiping the blood from her hands on her shirt and then using her sleeve to wipe the snot from her nose as Tina pulled her back toward the door.

Leena and Tina stepped out of the office into the hall to see unexpected sunlight. The munition had hit the building, leaving large holes in the roof. Bodies lay strewn about the hall while the able-bodied tended to each of them to save those they thought they could save. Leena ran toward the Governor's Office to ensure the governor was safe. As she entered the office, Tina following close behind, Tilda Arinson came barreling through the door with her arms full of files.

"Tilda!" Leena shouted.

Tilda looked at Leena as if she was a ghost, likely because she thought Leena was still imprisoned.

"Tilda, the governor?" Leena addressed her again.

"Gone. She was taken to a safe house a few hours ago," Tilda said as she walked past them in a daze, clutching her files and making her way down the long stairs to the front door of the building.

Leena and Tina followed, helping several people on the stairs who had been injured by the blast reach the bottom. Glass was everywhere, and sparks from small electrical fires seemed to pop and sizzle at every turn as they made their way to the front doors, which were no longer on their hinges.

Another explosion, a little farther away, shook the ground as they exited the building. Leena looked up as she walked down the long stairs in front of the building, turning to face the building and looking above it as she moved slowly, walking backward down the stairs.

"These munitions are not from the fighters. They must have bombers," Leena said. "They have bombed the city. We need to get to the base."

At that moment, they realized they had no transportation. The commander had dropped them off, so they had no way to travel the ten miles to the base except on foot.

"I guess we're huffing it," Tina said as they walked in the direction of the base.

Leena and Tina walked about a mile before flagging down a People's Army truck. Fortunately, the driver recognized Leena as the leader of their division and allowed them to ride along. The pair climbed into the back of the truck, occupied by ten soldiers who were armed for heavy combat.

The streets were in an uproar. Although some of the city had been bombed, and smoke filled the air from the devastation, the attacks seemed to be precise, intended to take out specific targets. It was not long before they realized the truck was not headed toward the base.

Leena turned toward one of the soldiers in the truck. "Private, where is this truck headed?"

The private looked confused as he believed Leena to be his lieutenant and in charge of the mission. "We're headed south, Lieutenant, to protect our southern border."

"South? Why would they be going south?" Leena asked Tina.

"Maybe they're just putting some resistance in front of the Chinese to buy them time," Tina replied.

"Yeah, that makes sense, but that is not where *we* want to be," Leena said.

"Well, we're in it now; might as well help out!" Tina said loudly over the sound of the truck as she reached for a rifle and handed it to Leena.

The truck came to a stop just shy of the southern fence. The army had stacked sandbags to create machine-gun nests about every fifty feet parallel to the fence line and about a hundred yards inside the line. Iron-tank obstacles, called hedgehogs, were strewn about the border to prevent the tanks from rolling through easily. The road itself was blocked by several old school buses, hedgehogs, and barbed wire to alter their path. There were clear lines between the hedgehogs on each side placed to lure the enemy into using that path where mines were waiting. It was a good defense but no match for the number of soldiers they would soon face.

Leena walked over to a machine-gun nest near the entrance by the school buses and sat behind the safety of the sandbags piled high around them. Five hundred soldiers guarded the southern entrance. Leena knew their fate even if they didn't.

"Soldier," Leena called out to a private, "where is your CO?"

"Captain Wallace, she should be over there," he said as he pointed to a small tent they had constructed about two hundred yards from their position.

"Tina, stay here. I'm going to go see Captain Wallace."

Leena walked across the dry soil that was cracked and lifeless due to a lack of rain. She knew Captain Wallace. She was a good soldier and captain.

Leena stepped into the tent as two guards turned toward her. Captain Wallace looked up from her lunch.

"It's okay," she said as the soldiers moved and let Leena inside.

"Lieutenant, it's good to see you. Did you come to help us on the front lines?"

"Not exactly. I just caught a ride, and it came here instead of the base. I assume the commander read you in on the plan?"

The captain put her sandwich down and took a sip of water from a tin cup. She looked at Leena as if to size her up—to determine if she was friend or foe. She grabbed a napkin and wiped the crumbs from her hands before standing and approaching her guest.

"Aren't you wanted on charges of sedition and murder?"

"It was treason, actually, but it was a misunderstanding. You can radio Commander Johnson to confirm if you'd like," Leena said confidently.

The captain stared at Leena for several long seconds and then her face changed, releasing her sternness. "I'm not sure it makes a difference. We could all be dead in an hour. So, let's get to it."

The captain rolled out a map on the table and pointed to a position about ten miles south of town. "This is where their army is massing. From what our spies tell us, they will hit us with a battalion of tanks, followed by about thirty-thousand foot soldiers. The tanks will clear a path, and the soldiers will follow behind them, using them for cover. Our orders are to provide enough resistance to make them believe our force is small and spread out. We give them hell with the mortars to try to take out a few tanks. If they get close enough, we fire on their soldiers' front line. But once those tanks breach our fence, we haul ass out of here in the waiting convoy. We have teams that will cover our exit from machine-gun nests strategically placed on the top floor of these buildings. Their tanks will probably dispatch them quickly, so it's imperative we don't dally. Does that make sense?"

"Yes, Captain," Leena replied. "Have you heard of our movement in Zone 7?"

"It's already begun. I heard you were behind that madness."

"Yes, I had a hand in it."

"Good thinking. It really is our only hope of stopping them. Let's get to work."

The captain turned to put on a bulletproof tactical vest, secured a belt with a firearm around her waist, and put on her cap. She grabbed an extra vest and handed it to Leena.

"This is a small; it should fit."

Leena put on the vest. It had pockets for extra magazines that she quickly filled with the ammunition available in the tent. Leaving the tent, she could see the enemy in the distance. A gigantic cloud of dust signaled that their march had begun.

The ground rumbled. The smell of diesel fuel and gunpowder was already in the air. Leena crouched in a foxhole that had been dug. Behind her, several teams of soldiers kneeled next to their mortar launchers, waiting for the enemy to come within range. The tension in the air hung heavy. The focus of the soldiers was indisputable.

Leena turned and looked behind her, judging the distance between her and the trucks that were waiting to provide their escape. She figured she could make the two-hundred-yard dash in about forty-five seconds.

Leena thought about her husband and wondered if he was there somewhere in one of the other foxholes or possibly positioned near the east gate as he had stated. She worried about him but knew he could take care of himself. He was not a soldier at heart, but she had seen him fight and knew when it came down to it, he was resilient and would not take unnecessary risks with his life.

The ground shook fiercely as the first tank silhouettes could be seen on the horizon. The sound of doom approaching became louder by the second. And then it stopped. The rumble. The sound. It all stopped.

"What the hell?" Tina said as she climbed out of the hole and strained to see why the approaching army might have ceased their death march. "They just stopped. Why would they do that?"

As she finished her question, several of the enemy's tanks fired, and Tina jumped headfirst into the foxhole with her comrades. Buildings a short distance behind them exploded as the tank shells found their mark. Leena turned to look at the soldiers next to the mortars who were now on the ground with their hands over their heads. The teams failed to return fire. The tanks were still out of range.

Several more shells landed, one destroying the school bus that was strategically placed to force them into a targeted path. A few hit near foxholes, causing some casualties. The Chinese kept firing, littering the field with rocks, shrapnel from exploding hedgehogs, and pieces of wire.

296 JOSEPH MICHAEL LAMB

The soldiers in the foxhole looked to Leena for orders.

"What do we do? Should we fire on them?"

"No, they're too far away," Leena shouted over the sound of the explosions. "We need to force them to move forward."

Leena stood up and ran to the closest mortar team.

"How far out of range are they?" she yelled.

"About fifty feet," a corporal replied.

"Take your teams and move. Get closer and bridge the gap. We must force them to move forward!"

The corporal shouted to the soldiers under his charge and about forty of them, armed with ten mortar launchers, began deconstructing the equipment and moving them along with their ammunition to set up between the chain-link fence and the hedgehogs. This made them vulnerable to attack, and they knew it. But they followed orders.

As they set their equipment back up, the Chinese became wise to their shift and began repositioning. The tanks were rearmed and began firing again, this time hitting close to the new location of the corporal and his team. Once set up, the mortars flew, dropping on several positions in front of and behind the tanks, and striking a few. The tanks then moved forward.

The continued blasts from the tanks changed the landscape. A one-hundred-yard section of the chain-link fence was destroyed, and several south-facing buildings sustained heavy damage. Smoke and fire filled the area around where the fence once stood. The tank blasts had blown the hedgehogs into a pile on one side, and the school bus and large vehicles were burning, pouring black smoke into the air.

The soldiers cried out orders to retreat. Leena turned to see soldiers leaving their foxholes for the trucks. "Tina let's go!" she called out as she leaped out of the hole and ran toward the convoy. Explosions continued to rock the buildings, the streets, and the open ground around them as they ran.

Turning her head back, Leena could see the tanks crossing the threshold of the city with soldiers lagging close behind. The number of Chinese was too many to count. The khaki color of their uniform with its red trim seemed to cover the ground as far as she could see.

She turned as she ran and began firing, as did several other People's Army soldiers. Many kneeled next to the trucks to provide cover fire as the men and women piled into the trucks, about forty soldier transports in all. As each one filled, it drove away toward Zone 7.

Leena and Tina loaded into the last truck as the Chinese soldiers began entering the city. The few soldiers in the back of the truck fired on the enemy as the trucks moved. A few tanks hit the mines that were planted and became disabled. The enemy used this to their advantage, however, by pushing the disabled tank out of the way and using that path to avoid other mines. This slowed them down a bit but protected them from additional mines.

The last truck picked up speed as Tina and Leena continued to fire on the enemy. Accuracy was not possible at that distance, but with the number of troops piling into the city, they felt it would have an impact, even if it was small.

They sat and wiped the sweat from their faces. No one spoke. The team knew the defense did not go as planned. They did not expect the Chinese to stop out of mortar range and pummel their positions. They lost many soldiers and many buildings.

The sound of machine-gun fire from the surrounding buildings filled the air, tearing a hole in the mob of army soldiers. Leena could see the devastation, but it only lasted about a minute. Tanks targeted the machine-gun nests and eliminated them with minimal effort.

Leena worried. She knew they had not slowed them down much. She hoped that her army, along with the camouflaged citizens, were already in Zone 7. If not, too much blood would be shed. She would certainly feel responsible.

Chapter 16

RETRIBUTION

The truck stopped about a mile from the north gate. Leena heard people shouting, the rumble of engines, the clanking of chains on the back of the trucks, and the faint sounds of enemy tanks a couple of miles behind them.

She pulled herself up and jumped down from the back of the truck. She could not see the enemy behind them but knew it was only a matter of time before they would be on top of their position. They would take their time, cautious of an ambush. She figured they had about thirty minutes.

Looking ahead, she could see a line of trucks. Not only the forty or so in her convoy but another hundred stopped, waiting to get into the north gate to enter Zone 7.

"Tina, something is wrong. Let's go."

They slung their rifles on their backs and ran toward the front of the line, passing soldiers, citizens dressed in People's Army fatigues, and sometimes children. As she passed each family, Leena urged them to go back into the trucks to avoid detection. She knew that if they found the families, her plan would not work. *Maybe that is what made the convoy stop.* She had to get there fast.

As they walked, their pace quickened to a trot and then to a run as they got closer to the gate. When it was in sight, they could see a large group of soldiers forming a line, with several others taking aim at a truck that was the first in line to enter the gate. They were shouting at those in the back to exit.

Leena ran to the CPU officer who was shouting.

"What is the meaning of this?!" Leena shouted, dispensing with any pleasantries.

The soldier turned and pointed his rifle at her. Instinct took over as she stepped into the aggression and blocked the barrel while delivering a punch to the soldier's face, grabbing his shirt as he fell to pull him back in the other direction and throwing him to the ground. She grabbed his rifle to ensure she was safe.

"Officer, I demand you tell me what is happening here."

"What is it to you? I will have you brought up on charges for assaulting a CPU officer."

"You idiot, don't you see what is happening here? There is an army on our tail that is about to come crashing into this wall. If we are on this side of it when that happens, we are all dead."

"I heard children in the truck. This isn't an army, it's an exodus."

"Soldier, you are making decisions far above your pay grade. Do you believe now is the time to question this decision, made by Commander Lawrence?"

"I guess not," the officer said, now backing down.

"Okay, get on your feet and get these trucks moving."

"Yes ma'am."

The officer stood and whisked the dust off his shirt and pants while he signaled for the convoy to keep moving. The trucks began pulling away one by one. Tina and Leena stood by the gate, making sure they got through without incident. They peered toward the end of the line to ensure the enemy was far behind.

Within ten minutes, she could see the end of the line of trucks and watched as they edged closer. The enemy was nowhere to be seen, and that seemed unusual. They must be regrouping, Leena surmised. Or they were searching the city as they moved.

Once the last truck made it to the gate, Tina and Leena grabbed the back of the truck and settled in for the ride. They had no idea where they were being driven but assumed Commander Johnson had worked all that out. As they passed the gate, they could see the enormous iron doors being swung into place and barricaded with a large bulldozer. The weight of the bulldozer would reinforce the door's integrity as a barricade. Leena knew as she watched, however, that it wouldn't matter. The hellfire that was coming would get through it. She had already seen the devastation their tank battalion had inflicted.

In the distance was the CPU detainment building, a temporary jail, processing center, and courthouse for the Aberjay. It was used to prosecute and hold criminals. Leena had spent some time there for breaking and entering, among other charges, a couple of years earlier.

The field she stood on was vast, filled with temporary structures—mostly army tents pitched to accommodate thousands. The ground was muddy, and everyone she saw had mud stains up to their knees. It was not the best venue, but she expected nothing more from the Aberjay. They didn't see the Miniyar as people but as a nuisance. Their workers. Their servants. Their cooks. Their property. But not human. They refused to acknowledge equal worth. It was a different type of discrimination—not racial but economic. The Miniyar were just poor people without the opportunity to thrive in the world. The Aberjay thought that was the natural order of things, that people should accept their fate. Every decision they made seemed to infuriate her. She still blamed them for her mother's death.

"The command center is this way, Leena," Tina said as she turned to walk in that direction. "It could be worse, I guess; it could be raining."

Leena smiled at her friend's sardonic wit. She knew Tina felt the same way she did about the Aberjay. And being in this place just enforced the distaste for their condescension.

Leena thought about Liv. She did not know what happened at the desalination plant, whether the Chinese took prisoners or killed them before destroying the plant. She hoped Liv was safe, wherever she was, but felt a knot in her stomach thinking about what might have happened.

Leena walked into the command center tent to find Commanders Johnson and Lawrence as well as about thirty other officers talking, planning, and preparing for war.

"Commander Johnson," Leena said as she approached, "I have come from the south gate."

"Lieutenant," the commander replied.

"Commander," Tina corrected him, reminding him that Leena was now the leader of the Crow, not his subordinate.

"Yes, well, we will figure that out later. What news from the south gate?"

"They rolled right over us. Used tank fire out of range from our mortars to pummel our positions and then pushed through with an entire tank battalion and about thirty thousand troops."

"Losses?" the commander asked.

"We didn't have time to count, but likely more than half our force," Leena replied.

"It seems they slowed the enemy enough. Thank you for the report. I will need your team here," the commander said as he pointed to a forward position on the map.

Leena could see the map of the city broken into colored zones: reds, blues, greens, yellows, and oranges. These were used to assign designated troops. The red zones were near the south wall of the zone where Leena would be posted along with a large contingent of her soldiers.

"Take this radio to stay in contact and get cleaned up. Then get out there. Three squads of your soldiers are already in place awaiting further orders. For now, I will call you Lieutenant if that's okay with you."

"Yes, Commander," Leena said sheepishly, slightly embarrassed.

"Commander, where did my soldiers end up?" Tina asked.

"They're here," he said, pointing again. "Right next to Leena's position. Your job is to guard the right flank. I will position you in a building on this street. Use RPG and mortar fire to disable as many tanks as you can when they head through the gate. We have some air support that will do the same. Once they break through the gate, it will be a flood. Do what you can to reduce their number and fall back to this location with Leena's squads once you feel you can't contain them. Commander Lawrence has given us the directive to keep the enemy from these areas shaded in blues and greens. Understand?"

"Yeah, I got it," Tina said, intentionally omitting his rank.

"Commander," Leena said quietly to ensure that others around the table didn't hear. "How did we do?"

The commander looked around and moved slightly closer to Leena to whisper. "About twenty thousand citizens made it into the camp here. We have put them to work to keep up appearances. Another sixty thousand made their way through the tunnels, but we aren't sure where they are now. We can only hope they are safe."

"That is only a little over ten percent. I was hoping for more."

"I know. We just didn't have time. They will be fine if they hunker down in their homes. Remember, the war is coming here." The commander then went back to his maps.

Leena and Tina left the command center tent and headed to the supply tent for more ammunition before getting cleaned up. As they washed their faces with buckets of water and changed their clothes, the sound of jets flying over the field shook the tent.

"Are you ready for this, Tina?" Leena asked.

"Ready to kick some ass," she replied.

"You stay safe out there. I don't want to lose you again."

"Aw, that is sweet. I love you too." Tina said it with a smirk and a tinge of sarcasm, but Leena knew they had grown fond of each other. They fought side by side for more than a year. Combat has a way of bringing people together. It's strange that a war, as violent as it is, can produce such bonds. Sharing a fear of death has that effect.

"Do you think your dad is out there with the troops?" Leena asked as she finished buttoning up her new jacket and vest.

"My dad is not a fighter. He's more of a philosopher. But if he's out there, I'm sure he is telling them what they are doing wrong."

"That sounds about right," Leena said. "Let's get moving. I want to examine our positions in the daylight before hell breaks loose."

Leena and Tina stepped out of the Jeep they had taken to the front. The conflict had yet to begin. The sky still occasionally cried out with jet plane crackles and roars, but the streets were motionless. The buildings of Zone 7 went right up to the wall. There was little space for open combat. This would be an urban conflict. The CPU had surrounded the few buildings on the main street leading to the gate with sandbags and barbed wire to create machine-gun nests. Soldiers sat on the ledges of just about every building within a half-mile of the gate. They were waiting. Waiting for the enemy to burst through the gate and give them a target.

The wall was tall and made of stone and mortar. It was no match for the tank shells, but it would slow them down. There were no turrets on top of the wall, so the only way to engage the enemy before they got through the wall was through mortar rounds. Strategically placed, the weapon could disable tanks to create a barricade on the other side, which would not stop them but might delay their movement a bit.

"I think this is my stop. I'll see you later," Tina said casually as she gave Leena a side hug and strolled to a building on the other side of the street. The Crow had already spray-painted a large crow on the side of the building, marking their territory. Leena laughed, knowing the graffiti would drive the Aberjay mad.

Leena turned to the right and walked past several nests of soldiers waiting for the enemy. She walked into the building and peeked into each room. Every window with a view of the street was set up as a nest of soldiers, some with large M60 machine guns and some with RPGs, obviously gifted to them by the CPU as the People's Army never had such armaments.

The building was six stories high. Leena climbed the stairs to the roof. She opened the door to the roof and walked out to see about twenty mortar teams in formation, ready to engage the enemy.

Leena spotted a friendly face.

"It's about time you showed up," Captain Lewis said in jest.

"Captain, it's good to see you," Leena said.

"Did you come directly from the stockade, or did you have time to do some shopping?"

"Hilarious. I can assure you the news of my treason was exaggerated."

"That's good to hear. I never pegged you for a traitor. A murderer, yes, but not a traitor."

They both laughed. It helped ease the tension. Both had seen many battles, but this one was different. This was a battle against overwhelming odds.

The building they stood on was about half a mile away from the gate. Leena could see the roofs of the buildings; soldiers were littered about them. Some with mortars. Some with RPGs. Even a few anti-aircraft guns had been assembled atop the buildings to provide defense against air assaults.

The building beneath them seemed to shake. Distant tank fire rang out. Leena tried to calculate how far. A mile, maybe two. She walked to the south end of the roof to get a good view of the gate.

"Take your positions," she shouted as she took a position at the corner of the roof. Most of the buildings around her were smaller than this one, giving her a height advantage and a good view. She could see smoke in the distance. She was not sure what the enemy was engaging on the other side of the wall as they left no soldiers behind.

On the radio that the commander gave Leena came the announcement that the tanks were approaching the gate. Everyone waited patiently for what would come next. Some seemed to even hold their breath, waiting for the hammer to fall, for the might of the enemy to be thrust against the giant wall.

"Begin mortar fire!" came the call from the radio.

Leena relayed the information, and soldiers began firing their mortars. All at once, their bombs fell on the other side of the wall, targeting the Chinese forces. The sound echoed as hundreds of mortars hit the ground. Leena knew the area they were shelling was where her apartment used to be. It brought sadness to her heart even though she knew the building was no longer there.

Tank fire began on the other side of the wall, and it was obvious the enemy's target was not the buildings but the wall itself. Stone and mortar dust filled the air as tank fire pummeled the structure. Within a minute, they could see a hole. Then another. The enemy was not content with a single hole to march their troops through but seemed to blast the wall in many places. Then it dawned on Leena: They were not all coming up that one street. They had taken positions across a mile of the wall and were pelting it with explosives to annihilate it entirely.

Leena was not sorry to see that as the wall had been a symbol of Aberjay superiority over the Miniyar for as long as she had been alive. She knew the Aberjay would likely rebuild it once this war was over, but at that moment, in that act of aggression and destruction, the enemy was on her side.

The mortar rounds silenced a few of the tanks, but it did not slow them much. Continued fire on the wall brought about a mile of the wall to the ground. The streets were littered with boulders, cement dust, and debris from the wall, which had stood for more than fifty years.

The building rumbled again as Federal Army tanks rolled past. Leena looked over the edge to see about forty tanks enroute to meet the enemy. The first two fired as they rolled while others began taking side streets that were wide enough, broadening their onslaught. As they found streets suitable for their advance, they turned toward the wall and returned fire.

The tank battle lasted for hours. There was not much the soldiers could do but continue to deploy mortars to the other side of where the wall used to stand. Most of the enemy tanks had made their way into Zone 7 and were trolling the streets, looking for targets. Some were easily dispatched by RPG fire, but others seemed to target buildings where soldiers were waiting to join the battle.

Leena noticed something curious. She could see smoke rising from the buildings that had been struck. She knew they were targeting the buildings to eliminate the troops who were firing on them. But there was a pattern. She could not place it. Something seemed familiar about what she was looking at, but she couldn't quite put her finger on it. But that made no sense. She had never been to this part of town before. What was it she was observing?

"Captain," she called out. A few seconds later, Captain Lewis joined her.

"What is it?"

"Look at the targets. Do you see the smoke rising from each building? Do you see the pattern? I see something familiar, but I can't quite place it," Leena said, desperately trying to describe the pattern that her mind had yet to process.

"A pattern? I don't know what you mean. There can't be a pattern, it's just..."

"Wait!" Leena shouted. "Do you have a map of the city?" she asked the captain.

"Yes, let me grab it." The captain ran back to a small table and grabbed a large map. Walking back to the edge of the roof, he held it up to try to ascertain where they were in relation to the map. This map was the same as the one in the command center, but it didn't show the same sections and colors as the other map.

"There," Leena said, pointing. "And there."

"I don't know what you're seeing," the captain said.

"They're only attacking the red and orange colors. They're not attacking the buildings in the other sections of the city."

"I've seen the map you're talking about, but I don't remember the colored zones."

"I do! I just saw it a few hours ago. They're not attacking the other colors!"

"What do you think that means?" the captain asked.

"It means someone is up to no good and working with the Chinese. Someone has made a deal. They sold us out."

"Sold us out for what? That makes no sense. Wait, what color was this building in?" the captain asked.

"Red," Leena said.

An explosion sent Leena and the captain to the floor of the roof, along with many other soldiers who fell next to their mortar launchers. A hole on the other side of the roof they were standing on opened up as if an invisible vacuum had just sucked it down toward the ground. When that side of the building collapsed, more than thirty soldiers fell to their deaths.

"Leena, get up," the captain said as he grabbed her hand and pulled her to her feet. "We need to get off this building. It's collapsing!"

Leena stood up and looked over the edge. She saw the tank that dealt the blow exploding, the result of an RPG from a nearby alley. The street was littered with stone, dust, tank tread, and bodies. She turned and ran toward the stairs, but they were on the side of the building that fell to the street. They would need to find another way down.

As she bent to help soldiers injured in the blast, Leena noticed the building next to the one she was on was about two stories shorter. The tank fire and collapse had lowered a part of the roof she was on, making it possible to jump safely to the roof of that building next door. The jump would be about six feet across and ten feet down.

"This way!" she shouted as she jumped down about eight feet to the collapsed part of the building. The part of the rooftop she stood on shook underneath her, giving the impression a collapse was imminent. She then slung her rifle on her back and, with a running start, leaped across the chasm to the other roof. She then stood and turned, motioning for others to follow. One by one, soldiers jumped to the lower part of the first building and then jumped across to the other building. About thirty in all made it, leaving Captain Lewis as the only one on the other side. He made the jump down to the lower part of the roof, but it collapsed as he was dashing toward the other building, sucking him down into the pit of fire, smoke, and debris.

"No!" Leena cried before turning away to shield her eyes from her captain's demise. "Dammit, dammit, dammit!"

Another explosion nearby startled Leena, forcing her to mentally set aside her shock over the captain's fate. She looked around to see her squad gathering their weapons and tending to their fellow soldiers' wounds. Many stared at her, clearly awaiting orders.

"Head down to the street. I'm not sure these buildings are secure any longer."

The squad found the door to the stairwell and made their way down the stairs with haste. The team used a side door to file into an alley. Leena quickly broke them into teams of ten.

"Team one: Exit the alley and move toward the gate to engage ground troops. Team two: Go west to the next street and rendezvous with us at the gate. Team three: Go east and do the same thing. Avoid contact with the tanks; they're targets for our air support. Got it?"

The soldiers nodded and cautiously left the safety of the alley. Leena could hear small-arms fire to the south, a clear indication that ground troops were entering the city.

Leena led her team down the street, hugging one side to stay out of the center, slowly moving past machine-gun nests, many of which had already been destroyed by tank fire. Leena realized that the earpiece for her radio had fallen out during the strike on the building. She pushed it back into her ear and could hear the command center calling out.

"Breach! Breach! Breach! Enemy soldiers have breached the gate!"

A tank rolled through the smoke about fifty feet from their position, with more than thirty Chinese soldiers flanking it. Leena signaled for her team to take cover, and they dropped into a machine-gun nest that had recently been abandoned. The M60 machine gun was still there, along with boxes of ammunition. Leena slipped behind the enormous weapon and began firing on the group of soldiers, easily eliminating about a dozen and forcing the remaining invaders to take cover behind the tank. They blanketed the tank with bullets, attempting to strike or flush out the soldiers behind it as the gun turret turned toward them.

"Take cover!" Leena shouted, and the soldiers hastily abandoned the nest.

The tank fired and struck a few feet in front of the nest, killing three and sending dirt, rocks, and parts of the building behind them flying through the air. Leena dashed right back to the M60 that had survived the blast and began firing on the tank again.

"RPG! RPG!" Leena shouted.

"We don't have one!" a soldier yelled back.

The tank turret was repositioned by the occupants of the tank as it moved even closer. Before it could fire, an RPG from two floors above in the building that provided them cover fired and hit the tank directly on the top. Fire engulfed the tank as the hatch opened and smoke poured out. Two men climbed out to escape the smoke, but Leena eliminated them before they could reach the ground.

The remaining Chinese troops had no choice but to continue without the tank and were mowed down by Leena's machine-gun fire once they were visible. When her M60 ran out of ammunition, only a few stragglers were left. She grabbed her rifle as her remaining team members took out the rest.

"Let's keep moving," she said as she checked the status of her wounded.

Leena caught a flash of red behind her. She turned to see Tina leading about twenty soldiers up the other side of the street. They ran across to meet Leena as she was patching up one of the wounded.

"Need any help?" Tina asked.

"Nice of you to join us," Leena said with a smirk.

"Let's go!" Leena commanded her troops as they kept moving down the street. The enemy was moving into the city in groups of about thirty to fifty. They tried to use tanks for cover, but the federal air support was tactically eliminating most of them as quickly as they breached the walls.

The People's Army was clearly outnumbered, but the smoke made it hard to navigate the streets, which provided some advantage to the local forces. Hiding in and around the buildings provided cover as they picked off Chinese troops who stepped into the street after abandoning their immobilized tanks.

They encountered several more groups of the enemy as they moved closer to the gate, and many more had already gotten past them. There seemed to be no line of defense. This was truly urban warfare, and because the lines were broken, the enemy could come from anywhere.

Leena turned to her soldiers as they stepped into a half-destroyed building near the front gate for cover. "I think we

314   JOSEPH MICHAEL LAMB

should seek higher ground and try to trim the herd. Keep an eye out for our teams who are taking the other route."

The soldiers under her command nodded.

Tina pointed to an apartment building across the street that was about three stories tall, offering a good vantage point for firing on the gate. "How about there?"

"That will work. Move out!" Leena said as the team regrouped and ran single file through the smoke and across the street strewn with stone, disabled tanks, and bodies.

They assembled in a room on the top floor as soldiers positioned an M60 in the window. They had about a thousand rounds of ammunition. All of the apartments had been evacuated because the building was so close to the gate.

Leena and Tina sat on the floor with their backs to the wall, pulling canteens from their belts and drinking all the water they had left. Eyeing the bathroom, Leena walked over and turned the knob to the faucet. Water, crisp and clean, flowed from the spigot. *Well, isn't that nice?* she thought. *Our water doesn't flow on a good day, and they have clean water in the middle of a war.*

"Freakin' Aberjay," she exclaimed.

The sound of the M60 rattling off rounds made Leena jump. After filling her canteen, she moved closer to the window so she could see the progress. The waves of troops entering the city were massive. Thousands. Not in a single line but seemingly in lines a mile wide. They were making great use of the huge holes in the missing wall.

The soldiers in the room kept firing, eliminating the enemy twenty at a time. Small-arms fire was returned, piercing the window and striking the ceiling of the room, but it didn't prevent the gunner from continuing to fire until they had to reload. They went through the existing ammunition and a corporal called for more on the radio. The resupply would not be quick, but it was essential if they were to hold that position.

The other two teams showed up shortly after they ran out of ammunition for the M60 and piled onto the first floor to provide a defense for them as the enemy swarmed around them. Leena knew that they were now surrounded and the only thing keeping them alive was that they were not a valuable target.

The soldiers operating the M60 yelled for more ammunition as the Chinese troops were beginning to refill the street below, replacing their fallen comrades. Leena's soldiers used small arms to continue firing, but they were not as effective as the big gun. After about an hour, the war had grown quiet. Small arms fire still rang out every few minutes, but the roar of the battle had subsided. Leena desperately wanted to know if they were making any difference at all, but it was difficult to tell. The enemy swarmed like roaches, and no matter how many they squashed, there always seemed to be more. It surprised her that so many were still alive.

The sun began to set. Leena tried to deliver a situation report on the radio. There was still conflict happening, but it was further north inside the city walls. They ordered her to hold her position through the evening hours. She informed her soldiers to settle in for the night, placing guards at the ground entrance and all of the windows. They would sleep in shifts. She knew the enemy needed sleep as well and would likely look for quiet places to shelter until morning.

Leena lay next to Tina on the hard floor. She nibbled on some crackers from an MRU. Her ears were still ringing from the sounds of war. She shifted uncomfortably and felt bruised down her left side.

She took the time to inform Tina of what she saw from on top of the building.

"What do you make of it?" Tina asked.

"I don't know. The buildings they attacked all held People's Army soldiers. Why? Did the Aberjay tell them to target only those buildings and then order us to guard them? What is the endgame here? To eliminate our people? It doesn't make much sense. Who cooperates with their enemy?"

"Those with similar interests," Tina replied.

"Similar interests?" Leena said inquisitively. "What would they have in common?"

Leena nibbled on another cracker, chewing slowly as her mind spun. *What cooperation would there be between the Aberjay and the Chinese? The Aberjay hate the Chinese. They constantly rail against communism.*

"Money," Leena said after a long silence.

"What?" Tina replied.

"It is the only thing they have in common. They both love money. Maggie said when she looked up the ownership of those buildings in Zone 6 that Feng Lao's company was a co-owner with the Aberjay on many properties here in Zone 7. Somehow that son of a bitch coordinated with CPU forces to ensure his army only targeted the buildings not owned by his company."

"That seems farfetched. Can you prove it?" Tina asked.

Leena stood up and walked toward the closest window. She peered outside to the street, looking up and down its length until she stared at one thing in particular.

"What are you looking for?" Tina asked.

"Come on, I have a hunch."

The two walked downstairs to the ground floor. Soldiers lay sleeping while others stood guard. They nibbled on rations and whispered in the corners. Leena and Tina walked out a side door to an alley. Carefully, they started walking to the street. The moon was a sliver, casting little light. The smell of smoke, gunpowder, and burned flesh was strong.

Once they reached the street, Leena and Tina ran about two blocks to a tank that had been destroyed early in the battle. She climbed on top to the hatch and dove headfirst inside.

"What the hell are you doing?" Tina whispered.

A minute later, she popped her head up out of the tank with a set of goggles.

"What's that?"

"Goggles. I saw them wearing them and was not sure why since it was during daylight. They're not night-vision goggles but targeting goggles. Here, look." Leena handed the goggles to Tina.

Tina put them on. "Holy shit! The buildings are painted different colors!"

"Is that proof enough for you?" Leena asked.

A few streets over, they heard the crack of a rifle being fired a few times, causing them both to jump.

"Let's get out of the street," Tina said.

Dropping the goggles into her pack, Leena walked back to the alley and the building that was sheltering them. She found her way to the top floor and laid down to get some shuteye. She knew the next day would be a challenge and, without proper rest, might be impossible to get through. She had to deliver this evidence to Commander Johnson. She didn't know if he could do anything about it, but the story had to be told.

Morning came as always, but instead of cheering rays of sunshine and birdsong, it was marked by the smoky fog of war and gunfire. Leena sat up, startled by the resumption of hostilities. She reached over and shook Tina to make sure she was awake and walked to the bathroom to throw some water on her face. She figured she got about three hours of sleep. Not nearly enough.

A corporal walked into the room.

"We have a problem, Lieutenant," he said.

"Commander," Tina corrected.

"Let's have it, Corporal," Leena said.

"The enemy troop count around the building grew significantly last night. They must have moved some in under the cover of darkness. We are surrounded and heavily outnumbered."

"Why haven't they busted in here and killed us then?" Tina asked.

"That's the thing. I don't think they know we're here. The enemy occupies every building around us, but they don't seem to realize we're here."

"Thank you, Corporal. Let's get a message to the command center and see what our orders are. Maybe they can throw us a lifeline."

Leena checked her rifle to ensure it was loaded and ready. She walked near the window but kept her distance because the sun was beaming through, and she didn't want to give up her advantage if they really didn't know they were there.

"Tina, is Wolf here with us?"

"Yes, I think he's downstairs."

"Go get him for me. I have an idea."

Tina left the room as Leena went to her bag and took out the goggles she had seized the night before. A few minutes later, Tina returned with Wolf behind her.

Wolf was a small man with a bushy brown beard, thus the nickname. He was a Crow and worked in the IT and Communications Department. He was well-known within the group for his ability to hack communications signals and plant bugs when necessary. He was also quite competent on computers even though they were not widely in use in Zone 6 because of the lack of internet connectivity and the fragility of the power grid.

"Wolf, I have a question," Leena said as she handed him the goggles. "Is there a program inside these goggles that makes these work, or do they get the information from somewhere else?"

Wolf took the goggles and looked through them, then turned them at different angles. He pulled a small screwdriver out of his pocket and popped off a cover that was filled with Chinese characters. He held them close to his eyes, investigating the insides of the device.

"There's a wireless chip in here. They are likely getting a signal from somewhere else. Maybe even a satellite."

"Wolf, can you hack that signal? I want to change the colors of the buildings."

"I don't see why not," Wolf said as he put the goggles on. "It will take me about an hour to figure out the encoding though."

"Get to work on it. Get it done as fast as you can."

"Yes, Commander," he said as he turned and headed back downstairs.

"Excellent," Tina said after realizing what Leena was planning.

"Let's give Wolf some time, and then we will figure out how the hell we're going to get out of here."

The corporal they spoke to earlier returned about an hour later. He had a confused look on his face and a radio in his hand. Leena also had a radio but had not been wearing her earpiece as the war had moved north of their position and the back and forth was only related to troop movements in those areas.

"What's the word, Corporal?" Leena asked.

"I got through to the command center on another channel. They said we're deep in enemy territory, about thirteen blocks. They can't rescue us but said they would send us some help, something they called an M squad."

"M squad? What the hell is that?" Tina inquired.

"I don't know, they didn't say."

"Okay, get everyone ready to go. We will keep our eyes open for this help they're sending. We should be ready to get out of here when it arrives."

"Yes, Lieutenant," the corporal said before turning toward the door.

"Commander!" Tina shouted at him as the corporal left the room.

"What do you think it will be?" Leena asked Tina.

"I don't know. A tank? A helicopter? A drone with sandwiches?"

They could hear gunfire getting closer. They looked at each other and ran to the window. They could see enemy troops running out of nearby buildings with weapons in hand, headed north. A few enemy tanks, likely the only ones remaining in the city, went by as well, rumbling in the same direction.

"Whatever it is, it's causing quite a ruckus," Tina said.

"Maybe this is our help. Let's get out to the alley," Leena said before leading Tina and the rest of the soldiers in the building down the several flights of stairs and exiting into the alley. They crouched to avoid detection and slowly made their way to the main street.

Besides the small-arms fire that was getting louder, they heard tank fire. It seemed to be coming from only four or five blocks away now. Leena ordered two teams to cover their retreat as the duo guided the rest of them down the street toward the battle. They engaged small bands of enemy soldiers still coming out of the buildings as they made their way north.

Leena signaled her troops to stop and hide behind sandbag walls as they were slowly making their way forward. She could see the battle now. The enemy was being overwhelmed with gunfire and explosions, likely from grenade launchers. But the allies were not human.

"Tina, look!" Leena said as she pointed.

"MIRO?" Tina said. "Since when do MIRO fight?"

"They're weaponized MIRO. I knew they were working on it but didn't know they'd made this much progress. There must be a hundred of them fully armed. They're making a mess of the Chinese. The enemy is retreating. Let's give them a surprise."

Leena waved, and the entire group moved into the street from behind the barricades and began firing on the retreating Chinese. Like falling statues, the soldiers fell one after another with little hope of successfully defending against the attack that was now coming from both directions. Hundreds of soldiers lay dead in the street, full of holes, and those who were still alive howled in pain.

As the line of MIRO came close to Leena, they stopped firing. Leena was shocked to see this new MIRO, tall and blue, with mechanical bodies and faces—yes, faces. Some sort of synthetic skin had been used for the head, giving them a very lifelike appearance. The mechanical parts of the robots were painted blue, and one MIRO, obviously the leader, had three white stars painted on the front. Leena was shocked when it spoke as all the MIRO she had ever seen had a very limited vocabulary.

"Greetings, Leena Zhen. I have been dispatched to assist you and your team."

"Thank you," Leena said awkwardly, never having had a conversation with a robot before.

"Please follow me, and we will escort your team to safety."

An explosion in a building behind them poured brick and cement down into the street. Turning around, Leena could see the few remaining tanks engaging. Seeing Wolf approaching, she yelled to him.

"Wolf, did you do it?"

"Yes, Commander, just give me the word."

"Turn it on!" she shouted.

Leena directed the MIRO to avoid engaging with the tanks as they began running up the street, using the building, disabled tanks, and cars, as well as sandbag nests for cover, as they avoided the tank fire.

Leena took the goggles from Wolf and after looking through them briefly, began running toward an office building for cover.

"What are you doing?" Tina shouted.

"Trust me!" Leena yelled back as she ran through the front door of the building with about twenty soldiers following. She frantically ran down the hallway, looking for an exit, and found an open door in the back. She ran out into the alley behind the building as the tank fired on the building, raining down more stone and brick.

With the group of soldiers behind her, she ran back to the street to get the attention of the tank and then ducked into another building. This time finding an apartment door open on the first floor, she burst through the cracked door and smashed the window, providing an exit. She jumped out the window as another shell from the tank caused the building to collapse on one side. She helped everyone get through the window, listening to the grunts of the soldiers, some of whom barely fit through the window.

The MIRO fired on the tanks with small arms only, knowing their bullets had little effect. Leena followed the pattern, getting the attention of the tank operators then ducking into additional buildings, drawing their fire.

Tina and many of the soldiers grumbled as they did not understand why she was intentionally drawing fire. Then it dawned on Tina that Wolf had changed the colors. The tanks were only firing on the buildings because they saw them as acceptable targets when, in fact, they were the opposite. Once she caught on, Tina found another set of goggles on a disabled tank and split the team into three teams, relaying the plan. The three teams led the tanks down several streets, which destroyed more than fifty buildings.

Leena watched, exhausted, as teams ran from building-to-building drawing fire. She was now near the command center, and the MIRO were still protecting their efforts as Leena had ordered them to do. She began the short walk, about ten blocks, to the CPU detainment building and the command tents behind it. The streets were littered with destruction, equipment fragments, and bodies. Fires burned everywhere. The Chinese had decimated the zone. She could hear more battles taking place in the north, but her will to fight was deflated by the treachery she had discovered. She could not continue. She craved justice.

As she approached the command center, holding the goggles she had retrieved from Wolf, soldiers ran with urgency to the west side, which was now taking fire. The war had come to them. The camp was in danger. She could see more weaponized MIRO marching toward the action and knew they would prevail. Small-arms fire had little effect on them, and with the heavy artillery mostly put down, the Chinese did not stand a chance.

Leena walked into the command center tent looking a mess. Black ash was smeared across her face; blood dripped from her legs, cut by shrapnel and window glass. She walked over to the planning table where the commanders and other high-ranking officers were still at work. They all turned as Leena approached.

"Thank goodness you're safe," Commander Johnson said as he approached. He planned to hug her, but seeing her face, he knew better. He had seen that expression before.

"Commander Lawrence!" Leena shouted.

"Yes?" he sheepishly responded.

"What are the colors for?"

"What?"

"What are the colors on the map for? What is their purpose?"

"I don't know what you mean. The colors show where we assign troops to allow..."

"Shut up! You shut your mouth! I don't want to hear any more lies. You tell these people what those colors are for!" Leena shouted.

"I really don't know what this is about. I already told you,"

"The colors designate which buildings are owned by the Chinese. Ambassador Feng, in coordination with Commander Lawrence, had their assets tagged so the Chinese would only destroy non-Chinese-owned properties. This invasion is not an attack. The actual attack happens after they are done, when the properties that are left triple in value. Before long, they will own the entire city."

"That is preposterous! Guards, take this traitor into custody!" the commander shouted as two guards came and grabbed Leena.

Commander Johnson stepped forward, "Leena, is this true? Do you have any proof?"

Leena took the goggles and threw them onto the table in front of Commander Lawrence.

"There is the proof right there. The Chinese have a centrally controlled blueprint of our city, and the goggles communicate to the tank drivers which buildings to target."

"Let me see that," came a voice from the corner of the tent. Captain Tina Smith, the CPU investigator, walked to the table and grabbed the goggles. She repeatedly looked through the display and then at the map.

"She's right," the captain said as she looked up at Commander Lawrence.

"You can't believe this traitor!" Commander Lawrence bellowed. "Tina, please, this is a trick. This is ridiculous!"

"Guards," Tina said to the military police who had Leena by the arm. "Take Commander Lawrence into custody for treason."

The commander continued to protest as the soldiers dragged him from the tent. The captain walked over to Leena and with a smile said, "Excellent work, Lieutenant."

"Commander!" Tina shouted from behind.

"I underestimated you," the captain whispered.

"I'm sure he didn't do this alone, Captain," Leena replied.

"Don't worry, I'm good at what I do. I will find his collaborators and put them all behind bars, assuming we survive all this," she said as she waved a hand toward the battle that was now raging less than a mile away.

"What's the status of the war, Commander?" Leena asked Commander Johnson.

"Good. With the MIRO in play, we're making significant progress. The British warships have just arrived off the coast and should have reinforcements here in a couple of days. I think we'll prevail."

"Quite a mess out there," Leena said. "There will need to be a significant amount of construction to get the city back to the way it was."

"Indeed," Commander Johnson agreed.

"I wonder where they'll get a large enough workforce to put the town back together?" Leena smiled and gave the commander a wink.

Leena turned away from the table and, grabbing a rifle from a soldier, walked with a limp toward the opening of the tent.

"Are you rejoining the battle, Commander?" Tina asked as she walked by.

"No... I'm going to find Liv."

Leena exited the tent. Tina and the other Crow who were present followed her out into the field. The sun shone brightly as they found a truck nearby that they could requisition.

"We will need some supplies for our trip if we are going to find Liv," Leena said as she pulled herself up into the cab. "And we need to find my husband."

"Not a problem," Tina said. "Let's rally the Crow as well!"

"Is that really necessary," Leena said.

"We go where you go," Tina replied as she pulled herself up into the passenger seat. "Besides, we can't let you conquer the Tullian without us!"

About The Author

Joseph Michael Lamb is an award-winning entrepreneur, business consultant, group facilitator, and author. He earned a B.A. and M.B.A from Southeastern University. Before beginning a career in writing, Joseph founded a technology firm in Atlanta, Georgia that he operated for nearly twenty years, selling the firm in 2018. From there, he founded a management consulting firm RedVine Operations where he provided business consulting and group facilitation services to small businesses.

Joseph writes in the science-fiction, thriller, and fantasy genre. His love of writing comes from his love for reading, which began in his early teens with the fantasy genre. While his early writing has been technical non-fiction, including a book he co-wrote in 2000 and as well as his first full length non-fiction book in 2001. His latest work is a fiction series 'Aberjay' which includes Aberjay Rising (book 1), Beyond the Miniyar (book 2) and Tullian Forever (book 3).

Keep in touch with Joseph or join the new publication notification list at www.josephmichaellamb.com

Also By

Enjoy other titles by Joseph Michael Lamb.
Be sure to visit josephmichaellamb.com for updated release dates.

Tullian Forever (Scheduled for release March 2024) – The third book in the Aberjay Series, Leena Zhen, citizen of Zone 6, now the leader of The Crow, a Resistance Force, steps out into the land of the Tullian to search for her friend lost during the previous conflict. Armed with her vitriol for her enemies and the love for her family, she must mount the last battle against the oppression of the Aberjay, the impending insurgency of Tullian raiders, and the unrelenting insidious plague that has ravaged the land. Will she be able to topple the powers that enslave her people and find true freedom?

Wellbeing (Scheduled for release late 2024) – A thriller that follows John Lancaster, a stock broker that decides to change his life and give up his career to become a writer, moving to the small town of Fountain. John soon learns things are not what they seem as his family begins to go through supernatural changes. His investigation of these strange occurrences leads to a truth that may destroy him and his family. Will he be strong enough to give up his good fortune to save the ones he loves?

Made in the USA
Columbia, SC
04 October 2023

23883285R00200